THE DISCOVERY OF JOY *a novel*

YVONNE ERWIN

Paperback-Press
an imprint of A & S Publishing
A & S Holmes, Inc.

ISBN-10:0692363432
ISBN-13:9780692363430

DEDICATION

To all of you who believed it me - you made all
the difference.

TABLE OF CONTENTS

CHAPTER ONE

Julie

"Julie Krueger?"

I whirl around beside my car to face an old man holding a bouquet of red roses. A Linda's Flowers van is parked behind him.

The January wind whips my hair into my eyes. Impatiently, I pull it behind my ears.

"Who wants to know?"

"Got a delivery for ya."

Oh, great. Rodney strikes again. I'll have to call the lawyer's office again and tell Claudine, the paralegal on my case, he's acting like a stalker.

The old man seems to think I'm a little slow – I should be ecstatic over getting flowers.

"I don't think so."

"You're Julie Krueger, right?"

"Yeah, but no, take those things away. I don't want them."

"You sure? Somebody special's thinkin' about you." The old man shoves the roses at me so I can take another look.

"Get them out of my face. I said I don't want them."

Shrugging, the old man gets back in his van and I see him toss the flowers over the seat.

As the delivery truck pulls away, I click my phone to silent just in case Rodney texts me.

No need to get my mom, Renae, all riled up. She'd be furious if she thought Rodney was getting in touch with me.

"I'm home," I call, banging through the back door. I'll be lucky if she didn't see the delivery truck out there.

Renae is coloring her hair that black as death shade she favors so much. She is obsessive, but at least the black is better than the red she tried once. *Oh my God*, Mark would be surprised if he knew she is really dishwater blond with a lot, and I mean a lot, of gray messed up in there.

Mark is my stepfather. He's the quiet type, never says much, or at least not to me. I'm twenty-three and I live with these two, in the basement of a bungalow in the middle of town.

"Mom," I say, stalking the kitchen for some chips or leftover takeout. I spy a miserable piece of cheese pizza at the back of the fridge and nab it. "You're gonna look like Morticia Adams."

My mom turns the kitchen faucet off and rolls her hair up in a towel. She's wearing her pink bathrobe and slippers. Her mascara's smudged under one eye.

"Well, my darling daughter. As usual, full of witty insults," she says, brushing past me.

"Mom, you can't really think it's gonna look good."

"I don't think it will look bad, Julie," Renae says.

Oh lord. It would be the end of the world if Mark saw all her gray hair, I'm sure. I shrug and take a bite of pizza.

I plant a kiss on the top of Alex's head. My son is fourteen months old. At the moment, he's in his highchair waiting for Renae to finish her beauty treatment.

"How's my little man?" I say, pulling him out of his chair and hugging him close.

Alex chortles.

"Mum mum mum," he says.

"Julie, don't you think you should take a shower before you hold him? I mean, you just got off work. You're bound to be all greasy and such."

"Of course, Mother. Of course. Wouldn't want to taint him or anything." I wait tables at an upscale restaurant in Springfield, Missouri. The way Renae acts, I may as well work in a leprosy camp.

I set Alex on the floor and retrieve a little truck from the corner.

"Mommy, be right back."

"That's not what I meant but… Julie, you can be such a child sometimes," Renae says while toweling her hair from the other room.

Down the stairs to the basement, I jog to my small world. I peel off my work clothes and turn on the shower. All I want to do is scrub off the grease and maybe smell good for Alex.

Renae thinks the world revolves around Mark. Well, him and Alex.

My dad left a long time ago. I was ten. I thought my dad would always love me, always come around for me. I thought my dad would always be there, somewhere, for me.

What a joke. My first birthday without him passed, and then Christmas and all the other holidays and special times I wanted to share with him. You know, father-daughter stuff. Renae made excuses. "Oh, he's very busy, I'm sure he just forgot. I'm sure he didn't mean to."

The truth is, my dad left Renae and me behind because he made a new family with my babysitter. A bit by accident, I suppose. But a baby was born just a few months after he divorced my mother and married his new wife.

I had no idea they were screwing. Neither did my mom, apparently, but the betrayal hit her hard. When Mark strolled into my mother's hemisphere, she latched onto him and didn't let go. They got married when I was thirteen, or fourteen. In any case, why wasn't I good enough for my dad?

Back to Alex.

Alexander, my baby boy. He is so sweet. I could hug him all day. He's just precious, from his little pug nose and his button mouth, all the way to his fat little toes. You'd love him.

I met his dad when we both worked at the Olive Garden. We were on the wait staff. His name is Rodney Moore and he's a lot older than me, fifteen years actually. When we met, he told me he was separated from his wife. Come to find out, Rodney was – and is – married to some hound dog named Angela, and they were never separated. That nutcase Angela was standing by her man, come hell or high water and I rather think she has been through both. Angela is devoted. Rodney? Not so much.

He started calling me. He left flowers on my car. He followed me around. And then the text messages started. Oh my God, the texts. Hotter than hell, sexier than bringing sexy back. Rodney begged me, he pleaded with me to see him. How could I refuse? I mean, he *was* sorta hot. He liked my reddish tresses, or so he said. He dug my pretty tits. He said he loved me. Angela meant nothing to him. She loved him but she knew he didn't feel the same way about her.

He said all that stuff, you know? I could just croak. Well, it was fun for a while but then it got dangerous and well, one afternoon, Angela came screeching into the TGIF parking lot where I was hanging with my friends, and punched me square in the nose. I had no idea at the time, but my life was about to change forever. I went from staring at a bruised, swollen face in the mirror to facing just one little pink plus sign on a bland plastic package.

Telling my mom and Mark was the worst.

They are convinced I'm troubled and need their intervention. They've been keeping me under house arrest since I told them about Rodney, and me being pregnant. Shit, like I'm twelve. Know what I mean? Every time these people get the notion, maybe the moon changes or something, there they are, filing ex partés against Rodney, of course, and Angela. Then the worst thing happened. Rodney filed a paternity action against me. He wants visitation with Alex, but I just can't let Rodney have time with my son. What if he didn't bring him back to me? My lawyer, Leon Martinez, seems to think this is all a cake-walk but it scares me shitless that Rodney could take Alex for an hour or a day or whatever and then never come back.

Renae's crazy intense about keeping Rodney out of my life. Just because he left notes on my car and flowers, and came to meet with my stepdad, and called my mother at the insurance company where she works. He just wanted to talk with her and all that sort of stuff. Of course, Angela started calling too and, by then, my parents had a belly full of hot crap and didn't want any more. I became the bird in the cage. So now they monitor my gas usage, my mileage, my cell phone bill (Oh, they would *shit* if they knew Rodney put me on his family plan and gave me a cell phone), my email, my entire existence. They think they have me under control and I let them think it. One of these days, I'll escape.

Rodney used to tell me, when we were together, "You're a Jaguar, baby." The car, you know? He loved Jaguars. He knew every way to push my buttons. My God, he just makes me hot. In spite of Angela. He does not love her. He told me so. She knows it.

Back to my life here, now. I have Alex. Angela could never have children. Rodney has two from a previous marriage and has custody of them. She is raising another woman's children plus here I am, or rather here Alex is, proof her husband cannot love her properly. Alex is proof her husband can reproduce without her.

I toss my bath towel aside and stare into the mirror. Renae is not that old and she's already covering up her gray hair. Am I going to be that desperate when I'm her age? I pull a comb through my hair, which is longer than usual, and inspect the freckles on my nose. Angela's darker than me, but I'm better looking. I'm not overweight. She isn't either, in fact, she's sort of like a stick with dark curly hair. I'm a curvaceous chick. I stare for a long minute into my blue eyes. Not bad.

I turn to the side and take a long look at my chest, sticking it way out, what I can see of it anyway. Yeah, them titties are sitting up there nice and pretty. No sagging here. Yay for me.

Alex is calling for me. Yet another text from Rodney is on the cell phone he gave me. He loves me. He wants to talk about Alex. I'll send him a text later when the folks aren't so close.

I bound back up the stairs to find Renae is finished messing with her hair and wandering around the house with a towel draped across her shoulders, singing Elvis tunes. She's holding Alex by the hand and, for some reason, he's got a towel around his shoulders too. Weird.

Being trapped in this house, in the basement, a

hostage of my mother and Mark, is making me crazy. I don't know how yet, but somehow, I've got to get the upper hand and get out of here.

CHAPTER TWO

Andrea

Early morning light spills over the comforter, leaving sparkling veins against the white. Sated with afterglow from the weekend, the first in months that Elliott stayed away from the hospital and with me. I feel like the luckiest woman in the world. We talked like we had not talked in months. Well, to tell the truth, we had not talked in months. Not since the incident.

It happened a few months ago when Elliott, my husband, locked me in our bedroom, rammed my head into the closet and took me from behind. We had been in an argument because he wanted sex. His children, Will and Dawn, were downstairs. I tried to keep it quiet – hopefully, they didn't hear any commotion coming from the closet or Elliott groaning. It was a cruel moment but it's gone. It's behind us and I can forgive him for it. Anyway, the birds are singing and my heart is pounding a tune right along with them.

Praise you Jesus, you've brought a miracle.

We made love last night, *real love,* for the first time

in many, many nights. I can't count how many, it's been so long. Elliott was insatiable, romantic and gentlemanly and demanding all at the same time. Our love was wonderful. I gave myself completely to him last night. A delicious interlude in our marriage.

Rolling over, I kiss Elliott's back. He is lying on his side, facing away from me. He flinches causing me to slobber down the side of his back. A little trepidation seizes me. I get up and pull my robe around me and check Elliott before heading downstairs, leaving him in a deep sleep.

Making coffee and taking it upstairs on a tray sounds *primo*. Elliott would like that and maybe it would prolong the weekend a bit. I pull the Starbucks bag out of the cupboard and inhale the raw aroma of unground coffee beans. I love the manly, luxurious and delicious smell. As the beans whir in the grinder, I think I hear Elliott getting up but maybe not.

Coffee perking, I scan the driveway for the newspaper, which hasn't arrived yet. Maggie, my little Yorkie, stares at me intently. It's her signal to be let out to the back yard.

I hear the toilet upstairs flush. Oh well, Elliott is awake. Coffee will be ready for him when he gets down here. I love mornings. Drinking coffee in the morning with my husband is one of my favorite things.

"What's the matter with my girl?" I chortle at Maggie while she wags her tail in earnest. She is anxious to get out. "Okay then," I say as I open the French doors off the kitchen and let her out. She is all fur and eyes and not a whole lot else, except for a wet nose when I am trying to type on the computer or read or something.

Coffee is ready. Maggie bounces back in from the late January cold. The newspaper should be here by now, plunked on the front step. I'm making my way to the front door to check when the doorbell rings. Maggie barks once, twice. Glancing at the clock in the kitchen, I realize it is 7:45 a.m. Who in the world is at my door at this hour?

"Uh, Andrea." It's Jennifer Lutjens, one of my husband's longtime friends. She's holding a video camera in gloved hands, her parka hanging off her shoulders. Her hair is bound up in a ponytail and she just can't help herself. She looks amazing. No, *freaking* amazing, like those snow bunny cover girls posing in front of a snow blanketed chalet in Switzerland with their white teeth and glowing skin. Those model girls with perfect figures who wear leggings like a fine glove and boots like they were meant to walk all over the damn mountain in nothing else.

But I don't know why she's here and why she's holding a video camera.

"Jennifer, hi. What's going on?" Looking past Jennifer, I see a moving van backing up to our garage. Behind the moving van, circling around in his Nissan Armada is Bob Smith, my husband's good friend.

"What's going on?" I say again. Before Jennifer gets a chance to answer, my husband is standing behind me, pulling Jennifer into the house. Bob follows behind.

"Hey Jennifer, thanks for coming," Elliott says.

On the heels of Bob Smith, Matt Lutjens, Jennifer's husband, appears. Nobody is looking at me. Nobody is speaking to me. My husband is dressed in jeans and a T-shirt. I see gray stubble on his chin.

Nothing about this scene is right.

"What's going on?" I say again. "Elliott?" He turns away.

"See here, this is how we're doing this," Elliott says to Jennifer. "Video everything, absolutely everything I'm taking out of the house. Okay?"

"Okay," Jennifer says and moves into position with her camera.

From that moment on, I realize I might as well not be here. I am less important than a speck of dust. What I am watching, what I feel, what I want, none of it matters. I am an unwelcome spectator.

"What's going on here?" My bewildered pleas hang unanswered.

Watching the three of them move Elliott's things out while Jennifer videotapes makes my stomach drop to my feet. I don't understand. I thought all was well.

"Elliott?" I hear my voice and I see my feet moving across the floor, following, trying to keep up, attempting to find something to hang onto and falling short. Elliott says nothing. Jennifer continues filming. Bob moves along, loading Elliott's things into the moving van.

When was this planned? The three of them move in tandem, loading up his clothing, his personal items, and then they take the TV from the bedroom and the furniture from the guest bedroom. The front door opens and shuts over and over again, allowing frigid air to billow into the house. Jennifer is videoing every moment of the debacle. It is so humiliating. I corner Elliott in the kitchen, tears in my eyes, as he pulls his U of MO coffee mug from the cupboard.

"What are you doing? Please, at least tell me what you're doing," I say.

He grimaces in disgust. "Andrea," he says, as though I am four years old. "I'm moving out. I'm leaving."

"Why?"

"I can't talk right now," he says.

"What is going on, Elliott? You have to tell me. Why are you leaving this way?"

"I have to, Andrea. I can't live like this anymore. I won't. I am leaving because of you." Then he walks out of the kitchen, slaps the backs of his friends and they all hop into their respective vehicles, backing out of the driveway one by one. And that's how my husband left me.

Tomorrow's my birthday.

And the day before my birthday, my husband loaded up his stuff and moved out. He left me staring out the front door in the cold at the departing vehicles, wondering if I was having a bad dream.

The tail lights are now out of sight. They've passed the curve in the driveway, through the trees.

The house is silent, a wreck of boxy spaces where stuff once sat. An echoing, accusing silence of recrimination and ending. Something over, something taken, something done, whether you like it or not.

Too shocked to even cry, I close the heavy front door and sag against it.

What to do now? Should I call an attorney? I only know of one I'd trust, Leon Martinez. He's supposed to be the best. Elliott's first wife used him in their divorce.

The phone book falls from my shaking fingers, the spine slamming onto my foot. I finally locate Leon's number in the yellow pages and grab my cell phone. Clearing my throat, I wait for a voice to come on the line.

CHAPTER THREE

Claudine

Oh God, I groan. *Please do not let this cost so much. Please.* What exactly is involved with a cracked shower floor anyway? How many pesos? Where will I get the money? I will take it out of savings, like everything else.

The cheap, plastic shower liner installed by previous owners is old and dried out. I do not know if I can do anything about the floor. Driving to work on a near empty tank of gas, I'm thinking about fixing a shower. Who I will find to fix it? When can I get this done? I already have a headache. Unmarried life is overwhelming.

"I don't need this right now," I say to the heavens.

The sky appears unyielding, grey and heavy with snow clouds. I don't have Jim Coulter to fall back on since our divorce. Jim owns a construction company, so he builds and besides that, he can fix anything. I have me, Claudine, forty-five years old, a family law paralegal in the town I've lived in all my life. I spend my time watching my house deteriorate, learning how to raise a sixteen-year-old daughter on my own, not prepared for any of it.

I'm the first person in the office today, which means I can start a pot of coffee and do a little internet research on shower replacement before anyone gets here. A quick check of my calendar shows one appointment, Andrea Sommerfield. She has been in to talk to my boss, Leon Martinez, a couple of times already. I remember seeing her name on the calendar. This will be my first meeting with her. I pull her notes from the miscellaneous files in the filing room. Husband is a prominent plastic surgeon, Elliott Sommerfield. In fact, we handled his first divorce – or rather, represented his first wife in their divorce. He was an ass. This ought to be interesting.

Back in my office, I pull my honey gold hair into a pony tail, winding a scrunchie around it as I peruse the notes. Andrea, 33, married Elliott five years ago. They have no children. Honeymoon in Bora Bora.

I bet she has never had to worry about a cracking shower floor. I wish that little catastrophe hadn't come to mind because now my stomach's dropped again and I am tired of being stressed out.

Rubbing my temples, I go back to the notes. Big house, lots of assets, little debt. Dr. Sommerfield has a thriving practice. Andrea hasn't worked in five years. No request for alimony. Odd. He walked out one morning with no warning. Friends, wealthy, well-connected friends, helped him. She was just served with divorce papers.

Skimming the notes, I read Mrs. Sommerfield was diagnosed as an alcoholic three years ago. Husband sent her to a treatment center in Minnesota, a place famous for treating celebrities and politicians. She admits to anorexia, has impulse control issues, trichotillomania. *What is that?* I look it up on the internet. Pulling one's hair out in times of stress... She wears a wig. Some physical abuse – he poured champagne over her head on their honeymoon and told her she was a cold bitch. During a trip to San Diego, he shoved her into an elevator. He slapped her around in a Chicago hotel and called her vile names. *I bet she didn't know what she was getting into. Rich, older guy must have been pretty flattering. It was supposed to have been a fairytale. Only now, he wants to be rid of her.*

My forgotten coffee's cold, so I wander to the kitchen and get a fresh cup. This new file intrigues me. A case like this hasn't come to me in a while. And I've never heard of trichotillomania. *Who pulls their hair out on purpose?* Can't imagine how that must feel. The internet says there is no medication for it and no cure. Leon's notes say Mrs. Sommerfield is in counseling. I make a note to get the name of her counselor. Better get the records from the treatment center too.

I move back to the assets. There is a pricey marital home involved. His practice, his building, his rentals, his stock accounts, everything seems to be his. She came into the marriage with a car and a small retirement from her last employment. Dr. Sommerfield made an offer after he left her apparently, $500,000, a car and the furnishings in the house. Obviously, Leon wants to do better. Besides, I bet he wants the chance to kick Elliott Sommerfield's ass like he did in the first divorce.

Kelly, our receptionist, slams the outside door. "Good morning," she calls out and clumps up to her office. Slowly, the office comes to life. My best friend, Beth, arrives, peeling off her scarf. She waves and walks on to her office. The phones start ringing and I hear people talking, but I am buried in a new case.

We represented Jackie Sommerfield, the first wife, probably twelve or so years ago. It was an ugly divorce. Ugly and drawn out, as in a four-year divorce. That case became a landmark for my boss, who won huge awards for wronged wives. In her case, Jackie wound up with a significant portion of the assets, $8,000 a month until death or remarriage, and $2,000 a month in child support.

While it was a huge victory for Jackie and a fine plume in Leon's cap, Dr. Sommerfield felt raped. He swore if he could kill Leon Martinez, he would. That case is also the reason my boss has represented so many of the soon-to-be ex-wives of men who can afford to drop that kind of change (and some wives who think they should be able to).

My pulse is beginning to beat a little faster. This is a case I can sink my teeth into, and I could use one of those. Things have gotten a little stale around the old law emporium of late: small files, clients with no assets and no money, boring stuff. This may be just what I need to get my head back into it. Another pull on my coffee cup and I drop back into to the notes.

CHAPTER FOUR

Julie

D*ING, ding, DING.* The green screen on my phone lights up.

"Hey baby. It's me. Rodney. Talk to me."

I can't talk to you. Just forget about it.

"Can't. Thought about you all night last night. Still love me?"

Leave me alone. I have to think.

"You love me. You know it. Do you like the flowers?"

I can't say anything right now.

"Why? Because you're Mommy's little baby living in her basement and you're scared? I want to talk about Alex."

What about him?

"He's my son too and you froze me out. I let you come back after a year and this is what I get?"

What? Are you sure you're not bi-polar or something?

"I want to see my son."

Let me think.

"I want to see my son, Jules. You can't keep him from me. I know my rights."

I can't talk right now.

"Oh sure. You're scared of your mommy. Get some balls, Jules. What'll she do to you? Lock you in your room, I mean, basement?"

Stop it. We have court next week. Let's just see what happens then.

"I want to see my son, NOW. You're not being fair. Angela's got a job interview tomorrow. We need to talk."

I'm going to work. Leave me alone.

4:17 p.m. *DING, ding, DING.*
Ack.

"Baby, talk to me. You know you want to."

I'm at work. Stop this. We can't talk now.

"Just had to tell you I think you're beautiful."

Now I know you're bi-polar.

"Why?"

Because you come on so heavy and then you say all this. You don't put someone you love through that. But I guess you wouldn't know that.

"Love you, baby. I think about you all the time."

Gotta go.

6:38 p.m.
DING, ding, DING.

"Jules. Message me back. I want to talk about our son."

7:14 p.m.

"Julie, Julie, Julie, do you love me? Message me back."

7:26 p.m.

"Okay, I won't bother you anymore tonight. Angela will be gone from 1 to 3 tomorrow. I'll be home. Waiting for you. So come by. Talk to me about Alex."

8 p.m.
"Baby, I love you."

Well, that's Rodney. I don't know if I want to talk to him or not. He winds me up so quick. He takes me to the boiling point in so many ways.

I click the phone off and slap it next to my alarm clock.

What a pain in the ass. I want Rodney but I don't want Rodney. I love Rodney but in all reality, I can live without him. Rodney fucking excites me. On the other hand, he drags me down, makes me want to drown myself. He's the father of my son, and I did everything I did with Rodney because I wanted to, and Alex was the result. But I feel empty, no purpose. *What is it I really want?*

I called Leon's paralegal, Claudine, this afternoon. She wants me to bring the phone by so she can take the texts from it. God, I hate talking to her. She is, like, so I do not know, sort of like my mother in a way. She tries to be nice to me, but I can tell she thinks I am a stupid little kid. Anyway, what would she know? I wonder how often she gets laid, stupid cow. She told me not to react to Rodney but, well, he is Alex's father and when we were together, we made plans for a long life together and I can't just throw all that away, just like that.

I have to be careful too because if Renae and Mark found out I have this phone, they'd be all up in my business. I could send him one message back.

* * *

It's a little after 1 p.m. the next day. I pull my silver Tracker into Rodney's driveway, heart thumping. Angela's Thunderbird is nowhere in sight, thank God. Rodney is coming out of the house. He's so tall. I hope Alex turns out to be tall.

Today is one of those blazing, clear winter days in the Ozarks. Brilliant blue skies and cold, harsh sunlight. The trees are denuded of leaves, except for the oaks, which never seem to lose their leaves. They just go brown.

It's cold even in the bright sunlight. I'm shivering in the car. Rodney walks to the driver's side and I roll down my window.

"Get in," I say. "We can talk in here."

He gets in, all six-foot three-inches of him, folding and unfolding his legs in my little compact Tracker. He leans over to kiss me and I kiss him back.

"Happy to see me?" he says.

God, it is always all about him. But the fact is, I am happy to see him. I was nervous about this because I hadn't seen him in two months and he might not think I'm so cute any more.

"I guess," I say, hands in my lap. "You wanted to talk about Alex."

"Yeah, where is he?"

Alex is strapped into his car seat in the back.

"I want to hold him," Rodney says upon seeing his son for the first time, ever. He reaches back to undo Alex's buckles and strap and I grab his arm.

"No," I say. "No. Leave him there. You threatened to take him away from me once. Just leave him in the seat."

Amazingly, Rodney does as I say, but he looks at Alex for a long time. "He looks like me," he finally says. "And a little like you."

We talk about my expectations for him to pay some support, buy some diapers once in a while, and be a decent dad, even though he doesn't get to see Alex as much as he wants.

"I only brought him this one time so you could see him, but I can't guarantee I'll do it again," I say.

The court procedure is just more than I understand right now, and why he filed the case to begin with I can't say, except to keep turmoil between him and me, Angela and him, Angela and me, him and my parents. All of the shit going full-tilt. He says he cannot pay support right now. Angela is at a job interview and his job is part-time. Maybe he's making excuses. I'm in the restaurant world too and I understand down sales and few hours. It doesn't matter though. Rodney should do the right thing by Alex.

"He's your son too," I say. "You have a responsibility."

"He's my son but I have to pay support and I don't get to see him? That's bullshit, Julie. You know that's bullshit."

"Well, that's the way it has to be right now. You screwed things up by threatening me and threatening him. You're the one who filed the case. You fucked everything up, Rodney."

"No, that's bullshit. You come around here with this crap and expect me to take that? I got custody of my other boys. I can do it again, Julie. Think about that. Angela's a great mom."

"Oh, don't throw that in my face, Rodney. You're full of shit. I gotta go." I start my Tracker. Pissed. "You need to get out. We clearly have nothing more to say."

He gets out and I start to back my car up but, well, Angela's Thunderbird appears behind me in the driveway. I start to back out and she pulls up so close to me, it would be impossible to drive past her without scratching my car all the way down the side. Rodney jumps back in my car and slams the door shut. Angela rolls her window down.

"Bitch," Angela shouts from inside her car, her black curls swinging. "You got a problem, bitch. You need to stay away from my husband."

"Angela, we were just talking about Alex. That's all, I swear." I so wish Rodney wasn't sitting in my front seat.

"You got a fuckin' problem, bitch. You lyin' bitch. All I got to say to you is stay away from my husband."

"I'm not here for your husband. Rodney, get out of my car. *Get out.*"

In an instant, Angela is out of her car, leaving the driver's side door hanging like a sloppy smile. She lunges through my car window and reaches for my hair. She is screaming and so am I. She grabs and pulls my hair and comes in with her other fist. *Ow.*

All I want is to get out of here with my son. I grab for her hands, uncurling her grip on my hair. Winter sunlight glares on my windshield and I can't see much, but what I can see is Rodney jumping out of my car, rounding the front end, climbing into the Thunderbird. Alex lets out a wail and then whimpers. Angela gives my hair one last jerk and gets back in her car. She backs up and speeds off. Holding my injured scalp, I jam my car into gear and drive, staring through a streaky windshield, bright sunlight searing my eyes.

It's the ugliest thing I've ever seen.

Fuck. *What in the shit happened? Did I ask for this?* What a bitch. What a fucking bitch.

CHAPTER FIVE

Claudine

Quiet tonight. I am home alone in my kitchen. Keri, my irrepressible sixteen year-old, has gone out. Again. She's with that Justin fellow who she thinks she is in love with but I wonder – well, I was sixteen once and I remember young love with her father. Watching her skip down the sidewalk and fold herself into Justin's little car, I whisper, "Be careful, my love, just be careful." Keri's so young. Her whole life is ahead of her and I am more than a little envious.

Left alone to unpack our groceries, I empty a new coffee blend into my coffee jar, inhaling the fresh aroma. It smells deep and rich and moist, like the earth itself. Let's see what this one's called anyway. Supreme Blend, South African and Columbian, rich, savory, dark. Oh yeah, I can attest to that already. I should get a newspaper and sit in front of the windows at the breakfast nook and drink my coffee in the morning, every morning maybe.

Sure I will. I will sit in my breakfast nook and read

the paper and drink exotic coffee blends and smile at the walls. I'll do that – either before or after I've sunk into the crying jag I've had nearly every morning since the divorce. It is debilitating. I don't want to grieve this way anymore but it seems out of my control. Why did Jim leave me? Oh yeah, because I am too controlling and too independent and I wreck his glorious sense of humor, and I don't applaud him when he acts like an eight year-old. Well, maybe I could have laughed a little bit more but maybe he just didn't seem too damn funny at the time. Misunderstandings. People growing up, moving forward at different speeds. *We were not so far apart though, were we?* Maybe it was me who misunderstood.

I turn and begin putting away the rest of the groceries, which are not much. Two steaks, which I bought thinking Keri and I might have a nice mother-daughter supper in the kitchen where we would laugh and talk and stir up good memories. But since she is out with her boyfriend, it will have to be another time. I put the steaks in the freezer and hope it won't be too long. She is always busy these days. Okay, well, I have some bacon. If I had lettuce and tomato – wait, no tomato. And the only lettuce is that shredded stuff you put on tacos. How about a bowl of cereal? Not crazy about that either, so I put the Honey Nut Crunches of Oats away.

Milk, eggs, chicken breasts, pre-baked baked potatoes. Well, I do have the old standby, peanut butter. Creamy, not crunchy. Jim always liked the crunchy and since his exit, I've turned back to creamy. Oh god, I wish I hadn't thought of that because right behind the new jar of creamy peanut butter, sits a half-eaten jar of crunchy. For crying out loud. I lean against the counter with both hands and stare at it, gritting my teeth. *Dammit, what are you still doing in my kitchen cabinet?* "You asshole," I whisper, pulling it out and chucking it with both hands into the trash can. Hopefully, Keri will not notice that.

The cracked shower pan is still on my mind. Remodeling the bathroom is one of those projects Jim and I put off until we could decide just exactly what we wanted, and thus, it never got done. And now, here I am stuck with it. How do people do it? How do people make ends meet on a limited income, in my case as a legal assistant in a small law firm? How do they live? My mind drifts back to Andrea Sommerfield, twelve years younger than me and a whole lot better off. Unless you count the fact that her wealthy husband is divorcing her. But the guy's a jerk and she is so nice and so pretty and, well, she would be a happier woman if she would just forget about him altogether. I can tell she will have trouble with that because she relates everything in life back to him somehow.

It was like that today in Leon's office, with Andrea sitting oh-so-prettily across from his big desk, her in the big leather chair, wearing her pink sweat suit, pearls and perfect makeup. She looked every bit like the young trophy wife.

You could have any man you fancy, I thought, watching her. *Why are you so enamored with this asshole, this prick, abuser, this nonsense boy?* I uncrossed and re-crossed my legs, jerked my skirt around and adjusted my notepad. She irritates me and I don't like the feeling.

"I took Elliott his mail today, to his office, and I put a plastic tub of beef stew, that's his favorite, in there with his mail. Sometimes I put his favorite candy in with his mail or something, you know, just to be nice. I can't believe I don't have any ill-will toward him. I mean, I should, but I don't. I guess it is God. Has to be. I just really feel His presence all around me and I'm at such peace, whatever happens," Andrea says.

I sat, taking notes. Leon stared at Andrea. In fact, he

seemed to be really, *really* staring. His black eyes were intense. Without looking away, Leon adjusted his god-awful tie, which matched nothing he wore, by the way. This movement meant he'd like to fire a boulder at somebody, but only people who know Leon well would know that.

"But, why would you do that?" he says.

"Do what?" Andrea asks, totally innocent or maybe just stupid, I'm not sure.

"Why would you take him food and candy? Why not just drop his mail off and leave?"

Andrea laughed. I wondered what was so damn funny. Hell would freeze over before I'd run by to deliver Jim any food or candy, or crunchy peanut butter. In fact, the memory of the bonfire I made in the fire pit out back when I burnt the clothing he left behind warms me just a little. Well, it was a nice fire, but I guess Andrea didn't have a thing for expressing herself through gasoline and matches.

"Well, I don't know," Andrea says. "It's just my faith. It's just really strong right now. And I was raised in the UK with heavy British influence and I think that's why I feel so liberated in this thing. I mean, Americans, no offense, are a little narrower than the British. We can be friends, even if we're not married any longer. I mean, that's the civilized thing, isn't it?"

"Sure," Leon says and I doubt he means it. Leon just might say "sure" to end a conversation he does not understand. Not that Leon is stupid. Oh no, not at all. Leon is damn brilliant. He rivals God. Leon is just, well, a little insensitive maybe? Condescending? Something.

As for the nuances of marriage, Leon was married and divorced long, long ago. So long ago he probably can't remember when it happened. I know he has an adult daughter living somewhere in southern California and she calls frequently asking for money. Leon always obliges, so far as I know.

"Who did you say your counselor was again?" he asks Andrea. She tells him. He looks over at me as if he just realized I am also in the room. "See if you can get a release so I can talk to her," he says and then, just as instantly, he forgets me. I nod and write it down. Release. Okay, sure.

"What's this thing, this trick-o-" he says.

"Trichotillomania," she says patiently. He repeats it twice but he gets it wrong both times. She says it again.

"What is that?"

"I pull my hair when I'm stressed. You should see my head. It's like a boy's buzz cut right now."

"Has Dr. Sommerfield ever seen you with your wig off?"

"Well, yes. It was right after I lost my job with the real estate company. He took me to Vermont, just as a forget-about-it all weekend and it was the nicest time we had, I think. We stayed at a Ramada and I had an entire suite to myself and he slept on a rollaway cot out in the living area. That evening, we were talking by the fire and drinking wine and we were kissing and I just kept moving my head this way and that because he was pulling on my wig and I was afraid he'd pull it off. I mean, I think he knew I wore a wig, but he'd just never said anything and so anyway, he finally asked me to take it off. I protested and he begged and I finally took it off and that's when he told me he loved me for the first time. I think that's when I fell in love with him." She smiles at Leon as if that explains everything about the entire universe, and I am torn between throwing up and crying.

No matter. Leon leans back in his chair and stares at the ceiling for a long minute while Andrea and I remain poised in our seats, waiting, afraid to breathe. Finally, Leon brings his gaze down from the ceiling and rubs his hands over his eyes.

"See, I think your traditionalist thinking is going to harm you in this divorce in the long run," he says. Crashing silence. Two pair of eyes, mine and hers, lock in on him but he clearly has nothing else he wishes to impart.

The god has spoken. Silly naves, putrid peons, pick up your staves and march on.

Giving Andrea a sideways glance, I wonder if she's as lost as I am. I don't recall much of the rest of that conversation with Leon and Andrea, except I spent the next hour after Leon dismissed both of us in the conference room with Andrea, talking about her income and expenses and what in the heck Leon meant about her traditionalist thinking being the culprit in this thing. I've known Leon for seventeen years but I can't always tell where he's coming from.

"That's just Leon," I finally say. "He says things sometimes that nobody can decipher. It's just the way he works."

Andrea's blue eyes narrow and she nods at me but she clearly does not understand what I just said. Like I can explain Leon? Nobody can explain Leon, which is the beauty of working for him.

What little instruction does come from Leon is rambled and layered with nebulous information, which keeps me sorting and categorizing for hours. Leon keeps a lot of information I could really use as his paralegal to himself, which often puts me at a disadvantage. How we've managed to work together all these years I will never understand. To look at him, physically, he resembles a tornado victim, rumpled, disheveled, mismatched clothes. Once or twice, a client, thinking Leon would appear in a thousand dollar suit, tie and impeccable shoes, gasped at me. "*This* is Leon Martinez? The great Leon Martinez? I would have thought he would have presented differently." I try to reassure people they're not paying for his wardrobe, just his mind. I know he's brilliant. He's the king of domestic cases after all. I just wish I could get more from him so that I could do my job better. I wish Leon would share, allow me some of the power of information.

But after that confusing office conference, Andrea finally pulls her sunglasses down from her unmoving hairdo over her eyes, wiggles her fingers at me and drifts through the heavy glass doors and into the sunlight beyond. I see her hop into her BMW and back out of the lot.

I wish life was better for Andrea. I wish she'd met a man who loved her unconditionally, and I wished she'd married that man, not Elliott Sommerfield.

It was a hard day at the office, I have to say. Staring down at the cast-off peanut butter jar though, I feel a little jubilation, some kind of victory. Just for a minute.

Noise. Unbidden noise, the beginning chords of "Layla." Startled, I'm jarred back to reality by my cell phone. Jim's name and number light up the screen. Jim, my ex-husband, now the husband of Lynn, who he left me for eight months ago. I suppose I should just let it go to voicemail but, I don't.

"Hey, Claudine," Jim says.

"Hey," I say. *Jerk.* Okay, I should be past that and most of the time I am. But today, just the sound of his voice, like the discovery of the peanut butter jar, rankles me.

"I'm just calling to let you know I'll be having dinner with Keri tomorrow night. Is that okay with you?"

Oh boy. Is that okay with me? *Damn you, Jim.* I clear my throat.

"Well, I'm sure it is. Um, just one question –"

"No, she won't be there. It'll just be Keri and me.

Father and daughter, like in the regular life." I sense the irritation in his voice but still, it has only been eight months and although I now have to get used to it because they are married, I still do not like the idea of Jim exposing Keri to Lynn. Not yet. Could he not have grieved over the death of our marriage just a little longer? Oh wait – Lynn is the reason our marriage is over. Not that anything happens in a vacuum, but I will say Jim cheating on me and leaving me for the woman he cheated on me with, well, that just had never occurred to me. Not a possibility. Not with me and Jim. We were solid. I didn't see any signs of infidelity. Magazine articles I've read always say the wife knows when her husband begins to stray. Maybe not directly, but in the back of her mind she knows. The wife recognizes the indicators, except I didn't. Did other people know? And if other people knew, why didn't they tell me? How did I miss all that?

There were times when Jim was late coming home from work, but as a contractor, I expected that and I was used to it. He was never away for days at a time. No surreptitious phone calls. I never smelled or saw anything on his clothes when I sorted them for the wash. Jim's mannerisms really didn't change that much.

Oh, we made love a little less than we used to, but I assumed it was because we were tired a lot. We were active, busy, raising a child. I didn't assume it was because he was making love with someone else.

But yet, I should have realized. The night we fought, that awful night he threw me on the couch face first, I should have known none of it was about me. It was about him and his choices. Or the choices he would make soon. After Jim told me about Lynn and left, I laid on that same couch for three days solid, watching Food Network and crying. The revelation was tremendously painful and made me physically sick. I was worthless. I blamed myself. I blamed him. I blamed Lynn. Mostly Lynn.

"Oh," I say. "Well, yeah, that was my question."

"You've got to get over this sooner or later, Claudine," Jim says. "It's not all Lynn's fault."

I shut my eyes to block out sudden tears. *Sooner or later*, as if we'd simply exchanged some unfortunate words. Not all Lynn's fault. *Well, then who was at fault anyway?* We were married, for Christ's sake. What did that mean? His total lack of responsibility in what happened is appalling.

We were Jim and Claudine, in love forever. We were invincible. I believed it. It was so.

Get a hold of yourself, don't cry.

"Okay, Jim. What time are you picking Keri up?" Leaning against the kitchen counter, I feel the pressure of the tile against my tailbone.

"About six. She already knows. We've talked this week." Oh, so clandestine talks also. I shake my head. *This is his daughter, for crying out loud, get a grip*.

"Okay, that's fine then."

"Okay. Well, I'll let you go. Have a good evening, Claudine."

I stare at my phone screen. I should be over this. I have no choice but to be over this. He is gone and remarried, and he did it the weekend after the divorce was final. I wipe my nose on the back of my hand and wander into the living room. It still feels so damn raw.

Some music is in order. Keb Mo. Good choice. I switch it on and go through the rest of my CDs. Melissa Etheridge. Oh my God, I love her music but tonight, tonight I'd sob my heart bare if I listened to her. I could not take Melissa tonight. Okay, so Keb Mo and some Adele will have to do.

Keri's still not home. Crazy, my daughter has more of a social life than I do. There's something wrong about that. Seems like the girl's gone nearly every night for something or other while old Mom sits at home, watching TV or listening to music or wondering how this case will go or that one. Andrea Sommerfield seems like such a sweet girl, even though she is hardly a girl.

I started emailing Andrea after Leon assigned me to her case when I needed information from her. So much easier and faster to do it that way, right? She responded immediately. If not for this lawsuit, we could be very good friends, I think. Anyway, I muse back to Leon asking her about her stay at the treatment center earlier today.

"Oh," she said. "That happened three years ago. Elliott had isolated me to the degree that I just didn't go anywhere. I sat in the house and waited for him to call, which he seldom did, or waited for him to come home, which was often late. He didn't want me to work, saying my availability for him and his children, when we had them with us, was more valuable than what I could make at any job, which would be a pittance. Anyway, I was becoming more and more depressed and feeling more and more isolated because everyone I knew worked during the day. I had no one and nothing to do. So I discussed this with him many times and his answer was always the same. He felt I'd be more valuable at home. And, there was work and there was golf and flying lessons and this and that and well, I drank and I took all those pills as a cry for attention from my husband."

Leon is listening. I am writing furiously.

"And then, what?" Leon says.

"And then, I was in intensive care for three days, mostly in a coma. My parents were there the whole time. I didn't know this at the time. They told me later but, Elliott and Matt Lutjens were conferencing the whole time about me being schizophrenic and such and when I got out of the hospital. Elliott took my car keys and my credit cards and everything I had, basically. He confiscated my passport and told me we were going to the treatment center and there was no debate. I was being checked in that day. So, I went, did the twenty-eight day program and came back. That's pretty much it."

"I need to see your treatment records. Claudine, make sure we get those records." He turns back to Andrea. "What has he offered you so far?"

"Five hundred thousand, my car, some of the furnishings in the house."

Leon is scratching furiously on his notepad. Then, he drops his pen on the pad and stares at Andrea.

"All right. See ya later." He extends his hand and it is over.

Dumbfounded, but dismissed anyway, Andrea and I get up and leave.

Why am I thinking of case work on my time off anyway? The answer to that question is easy. I do not have a life. Other people have lives. I know they do. Other people are going out to dinner or theater tonight, or a basketball game or just having drinks with friends. I used to be one of those people, but lately, I am doing none of that. Other concerns are crowing my mind, like a cracked shower. I have a cracked shower and a whole new dilemma about making something right.

The CDs switch out. I'm sitting on the floor with my wine glass, leaning against the edge of my sofa. Keb Mo ends and Adele begins letting her heart fall. God, I wish I still had a husband. I've lost my insulation from the world and it's scary. I have no sounding board now, no buffer, nobody standing between me and what-can-happen. And besides that, we were happy. We really were, or at least so far as I knew. But now, I am on my own, being a big girl. *So, big girl, what in hell are you going to do about that damn shower?*

CHAPTER SIX

Julie

Yay Team Julie, you fucked up again. My mom and Mark accepted service of a subpoena and petition on my behalf this afternoon while I was at work. Angela is suing me for assault. She says I broke her nose. Hell, I don't remember touching her. Renae and Mark are pissed. So am I. *Damn Angela.* Why did she have to open this can of worms anyway? Thanks to her, I am gonna be put through hours and hours of explaining and more questioning and more explaining and more rules. Maybe Rodney is right. Maybe I am just a scared little rabbit, living in Mommy's basement. Renae, not one to take anything sitting down, has taken charge once again. The other day, we went to see Leon Martinez, my attorney on this paternity suit Rodney filed.

"Why, tell me why, would you deliberately put yourself back into a situation that has caused you and your family so much turmoil?" Leon asks me. I clamp my lips shut. Old news, dude. I've heard it all before and, quite frankly, I'm uncertain why he's talking to me this way in the first place. Claudine is in the corner, taking notes, as usual. She is not looking at me, which makes me wonder what she's thinking.

Leon asks me again. "I mean, why? Why would you do that?"

I say nothing and stare at his eyebrows. Renae speaks first. "No one is more disappointed in Julie than her stepfather and me, Leon. This is really quite upsetting to us, that she would have contact with him and not tell us and then this whole incident with Angela. It's just very, very upsetting to the household."

"I understand that," Leon says. "I'd be upset too. I mean, really, if my daughter, who is just a little bit older than you, pulled this crap, I'd be a whole lot upset. You have to admit, Julie, this is not, this is *not*, exercising good judgment."

"I know this whole thing is my fault," I say, anything to get them off my back. "I made the decision to see Rodney and to let him see Alex. That was all I thought it was going to be. And then Angela came home and you-know-what hit the fan." I shrug. *Don't they get it?*

"I'll say it hit the fan. I mean, you have to know this woman hates you and here you are, sitting in her driveway with her husband in your car? That is just not smart."

I wish he would stop. I'll hear it for sure when I get home and it won't end until it ends. *Crap.*

"When Rodney and I were together, we used to talk about how it would be for our son," I say, but Claudine lifts her head from her note pad.

I catch an accusing look from Claudine. That figures. Look at the old hag in the corner, self-righteous cow.

"We have a child together. We planned on a life together." Claudine stares at me and then at Leon and then goes back to staring at her notepad. Her cheeks are flushed. *When was the last time you got a little, Claudine?* Not that it matters. Claudine concentrates on her legal pad.

Leon looks across the table at me. "What you have done is put yourself into the middle of another lawsuit. One you will probably lose, and then what? Have you thought about what happens after that?"

"Not really," I say. "I figure I'll just go on raising my son."

"Okay," Leon says. "Okay. Now, let's talk about court this afternoon. What do you expect?"

Renae speaks up. "We expect that since Rodney will probably have a pretty good income tax refund coming in, he'll waltz in at the last minute with an attorney who will put Julie through hell all over again. He's good at that. And by the way, Leon, I never told you this, but Rodney actually asked me once to hide his son from his ex-wife. We are fearful of what he might do. We use no outside daycare providers so Alex is with family only. We want no chance for Rodney to be able to kidnap him." Renae swells with this information as I stare at the table.

"Have you had anymore contact with him?" Leon asks me.

"No," I say. "None." My expression is sincere anyway.

"She hasn't," Renae says. "I check her cell phone bill every month. I'd know if there was."

Whatever.

Leon looks at me and then looks down at his notepad. "Well, we're going to go in there this afternoon and ask the judge to enter a parenting plan and order some child support. Are you ready?"

"Sure."

"Okay. See ya later."

The hearing was a disaster from start to finish. Rodney was a no-show and the judge was just about ready to enter my parenting plan when Rodney burst into the courtroom, hauling Angela with him. My stomach fell. Rodney argued with the judge. He claimed he got no notice of the hearing and the whole thing was unfair. He was lying, but the judge agreed and scheduled another hearing in a few months. I'm sick of court. I am sick of my parents bugging me and I am sick of my whole life being screwed up. I wish I could disappear.

7:03 p.m.
DING, ding, DING.

Angry words framed in little green balloons on my phone screen.

"Hey, what's your deal? That was a bullshit ambush and you know it."

Leave me alone, Rodney. It was just court.

"If you want, I'll just sign over all my rights to you. Is that what you want?"

Get off my back.

"It's just so not fair. He's my son too."

You don't have to remind me. Goodnight.

"Jules, I could see it in your eyes. You still care."

Stop it, Rodney. Just stop. It is so over.

"I don't think so. I could see it."

What did you think was going to happen?

"I thought the judge would let me see my kid. Without you. In my home, with my wife."

After what you've done? I doubt it.

"That's the pot calling the kettle black. You were there too."

What do you mean?

"You smoked dope while you were pregnant. I remember."

I'm not fighting with you. You know you terrorized

my family and drove my mother nearly out of her mind. You made threats. You stalked all of us. Not just me. You're not right.

"Alex is my son too. Angela would be a fine stepmother."

Don't even go there. Stop playing games.

"No games, sweetheart. Hey, Angela's wanting the phone back."

Fine. I'll take it to my attorney's office. Next week.

"Why next week? Why not tomorrow?"

Because I work all week. Banquets. Gotta go.

8:40 p.m.

"Hey Jules. Just wanted to kiss you goodnight. Consider yourself kissed. Tenderly."

Stop that. It's over. So way over.

"You like it. You know it. Goodnight, baby."

Can I stand up to this? Will I cave? Because I see myself caving to Rodney. Big time.

Maybe if I keep telling Rodney things are over between us, I'll be convinced it is over. Part of me wants it to be over and part of me wishes we had never gotten caught. Part of me wants him so bad it hurts. Part of me wants as far away from him as I can get.

If we were back together though, would anyone leave us alone? Renae? Not a chance. Angela? No way. As much as I would like to lie in his arms again, it can't fucking happen. I used to dream of an idyllic world, where it was just Rodney, me and Alex, and we were happy all the time and nobody bothered us. Of course, that is just a dream.

It is just a dream and it's the dream I have kept alive for a long time, but I wonder now, do I still want that dream? Rodney and me and Alex together forever and ever?

Yawning, I lay down in the bed next to Alex's little bed and somehow, I drift off.

CHAPTER SEVEN

Andrea

Dear Elliott,

I'm sitting here alone this weekend, actually happy you're away for a few days. I'm so hurt and angry with you right now, maybe a bit of space is what we need.

I am your wife, Elliott, your wife. I am the keeper of your heart and soul and you are mine. How ugly it was to hear those words come out of your mouth this morning. Lying back in the tub, I had this vision of slapping my washcloth across your face. Do you really feel good about yourself when you call me a "bitch" and a "whore"? No, not just "whore," "fucking whore". Do you think it makes me want to be intimate with you? You haven't been so cruel. I wanted to say I just really missed that.

I trust all things work together for good for them who love the Lord and are called unto his purpose. I pray for you daily, that your heart will soften toward me and we will be truly husband and wife again because this marriage will never be a marriage otherwise.

A.

I found this letter this morning in Elliott's closet. I think I wrote it last October when Elliott and Matt went to Colorado on a boys' trip. I also found my passport lying on the shelf. What is that doing in there? He gave it back to me after I returned from the treatment center, on the condition he would always be informed if I planned to go anywhere. It seemed like a non-issue at the time so I agreed. Why would I be going anyplace without him anyway?

Thinking back, I should have seen the signs of things to come, but I was so wrapped up in Elliott I just pushed all my misgivings aside. I truly wanted to love him forever.

Our honeymoon. What a fabulous, sexy, beautiful trip that should have been. Who doesn't want to go to a tropical island with the love of their life and have their own little romantic hideaway? I anticipated us getting to know one another in so many intimate ways and really enjoying each another as a couple, a couple who would be in love forever. But the morning after our wedding, when I woke up and spied the pool through the sliding glass doors and Elliott wanted to have sex, I should have known better. I paid for all my hopes and dreams in one day, all day. Elliott grew more surly and sullen as the day rolled on.

I was sitting outside on the patio, smoking a cigarette, drinking a glass of wine, when Elliott stumbled through the patio doors. He was not completely drunk but he had been drinking a bit and he was angry. I remember he had a bottle of champagne, the complimentary bottle from the resort, in one hand. He came around to the front of my chaise lounge and straddled it, bending over into my face, smelling of whiskey and Coke. His eyes, I will never forget his eyes. They were the eyes of a complete stranger, a mad man.

Fear began trickling up my back.

Elliott's cheeks were red and wrinkled, his eyes were bloodshot. I could see I was in trouble.

"You fucking bitch," he said, practically hissing. A little spittle fell from the corner of his mouth onto my bikini top. "You cunt, you whore."

"Elliott, please," I said. "Let's don't do this."

He stood straight, still straddling the chaise and roared at me, unwinding the wire on the bottle. Then, he pulled the cork on the champagne and threw it aside. "You're the coldest woman I ever met, Andrea," he said, and poured the bottle over my head. I jumped to get away and he threw me back against the chaise, his hand around my throat. He dropped the champagne bottle and took my cigarette from my hand and stuffed it into my wine glass.

"See?" he said. "See? If I don't get it from you, I'll get it from someplace else." He lifted himself off of me then and stumbled back into the hut saying, "damned cunt" all the way. Then I cried.

I told Claudine about all of it. Everything. She seems so understanding. I am drawn to something in her. Maybe it is her lack of pretense. Maybe it is just that she is a sincerely nice person. I do not know exactly, cannot put my finger on it just yet. I don't think she is wealthy by any stretch of the imagination but how could she be working for someone else? And even though I am sure Leon Martinez is quite generous, I just do not see the entitlement of the wealthy in Claudine. At any rate, she listened and let me unburden myself with the patience of a saint and told me I would make it. Just hang in there. Keep your chin up. "For someone who's been through so much, you've handled it so well," she said the other day. It is a miracle. That is exactly what it is.

Ironically, Elliott thought our first year together was the best. I thought it was hell. We took several trips that year. The one to San Diego sticks out particularly, not because we experienced such a wonderful, loving connection. Elliott was in a mood first thing that morning. I sensed an episode coming. He planned the trip in advance but at the last minute, something came up at the office and he worked late to get it covered and our trip was in jeopardy. I really would not have minded staying home a few days until the crisis was over, but Elliott insisted we go anyway, as soon as he got the work situation under control. So he hadn't slept much the night before we left and neither had I. He wanted sex. I wanted him to sleep because we had to get up so early to make our flight and he hadn't gotten home until after eleven. Elliott tossed through the night, tense and exasperated. It seems most of our arguments involved sex. I remember lying awake, listening to him mutter, "bitch, fucking bitch" over and over again.

The next morning, Elliott woke up red-eyed and surly. He threw our luggage in the car and demanded I get in so we could get to the airport. All the way through the airport, he pushed, glared and snapped. I apologized behind his back as we rushed through the airport.

Things got so much worse once we got to San Diego. When we arrived at our hotel, he threw me against the wall in the elevator and snarled. "Dammit Andrea, why do you have to make it this way?" He grabbed me by the shoulders and slammed me into the elevator wall.

"Elliott, please, baby," I said, stinging tears in my eyes. "Please, let's just have a good time, okay?" I hated myself for begging. Perhaps the trip could be salvaged. Elliott turned away.

Once we were in our room, Elliott seemed fine. He threw himself across the bed, crossing his ankles, cradled his arms behind his head and, in a perfectly congenial tone, said, "Well, what do you want to do first? Are you hungry? I'm starved."

The rest of our week in San Diego was sweet. Elliott was attentive, good humored and gentle. Although I was receptive on the outside, my insides were churning. Uncertainty, mistrust, a sick feeling I was letting myself be one of those women whose motives were a mystery to me. Those women whose husbands beat them and they stay. They just stay. Could this be me? In five years, ten years, whatever, would I be one of those bitter, used up women, the ones who seem to think they got what they deserved? Every time Elliott said something to me for the rest of our trip, before I responded, I would summon up a prayer. *Just give me the wisdom to answer* was my constant prayer, my constant whisper. *Just give me the wisdom to reply.*

We arrived back in Springfield late in the evening on our last day of vacation. Elliott retired to the family room to watch porn and drink. I went straight to bed and slept until morning, exhausted from my pretense all week. I knew I was a disappointment to him.

As I folded the letter up, ripping it into neat shreds, I remember how it was all such a mistake, the trip. Nothing really changed. Nothing at all.

CHAPTER EIGHT

Claudine

Julie Kruger is on the phone, talking about Rodney texting her over and over again at all hours of the day and night. I'm transfixed by snow drifting past my window and I wish I was home right now, cup of tea in hand, feet to fire.

"And my parents don't know about this phone so I've really got to be careful. There's something else they don't know too."

"What's that, Julie?" Why doesn't this girl just come clean? All these lies she tells, or maybe all these truths she withholds, are not helping her at all. My forehead drops into the palm of my hand. The pleasant dream of hot tea and a warm fire dissipates.

"Rodney threatened to kidnap Alex about six months ago and I never told them. They don't know and I don't want them to know, but I'm telling you so somebody does know just in case anything ever happens."

"This could be a serious threat, Julie. Your parents should know."

"Well, it's not like I think he's actually gonna do anything? It's like, he comes up to my work, like every couple of days and he sits in my station and just watches me. I don't think he even knows what he wants. I think he texts me just to mess with me, just to keep it alive, you know?"

I roll my eyes at the ceiling. Sometimes, this girl seems more like fifteen years old than twenty-three.

"And then all this texting shit. It's really a hassle, you know?"

"I tell you what. I'll talk to Leon about the texting. Since Rodney isn't represented, we don't have anyone to contact but him on that. Leon may want to send a letter." Tapping my fingers on the edge of my desk, I wonder if Leon will want to send a letter. One never knows with Leon. He could direct me to draft some sort of prohibitive pleading. I can see it now: Defendant's Motion to Prohibit Text Messaging from Scumball Plaintiff and Father of Her Child. Oh yeah, one thing about Leon is he can be damned inventive.

"Oh. Well, okay. That's fine, then."

Thankfully, when I talk to Leon, he just wants the conversation over. A letter is all that is required. Will it work? I don't know but at least Rodney's being put on alert.

If Julie would behave better, it'd help too.

When I glance out my window again, the once cozy snow fall seems to have changed into a rock hard acrylic blanket. I'm not sure a hot cup of tea would help at all.

CHAPTER NINE

Claudine

"Claudine," Kelly says over the speaker phone. I raise my head from the Sommerfield financial statements under my nose. I swim back into reality slowly. The tone in Kelly's voice is kind of like, *you're not gonna believe this, you gotta take this call.*

"Mhmm?" I say.

"Angela Moore is on the phone and she wants to talk to you." My eyes immediately hit the phone. No kidding?

"Put her through."

Beep, beep.

"This is Claudine,"

"Hey. This is Angela Moore. My husband is Rodney Moore and you all represent Julie Kruger." Her voice is like gravel on steroids. She coughs. It is a smoker's cough and I get a mental image.

"Yes," I say.

"Well, I just want you all to know I'm calling about your letter and you all need to know basically, when

Rodney's calling this cell phone, he's basically calling his own phone. See, we added Julie to our family plan because she wanted it and that phone belongs to us and I want it back. We keep trying to get it back from her but she refuses. Now I don't care how we do this so long as it's civil, but my husband can come up and get it from you all. Just so long as it's civil."

"Okay. I'll let Leon know about that."

"And you all need to know, this girl has got a problem. She needs to quit responding to my husband. She's got a real problem. She lies, just so you all know. She lies."

"Okay."

"So, I don't care how we do it, we just want the phone back. So long as it's civil."

I hear a long expulsion of air, like a drag on a cigarette.

"All right, I'll see what I can do."

"Whatever. Just do it. Get our phone back from that classless, lowdown little ho." *Click.*

Nice talking to you too, Angela.

Back from lunch, I find a cell phone lying in my chair. Setting it aside, I think about Rodney texting Julie and her agreeing to bring the phone back, which was no small feat on my part. It took a little begging. No doubt we will find a bunch more messages on this thing. I make a note to have Kelly do screen shots of the texts before returning the phone to Rodney. I know she'll love that little project. If it proves to be salacious, Kelly will dig it.

Kelly brings her screen shots of the messages to me, grinning widely. She hands me my reading material for the next hour or so and as I scroll through the messages, I'm astounded. Fourteen messages from Rodney to Julie in less than twenty-four hours. What a sicko, I think at first. But it almost seems to me the three of them, Julie,

Rodney and even Angela, actually enjoy this scummy threesome they created. They seem to be dependent on it. The lawsuit will end, sooner or later, but the convoluted logic of their relationship will continue, probably for the rest of their lives. I can see any one of them nurturing it, egging it on through the years.

What about the little boy? I feel sad for him. He deserves a normal life with a normal parent. I feel sad for Julie's parents too. Driving home from work one day, I happened to pass their house and I saw Julie's stepfather walking in the yard, holding the little boy's hand. The stepfather seemed burdened to me, unnecessarily burdened. I wonder if Julie will ever find the courage to break her bond with Rodney. I think of my own daughter, pretty Keri, with her wavy golden hair and enormous blue eyes. Will she fall for some jerk someday? End up bearing his child and causing herself a brimming pot of misery? Will she make poor decisions? I shudder. I hope my daughter will use good judgment.

The texts are pretty clear. Rodney's initiating them all but Julie responds, every time.

It is no surprise when Rodney shows up in our front lobby, demanding to see me. I ask Kelly to quickly prepare a receipt for the phone. One thing I do not need is him or Angela accusing us of keeping it from him.

"I want my phone," he says and not too kindly. Studying his face, I see no resemblance to the handsome, dark haired man from the internet photo Julie gave to me. So this is Rodney Moore, I muse. The married serial dater, hopeful internet hooker upper, self-described heartthrob. Not so remarkable. To begin with, he is blond with dark roots. His skin is greasy looking. He's tall but not built all that well. This is the man Angela thinks she cannot or will not live without? This same man Julie cannot or will not seem to break away from entirely? Two women can't seem to stand to be without this guy, who impresses me not in the least.

"Of course," I say. "You may have it but I need for you to sign this receipt first."

"It's my phone," he says, snapping. "All I want is my damn phone." But, he grabs the receipt out of my hand and asks for a pen, which I hand to him. He hurriedly scribbles his name and hands the receipt back. I give him the phone. He stomps out the door, clearing his throat like an animal. Nice. *What did Julie see in him to begin with?* Whatever it is that drew these two people together is lost on me.

"Nice guy," Kelly says, watching him roar away in a Thunderbird. "Classy, that one."

"I'll say," I say, heading back to my office. "Ain't he a peach?"

"All the jerks in the universe land here eventually, it seems," Kelly says.

CHAPTER TEN

Andrea

Dear Elliott,

What you need to know is I never, ever doubted you. I love you. You know that.

I was driving down the street today, with my Starbucks vanilla latte in hand, and I felt so extremely thankful for being able to simply stop and pick up anything I wanted. A Starbucks. I'm thankful I can spend $20 on a candle, just because it would smell good in the bathroom. I'm thankful for the expensive sheets we sleep on every night and the personal trainer and all you provide for me. So many women would give their eyes, teeth and more for this lifestyle. So why is it I'm driving past all these little two bedroom houses and feeling envious because the interiors are furnished with love and memories of good times and the possessions are cherished because of love alone? I need more from you, Elliott. That's what I've been trying to tell you, over and over again. When you say I'm obsessive and possessive, it hurts me because you do not see I'm suffering from the worst kind of loneliness. We don't spend enough time *together as husband and wife. You don't talk to me like you used to.*

When I came back from the treatment center, you became so distant, so politely impersonal. I'd failed you. All the misery I endured until I could take no more was of no interest to you. Do you even remember telling Matt in my parents' presence that I was schizophrenic? Do you remember my father confronting you and saying you did not act like a man in love with his wife? You were protecting yourself. Do you remember slamming out of the house in the morning, shouting, "This is not a marriage. This is not what I bargained for." Did you know I waited until that last slam before I hid my face in the pillows and sobbed? Does any of this mean anything to you, Elliott?

We can put our marriage and our life back together. For that, we will need faith. We will need time. But we can do it, I know. Please don't think I doubt you. I can see why you hired Shelby. It's just that she's so pretty I was just a bit insecure for a minute. I didn't mean to accuse you of anything.

Let's work on our union anew.

All my love,

A.

Cleaning out my desk drawers today and I find another letter I wrote to Elliott. I remember when I wrote this one. It was right after our trip to New York City last spring. Another anticipated trip that ended horribly.

You know, I had never been to New York City before except to change planes, but that city fascinated me. My dream was to see it for myself and taste the juxtaposition of cultures and histories and the quintessential busyness, the noise and the smells. It would be a whole new experience for me and I was excited. Elliott and I needed time away. The trip seemed like an answer to my prayer.

Elliott came home from work at lunch, something he never did, and said, "I have a surprise for you." He sounded so giddy. It just took me away.

"Get out, what is it?" I grabbed him around the waist and tipped my head back so I could look into his eyes. He seemed so happy. His eyes were sparkling and he was looking at me. *He was looking at me.* I did not realize at the time that he was not holding me back. I was just so happy to be holding him. And he had a surprise.

"I want you," he said, tapping the end of my nose, "to call and get flights to New York City for – next week."

Jumping up and down, holding his hands, I shrieked. "Are you serious? We're going to New York City?"

"Yeah, baby. New York City," Elliott hollered, just like the hot sauce commercial. It was a moment of excited mayhem. "You and me and New York City, baby." He hugged me then and kissed the top of my head. I was so happy.

New York City, the place I'd dreamed of going to and experiencing like a native. New York City with Elliott. He was so happy that day, I had no idea anything could go wrong.

It started in the airport.

"Look at how you're dressed," Elliott said. He was visibly agitated.

"What's the matter with how I'm dressed?" I asked, looking down at my sweat suit and sneakers.

"The men here are undressing you with their eyes," he said, walking furiously ahead of me.

"Elliott, what are you talking about?" I called, literally running after him in my shapeless pink sweat suit. He finally slowed down as we got to the street, hailing a taxi.

"You're just so – so – provocative, Andrea. Don't you know any better?" He curled his lips in an expression of disgust. I was dumbfounded.

The rest of the day was just plain wrong. We left the Four Seasons and taxied all around Broadway, finally getting out so we could walk around and see the sights. We had tickets for *Mamma Mia*, which I had been aching to see. But my stomach hurt now and I felt at any moment something could happen. Elliott's mood was surly at best. I tried to seem chipper but the beauty of the day was tainted.

He began arguing with me. I said I wanted to stop at a vendor and buy cigarettes. He started with a lecture on how I should not be smoking in the first place. He refused to stop at the store. To compromise, I told him to go on and I would stop at the store and meet him in the room. Finally, he slapped my ticket to the show in my hand and vanished into the throng, leaving me alone on Broadway.

Being alone in an unfamiliar city is not exactly new to me but this city was so intimidating. People pushing and shoving, all trying to get to some unnamed spot as quickly as possible while not spilling their expensive venti lattes down their even more expensive shirts and jackets. Someone pushed by me, shoving my shoulder back without stopping to apologize. I stumbled around a while, trying to get my bearings and finally wound up on the subway.

The greenish glow of the underground lights made me nauseous. And I was hungry, not having eaten all day. *How would I deal with Elliott when I arrived back at the Four Seasons? Would he even be there?* My stomach clenched and unclenched as I ran through all the various possibilities. What if he left the hotel? Somehow, I knew that was not a possibility. What would be his frame of mind? My palms were sweating. I felt cold and hot at the same time. Apprehension roiled in my stomach. What if I just did not return at all? But what would I do? Where would I go? *Come on, Andrea, you're in New York City. What are you thinking? You do not know a soul here.*

I had credit cards. I could go someplace else. But inexplicably, I was drawn back to the Four Seasons, back to Elliott.

Finally, I returned to the vicinity of the hotel. I could see it from my drop-off spot. Putting off the inevitable, I wandered into a Hallmark store and purchased a few greeting cards for friends and family who had not had the luxury of this marvelous trip. Marvelous. Ha. If they only knew. The Hallmark store was next to a bakery so I went in and bought Elliott his favorite desert, a Neapolitan. I walked slowly back to the hotel, dreading every minute. Every footstep led back toward hell.

He was lying across the bed, flipping TV channels, when I came in.

"Where've you been?"

"Just a little sightseeing," I said, trying to smile. "I brought you something."

He unwrapped the Neapolitan and threw it at me. It briefly touched my shoulder before thudding into the wall behind me, pastry and creamy filling sliding down the wall. "Damn you, Andrea." It was all he said as he rolled over on his stomach. I climbed onto the bed then and tried to hold him. I could smell the whiskey. "What kind of life is this anyway?" he mumbled. He rolled a little bit but I managed to hang on.

"Elliott, come on. Let's don't do this. Let's start over again. Okay? I mean, what a fabulous trip in a fabulous city."

He rolled over to face me. Tears were rolling down

his face. "I'm sorry, Andrea. I don't know why I get this way," he said, sobbing.

As I held him in my arms, I said all I could to sooth him. He fell asleep but it was a long time before I did.

The next morning, the mood was no different. Elliott woke up with his jaw clenched, lips pressed in a tight line, stomping from the bed to the shower and back to the bed. We stayed in the room all day long because he refused to leave it. Finally, he decided to keep our reservations at Le Cirque so we showered and changed and taxied to the restaurant.

All through dinner, Elliott became angrier and angrier. I was becoming more and more nervous.

"I just wish I could drink a glass of wine with my wife without her falling off the wagon is all," he said, loud enough that people around us could hear without any effort. Looking around, I could see people at various tables turning their attention in our direction.

"You know I don't drink," I whispered. I reached across the table to take his hand. "Elliott, people are staring at us."

Undaunted, he continued. "Why can't you just take a little? Just a sip? Oh, I forgot. You'll end up at the fucking treatment center again."

"Elliott, stop," I said. "If you don't stop talking to me like this, I'm leaving."

"Well, go then. Just go."

I did.

Miraculously, a taxi was waiting at the curb as I fled the restaurant.

Back at the hotel, I started packing my bags. Elliott got in just as I was walking out the door to the elevator. His face was red with fury. He grabbed my arm. "Where are you going?"

"I'm going home," I said. He was squeezing my arm. "Stop it. Elliott, you're hurting me."

"You are not going anywhere." He tried to pull me back toward the room.

"Stop it."

He was squeezing harder.

At that moment, one of the hotel staff stepped off the elevator and saw us in a clutch. I wrenched free and stepped into the elevator, dragging my bag behind. "Is there trouble?" The fingerprints cn my arm told it all. They were bright pink, almost red. No doubt marks would be left behind.

"Please take the elevator down," I whispered. Elliott attempted to step inside but was stopped by my accidental savior. "Stop there, sir, or I will call hotel security." Glaring at me, Elliott stepped back but that one last crushing insult, that one last verbal cut, came through the doors as they closed. "Fucking bitch."

As I sagged against the elevator wall holding my hand over my mouth, trying to avoid the horrified stare of the elevator man, my stomach wretched but my mind declared my freedom, at least for the time being. My heart sent another prayer, another plea. *When would God hear? Would it ever end?*

CHAPTER ELEVEN

Claudine

Keri is home early. Looking through the living room windows, I see Justin's car parked at the curb for a long moment and then she climbs out, running for the front porch. Justin drives away and I hear the front door slam. I thought they were playing tennis until four and it is now just after two.

"You're home early," I say and then I see the tears. My daughter is panicked. She comes to me and I take her in my arms, shushing and stroking her hair. She is shaking in my arms. For a few minutes, she is my little girl again. I can tell she has scraped something besides her knee this time, though.

"What is it, baby?" I whisper.

"J-J-Justin broke up with me," she says, sobbing. I walk her back to the kitchen and help her up onto one of the counter stools. Her face is flushed and her eyes are bright with tears.

"I'm sorry." It's all I can say. I am thinking of the humiliations of a sixteen-year-old girl, the heartache and the heartbreak and how I would like to damage Justin's face. She's only sixteen and already life is taking shots at the goddess within my daughter. I hurt for her. Somewhere in the back of my mind, I am also thinking about how these things too, shall pass.

She rubs the tears off her cheeks. "He wants to date other girls. He's already asked Amanda Quick out for next weekend."

I nod. Been there, done that. "You mean he gave up your company for Amanda Quick? She's not near as pretty as you and not as smart either," I say, stroking her hand, which is stretched out on the counter. Her fingers are long and lean, like her father's. "Piano playing fingers," he used to say. He paid for four years of lessons and we journeyed out to recital after recital until Keri informed us she was just tired of it. Still looking at her fingers, I am once again startled by the hollow thud in my stomach that reminds me I lost her father.

Keri rolls her eyes at me. "His loss, right?"

I rally.

"Very right. You'll meet other boys and, in time, you won't remember who Justin is, except that you shared a sweet romance once. But you'll be over him and the world will be good again."

"I know. It just hurts. Oh, by the way," she says digging her cell phone out of her pocket. "Dad wants you to call him. He wants to talk to you about the shower."

"What does he know about the shower?" Surprise mingled with irritation flashes through me. Jim wants to talk to me about the shower? What in the world for?

"He saw it the other day when he dropped me off. You were out with Beth someplace. I just forgot to tell you."

"He saw it?" The thought of Jim going up the stairs, seeing my personal things in my bathroom, which once was his bathroom too, feels instantly violating. Not that Jim's never seen my personal things but Jim and I aren't sharing a bathroom anymore – what right does he have to march in there and start snooping around just because the opportunity presented itself? Keri looks sheepish.

"I told him about it and he wanted to take a look at it. I'm sorry, Mom. I didn't think you'd mind, really."

"Oh, it's just sort of an intrusion, that's all," I say.

"Are you gonna call him?"

"No, I am not going to call him."

"Why not? What would it hurt? I mean, you got everything," Keri says and then her face flushes with horrified embarrassment. And shame.

What have I got? I want to shout at her. *What have I got? I got a one-hundred-plus year old house that has something going wrong with it all the time, a mortgage and the memory of a man who did not love me enough to stick it out for the rest of our lives like he promised. I have the vision of him and his new wife in their new brick ranch home in the new, perfect treeless suburb and their perfect life together, free of all bumps and humps. That is what I got.*

And little girl, you don't understand because you've never given your life, heart, body and soul to someone for all time and believed it would last 'til the day you died and you could trust him all the way, come hell or high water.

The urge to slap my daughter across her face almost takes over me but for the fact she is a kid and how would she know anything about life? And she's staring at me like she expects to get slapped. The anger instantly subsides. Now I am the one who feels ashamed.

"Oh Mom, I'm sorry. I shouldn't have said that. I was feeling mean."

"I'm feeling mean right now too," I say. "But it's okay. But –" I say with one finger lifted. "I am not calling him."

"Okay," she says, resigned. Brightening, she says, "I'm famished. What can we eat?"

Teenagers.

"You mean what will I fix you? How about some turkey on that sourdough bread you like so much? A little lettuce, some tomato, blue cheese mayo, slice of pear, Swiss cheese – sound like a deal?"

"Deal," she says and fetches two bottles of Sprite out of the fridge. "Mom, you know, I worry about Dad sometimes. I mean, he's married to her, and they've just bought that house and it's like they have everything they want." This makes me wince but at least I am busy putting two sandwiches together, working my hands right now and darling daughter does not notice. "But it's like he just doesn't have anything. Nothing real. Something's missing. I like our house so much better, even though it's old. I like the flowers you put out in the spring and the big windows and sitting on the front porch. I like our big trees. They don't have any trees at all where they live. It just doesn't feel right."

Stirring blue cheese crumbles into mayonnaise. Slicing a pear so thin, I could see through it. Heating the pan, buttering the bread, assembling the masterpiece. Throwing it all down, allowing the bread to brown up and get golden brown. I'm happy with these simple acts.

Down on the plate with the sandwich, some chips and a pickle. *Pretty*, I think, as I offer the plate to my daughter, who is eager to eat.

"I know, baby."

I watch her toss her blonde locks over her shoulder, and I wish I could protect her always, give her the best advice for her world to make sense and make the world a better place for her. I wish all this, knowing all I can do is love her and give her what I can, hoping it is enough.

She is so beautiful and so young. Am I enough, do I

know enough, to guide her through the yet unseen times of her life? Oh boy. It's a hard task but I'm her mother. I've been given this and no one else.

It pleases me Keri loves this old house and all its character as much as I do, in spite of its issues. Knowing Jim lives in a cookie cutter subdivision doesn't surprise me. I'd always suspected Lynn would turn her nose up at character-driven homes, being more driven toward commercial properties.

"Having things doesn't necessarily guarantee you'll be happier than anybody else, that's for sure. Your dad made a choice and life is different for him now. He may be happier than it seems to us." Keri's nibbling on the edges of her sandwich, a habit from babyhood. "I like our house too," I say. "I think I like it because so much love went into it."

"Uh huh, me too."

"You're not comfortable with Lynn?" I say.

She makes a face, still chewing. "It's not that she's not nice to me. She's just sort of a cling-on, sort of a weirdo. Dad and I can't have any time to ourselves without her coming around, trying to be a part of it. I think it bugs Dad sometimes. She seems like a phony baloney. Her boys are okay. We play basketball and pool and stuff but I don't know. I think she's trying too hard."

"You don't like her?"

"Not really."

Petty though it is, a little satisfaction washes over me. Just a little and I let myself enjoy the feeling for about ten seconds before I banish it. After all, I am an adult. But later, when Keri wanders off, cell phone to ear, chatting with her friend, Brandy, I do a little fist bump in the air before I clean up our lunch.

The house is quiet again. The only presence here now is mine. My husband, or now ex-husband, remains the invisible specter in the room.

Jim Coulter was the love of my life. Jim and I have known each other since we were ten. I think we knew we would get married someday even back then. We went from riding bikes and exploring the woods around our homes to teaching each other how to drive and dancing to the car radio in the dark and, sometime after that, we moved to seriously making out in our own private spot at his dad's cabin. We believed we knew life for what it was and nothing in our world would ever change, and then we walked hand in hand to the marriage altar. I thought we would be together forever. We wanted the same things out of life. We wanted security, we wanted children. We wanted a home and beautiful things and vacations and pretty pictures of our happy life to show for it all. We loved each other easily. There was never a time I didn't look forward to seeing him at the end of the day and he felt the same about me.

The security part came pretty easily. Jim had a talent for creating it. He opened his own construction company right before we got married. Times were good. Business was heavy. We bought our one hundred-year-old house with the wide front porch the same year. I worked at the law office. We started talking about children almost immediately. We both wanted four or five, at least.

After four years of trying everything and still no baby, we began to wonder if we would ever have children. I was a rhythm method expert and took my temperature hourly. If the temp was right, I would haul Jim to the bedroom, whether we had been there the hour before or not. He was sort of starting to resent that a little, I think. The problem became it wasn't so much fun as it was work for him after a while. I ate eggs every single day because some old woman told me it would increase fertility. No results. I was getting stressed. I was stressing Jim out. One day during a loud and nasty argument in the kitchen, a fight about nothing memorable, he grabbed me and hoisted me to the counter, ripping my panties off from underneath my denim skirt.

The intensity, the drive, was like nothing we had done to each other before. He carried me to a kitchen chair and I straddled him bringing him deep into me, straining and grinding to meet that one blinding moment, grasping his hair in my hand. He was like a madman, crushing my breasts, our sweat popping and sizzling on each other. When the moment of release came, something deep inside of me felt a spiritual connection. I felt the sperm shoot toward the egg and pierce it. I felt creation in my own body. "We did it baby," I whispered, holding his face in my sweaty hands. "We really did, this time."

"I love you," he whispered. Spasms of joy jolted through my body.

The pregnancy was easy. I never felt better in my life. With every month, as my body swelled to hold and nourish the child inside me, Jim told me I was more beautiful than ever. He rubbed my feet nightly. Sweet, sweet man. It seemed a short nine months and in fact, Keri was born five days beyond her due date, but I didn't mind. I was in love with being pregnant, I was in love with my unborn child and I was madly in love with my husband.

Keri was born on the hottest day of the year the next summer. She came quickly, which should have told me something. This child, this mini-goddess, was meant for great things. Jim and I, we loved her. We nurtured her. We taught her everything we knew, as if we really needed to. My daughter tends to just know. And now her heart is broken but only for a minute.

The thought of love reminds me I have not had sex in a very long time and my body is beginning to ask for it in little ways. Like the other day when I stood in line at the grocery store behind a college-age boy and my eyes were directed somehow to his posterior, clad in faded jeans. When he shifted, I noticed tears at the knees, which suddenly seemed completely erotic to me. And then, checking out the mailman. Oh, for crying out loud. The mailman. Well, it's the truth. I have not had a man's hands on me in a long time. I have not had my hands anywhere near a man since before Jim left. With a deep sigh, I clear the table and load the dishwasher.

It's hard to think sometimes. It's hard to feel and equally as hard not to feel. There should be some sort of therapy for what I'm feeling. Not some kind of drippy talk group, either. That might be a silly thought. I cut it off and wipe down my counters and wander to the pantry. Time to change the channel. This vein of thought is getting me nowhere.

Flour, sugar, yeast, cinnamon, brown sugar, I have them all. Milk, egg, warm water. Warm, sweet sugary cinnamon rolls. I could work the dough up in no time and bake them off in the morning.

Before long, I am up to my elbows in flour and sugar. I mix, I knead, feeling the soft pliable dough under my palms, more flour, turn, knead some more, turn, finally pull the dough into my hands and form a ball. My oiled bowl is ready and waiting. I drop my dough ball in and swish it about, roll it over so it's completely covered in oil. Draping a towel over it, I slide it into the oven and set a baking pan with hot water in it below. I am not thinking about Jim. I am not thinking about love or sex or anything remotely romantic. I am not.

I can't lie. I wish so hard nothing had changed. I reflect on how Jim might walk into the kitchen right about now to find out what I am up to, like in the old days. I imagine his warm, strong arms circling my waist and his breath on my neck, his sweet lips touching the back of my neck, coming around – I think about what might happen right after.

Stop it. Stop it right now.

I wish Jim hadn't done what he did. Cold pangs of sorrow punch me in the gut. I wish our marriage hadn't faltered and died. I wish he was still here, my husband, my true love, and I wish I didn't feel so damned empty and useless. I wish I didn't feel so cast away.

I sit at the kitchen table for an hour or so, staring out the French doors at the burgeoning dark, my mind wandering from one random thought to the next. I realize the dough should be ready to roll out and smother in butter, cinnamon, brown sugar and a little flour.

It's mechanical, this work, but I love it. I punch the dough down, pour it out of the bowl onto my floured board and I grab my marble rolling pin (a gift from my husband), and begin to roll the yeasty dough out over the floured board.

I say the work is mechanical, meaning I know it, but it's therapeutic too. I feel my arms and neck relax, easing into the rhythm of rolling the dough, watching the edges to make sure they don't get too thin, smelling the wonderful yeastiness of it. My spirit is rising up. I am becoming enthused about creating this bread gift. My mind is giving in, letting go of sorrow.

Okay, good texture, good thickness. Bring on the butter, slather it on. Drop brown sugar and cinnamon over. I begin rolling the dough up, cementing the edges with water. I am tender but strong with it. I slice the rolls and lay them gently in the greased pans. I'll let this rise until tomorrow morning when I'll bake them off and present them, steaming hot, to my daughter for breakfast.

One thing I know about me: I can provide damned good food to the people I love. It was a given all those years with Jim. It's a given now.

Well, all these declarations are fine, and it makes me happy to linger in the world of dreams for a while but practical matters are surrounding me now. I wish I didn't have to leave my peaceful, gentle fantasy world, but I do.

Keri is sleeping, golden tresses spread across the pillow.

I lay in bed, giving myself a few more minutes in pleasant reverie and make a mental note about baking the cinnamon rolls in the morning. A dog barks somewhere in the distance and I fall asleep.

CHAPTER TWELVE

Julie

Rodney is sitting in my section at Hemingway's again. This is the third day in a row he's shown up at the restaurant. He really doesn't do anything but drink coffee and watch me, but let me tell you, the whole thing is creeping me out. I told him the first day he walked in not to come back. Obviously, he didn't listen.

I stop by his table on my way to the kitchen. "Why do you keep coming in here?"

He shrugs. "Sooner or later, you'll realize what we have together is important. Maybe I'm just hoping for that," he says.

"I want you to leave," I say. "Don't come in here anymore. It's my job." I can't afford to lose my job. What is wrong with him anyway? He doesn't care about anything I care about, that's what's wrong with him. He has no clue.

He slides out of the booth and stands up. "Okay. When can I see my son?" Back to that. I stare hard at him.

"Maybe when you grow up and show a little sense."

He laughs and walks away. My manager, Caroline, walks over.

"Who was that guy? Hasn't he been here a couple times this week?"

"Nobody," I say. "Just a bad memory."

"Oh." She nods wisely. "I got a few of them myself. Chin up, sugar." She pats my shoulder and moves on.

All day, a creepy feeling stalks me like a shadow. I feel like he is in the corner or just around the next station, watching, watching, watching. *He is just messing with your mind, Julie,* I say to myself. *That's all, just messing with your mind. Keep moving on. Just keep moving on.*

When I get off work, I find a dozen roses lying on the hood of my car. It is enough to make me scream. I did gasp a little, but the roses are beautiful. Deep red, just the color I like. There is a card. I pull it out, although I already know what it says. "All my love forever, Rodney." What a dumbass. The roses and the card land in the dumpster behind the restaurant. How dare he mess me up like this. What does he think he's doing? Why is he doing this to me? Why can he not just go away and leave me the hell alone?

I'm not about to tell Renae or Mark about the flowers. I haven't told them Rodney has been hanging out at my work either. Right now they seem pretty calm so there is no reason to get the waters ruffled again. They'd go all berserk on me and insist I get another restraining order, as if we have not had enough of those already. There must have been a dozen between Renae and Mark and Rodney and vice versa. One between Rodney and me. And then there is Angela. I remember how she sat in the hallway at the courthouse when Mark, Renae and I went in to the judge on our restraining orders. I remember how she sat on the bench shouting obscenities at us. He ought to be buying roses for her, not me. I have my doubts that Angela ever gets flowers. No wonder she hates me. No freakin' wonder.

I am playing with Alex in my basement habitat when the door flies open and Renae is on the stairs, her eyes wild and wide. She startles me. This cannot be good.

"Julie," she says. "I want to talk to you." She is holding a dozen blood-red roses in her arms. Oh my God. It cannot be. It just cannot be. I am paralyzed on the floor. What has he done now?

"I found these on the picnic table when I came home from work. I read the card." She is holding it in her other hand, tear stains on her cheeks. "To think he's even coming on our property, uninvited and unasked for."

"Mom, I'm sorry—"

"Is this your only communication with him?"

"I'm not communicating with him at all. He sent me the flowers, remember?"

Renae sits on the stairs, the flowers flop between her knees. She looks at me and I feel pain at her pain. "Angela called me today at work. She told me that Rodney's been coming to your job and the two of you have been communicating. Is that true?"

"He's been coming to my work, yes. To say we've been communicating is false." Alex is clambering up the stairs to Grandma. She picks him up and holds him on her lap. I want him to always be oblivious to what's gone on between Rodney and me. If only that could be so.

"Mummmm." Alex hums.

"How do I know you're telling the truth? This wouldn't be the first time you've kept something from us."

"Look, Mom, I sent him away. I've been telling him

to leave me alone since the first time he came up there. My manager knows. It's not the end of the world. You know, we do have to communicate for Alex's sake. That's the only thing I would talk to him about."

"Julie, please. I feel so much danger from him. Mark and me, *we* feel so much danger from him," she says. "How can we protect this little guy?" She is holding Alex close, almost too close I think. Alex chortles, pulls on her hair.

"How about if I call Leon in the morning? Would that make you feel better?"

Renae stares off into space. "I don't know. Nothing makes any sense. I thought we were going to let this case slide until Rodney got tired of it and it got dismissed. Now we're in so deep – I don't know. Yes. Let's call Leon in the morning." This means she will call Leon in the morning. No way around that.

Leon sees us the next day. Claudine sits in the corner, as usual, with her face over her notepad.

"So, tell me what's going on?" Leon says. He's looking at me but Renae answers. His eyebrow hairs hang over his eyes. Repulsive. He's old. I should remember that.

"We've had a couple of incidents, Leon, and we're alarmed. We just want someone to know what's going on in case something else does occur."

"So, tell me about that, these couple of incidents." Leon is now stretched across the table, head in hands. Renae does not notice. She is too caught up in her story.

"Well–"

"No," Leon says to her and points at me. "You."

"Rodney's been coming to my work, sitting in my section, watching me. That's the first thing. He's been up there three times in the last week."

"And what does he do when he's sitting there?"

"Not much. He watches me, mostly."

"Okay, so he's sitting there watching you and you say he's done this three times in a week?"

"Yes," Renae says. "He's been up there three times this past week." I am staring at Leon. His skin is craggy. I realize he is an old man and he is probably tired of cases like mine. I'm probably just a pain in the ass kid who should know better in his eyes. Leon seems just tired, period.

"Tell Leon about the roses," Renae says.

Leon ignores her. "You say that's the first thing. Okay, what's the second thing?"

"Well, he left a dozen roses on my car yesterday, which I found when I got off work. There was another dozen roses left on our picnic table last night. Angela's been calling my mom at work, telling her Rodney and I have been talking, which we haven't, except I've asked him to go away and leave me alone. He wants to see Alex, or so he says."

"Where did you say he comes and watches you?"

"My job, my work."

"Leon, we didn't know about the first dozen roses, the one on her car. Julie didn't tell us about *that*." Renae's eyebrows are raised to me but she goes on. "I guess we're just at a point where we don't understand what's going on here. I mean, Rodney filed this lawsuit to declare paternity and it was our understanding we would simply let it alone until it just went away. Now we've been in court. We're working on a plan to allow him visitation, which wasn't our intent in the first place. It's just too dangerous, Leon. He will try and take Alex and we'll never get him back. We've all tried so hard to protect him. Now we've asked for a trial setting. We just don't understand, that's all." Renae's voice is rising. I see Claudine look up at Renae. I'm not certain but I think I saw a flash of concern in her eyes. *Oh Claudine, don't get overly involved in Renae's shit.*

Leon straightens in his chair and lays both hands on the table. He looks at Renae for the first time since we have been there. "The judge was going to do that anyway," he said. "Here's what I think we should do. We should ask the court to appoint a guardian ad litem. A guardian will represent your son." He nods at me. "And will protect the better interest of the child. Rodney is not going to take off with him. I mean, really, do you really believe he would do that?" Claudine is staring at Leon as if he is on fire. Now I know what she is thinking.

"Yes, we really believe he would do that," Renae says. "That's our first and foremost concern. You may remember I told you some time ago that Rodney actually came to me and asked me to hide his son from his first wife. The man simply does not know boundaries. He'll do whatever he feels is necessary to further his aims."

"I think there is a danger, yes," I say. Leon has no idea. What if Rodney took Alex away? What would happen to my baby then? I'd never get him back, that much I am sure of. "I think there is a huge danger."

Leon is looking at me. "In my experience, I have seen little of what you're describing to me. I don't believe it's a danger. And if he did take off with Alice–"

"Alex," I say.

"–we would get Alex back. It might take some time but we would get Alex back."

"I understand what you're saying," I say. "It's just a risk I'm not willing to take. Rodney is a proven criminal. He's a thief, he's passed bad checks and all that stuff." I stop just shy of telling Leon about the pot. I do not need to cause another upheaval for Renae, although if she read Rodney's ex parte against me and I am sure she did, she knows.

"I don't believe it's a danger. Now if you do feel in danger, call 911." Leon stands up. "Nice to see you again." He shakes my hand. He shakes Renae's hand.

"Thank you, Leon," Renae says automatically. They walk out together. Claudine is standing up, ready to usher me out.

She smiles at me. "Everything you've said today is documented," she said. "It will all be in the file in case anything comes up that has to be investigated. I know it's not much, but it's all I can do. Take care of yourself," she says. "We'll talk again soon."

"Is he always like that?" I ask. "I don't feel like we got anything accomplished today."

Claudine stops smiling and seems to be choosing her words carefully. "It may not seem like much is happening but he's fully engaged. Don't worry. He can take care of anything."

"He's been practicing a long time," I say.

"Thirty-five years," Claudine says. "He's seen a lot in his career."

"Okay," I head for the door. She isn't going to tell me anything else anyway. "Thank you, Claudine."

"You are welcome. Have a nice day," she says and departs down the hall into her office. I catch up with Renae and Mark at the door, not feeling fully reassured but at least I've talked to someone. It'll all work out, right? Just so Alex is safe. That's all I care about. Just so Rodney never takes him away from me and just so I don't have to worry anymore. That's all I want in the world. Can Leon make that happen? He's all I've got so he better, he just better.

CHAPTER THIRTEEN

Andrea

Oh lord, my paper for Psychology II is due next week. Going back to college has given me a whole new lease on life. It's such a welcome outlet. I need to go and get my books for next semester today though. Cannot forget.

Becoming less financially dependent on Elliott is important to me. I thought if I got my doctorate, I could go to work at any mental health clinic in the area and he would not have to support me any longer. He has been good to pay the mortgage, utilities, insurance, personal trainer and everything else I need every month. He gives me an "allowance" of $1,000 per month for food and sundries, but I am ready to get out from underneath his begrudging benevolence. He's not a saint anyway. He is only doing it because his lawyer, Rita McAllister, told him to. He has to look good in front of the judge. Little by little, I'm learning how these legal things work.

I told Claudine the other day about my classes and my dream of becoming a psychologist. That will come when all of this is behind me. Not surprisingly, Claudine is supportive of my goals and ambitions. I also told her about Elliott's reaction when I told him about my long-range goal.

At first, he was supportive of my taking classes but it was almost as if his thought was, "Let the little woman take all the classes she wants if it makes her happy." I don't think he actually believed I would ever accomplish anything with a degree. When I finally told him I planned to become a psychologist, he sneered. "So they'll call *you* Dr. Sommerfield?"

That was disappointing.

No time for gloomy thoughts. I pick up my bag and cell phone and head out to school to pick up my books. Here it is, a lovely day, warm for the beginning of March, but we didn't have much winter weather this year at all. Some rain, sure but no snow and above normal temperatures most of the season. The forsythia bushes are budding out all over town, yellow blossoms decorating every street I turn. I even see a magnolia tree bursting with blooms on one street. The air is heady and muddied with the perfumed promise of spring.

Heading north on National Avenue, I notice a gold Mercedes in the opposite lane. It is Elliott's good friend, Matt Lutjens, which reminds me of something else. Rumor has it Jackie got married this past weekend. Without thinking, I grab my cell phone and text Matt: "Been to Paris yet?" I set the phone down, giggling. Elliott and Matt had a joke between them when Elliott and I were living together: if Jackie ever remarried, Elliott would send Matt to Paris. Although Rita McAllister had started out with Elliott's divorce case, Matt made an appearance later and the two of them co-counseled. I know Matt will get the joke.

No response. Big deal. I thought it was funny.

My books are available and I push my credit card across to the registrar. She puts my card through but on second thought, I decide I better call Elliott and make sure he knows I'm charging them. Of course, he doesn't answer his phone so I dial the office. I'm put through to his office manager, Susan.

"Hi Susan," I say. "It's Andrea. I just wanted Elliott to know I'm picking up my books for next semester today and I've put them on the credit card." I can see the registrar looking at me, holding my card. I am looking for something to sign but there is nothing.

"Oh Andrea, Dr. Sommerfield has cancelled that card. You won't be able to use it any longer."

What? Cancelled my card? How could he do that? When did he do that?"

"Well, does he want me to pay for these and reimburse me then?" The registrar is still staring at me. A short line has gathered behind me. It's mortifying.

"No, he wants you to sign a voucher with the school and have the school send him the bill. He'll pay it upon receipt." People are shuffling behind me. I feel like a wart in the middle of somebody's face.

"Voucher? Let me check and see if they do that." I put the phone to my shoulder and whisper to the registrar. "My husband would like me to sign a voucher and have you send him the bill. Is that okay?"

The registrar frowns at me. She purses her lips and says, "Well, I guess we'll have to since your card is invalid." She *tsk tsks*.

Back to Susan. "They'll allow me to sign a voucher. Do you know why he wants to do it this way?"

Susan sounds irritated now. "He wants to keep track of his finances, Andrea. Have them send us a bill." She hangs up.

Oh my God. How embarrassing. The registrar hands me a voucher and asks for the pertinent information on my husband. They will send him a bill but I'm curtly advised if he does not pay promptly, the responsibility for the bill will be mine. My books are pushed across the counter to me and the registrar glares self-righteously as I gather them up and excuse myself from the small crowd now gathered behind me.

I treat myself to a vanilla latte at the Starbucks drive-through on my way home. It's a sense of personal satisfaction at having gotten my next semester's materials, although it didn't go down quite as I had hoped. So Elliott's keeping track of his finances is he? I remember his biggest complaint about Jackie was she spent too much money which, considering how much money there was to spend, was not a significant complaint in my book. He once compared my spending habits, which I thought were pretty thrifty, to Jackie's and he found us to be similar. I guess if my spending was his chief complaint, I would be getting off easy.

Both hands on the wheel, I brood on Elliott's complaints about me as I drive home. He will say in court, I suppose, I spend too much money. Truth is I barely spend any money except on my classes. That will be the least of it, I am sure. Elliott will say I am a drug addict, an alcoholic, that I have impulse control problems and pull my hair out. I am not a drug addict. In fact, I stopped taking all the medication my psychologist prescribed for me and I feel fine. No cravings, no withdrawals.

Now, I *am* an alcoholic but, an alcoholic who no longer drinks. I had been drinking to cope with the dark emotions churning through me during my marriage. Since I cut alcohol out of my life, I have become a stronger person, more fulfilled and content. About the hair pulling... Yes, I pull my hair out and I have since I was fifteen, which in most people's books might seem pretty disturbed. I wear a wig and have for forever. I've been told I have a disorder, a psychological disorder and I believe it. And I prefer the wig.

But seriously, the big hulking issue, it's none of those things. It's sex, or the lack of it in Elliott's mind. Elliott is a highly sexual person. When he makes jokes, often his jokes are about sex. When he gets together with his friends, the conversation often goes to sex in one way or another. His opinion of me is I am a cold bitch. I don't remember laughing much at his sexual jokes and innuendoes. Maybe I was just tired of feeling I was the butt of every joke.

Once home, I put my books and my latte down and go in search of Maggie, who no doubt wants out again. I let her out, taking in the sunny patio and the quiet contentment I feel at just being. My phone is ringing. It is Claudine.

"Hi Claudine," I say. "Isn't this a gorgeous day?"

"Indeed, this is fabulous weather, isn't it?" I am instantly cheered.

"What can I do for you?"

"I need to talk to you for just a second. We got a fax a minute ago from Elliott's attorney and I need to ask you a question about it."

"Okay, sure."

"What they are saying is you've been contacting Matt Lutjens on his cell phone."

That seems ludicrous to me. Why would they care?

"Well, yes. Is that a problem?"

"It could be, depending on what you were contacting him for. It's just a little concerning because he was Elliott's attorney last time around and we feel he'll get into this case also, so he probably feels any contact with you is a conflict for him. They also say Matt doesn't want any further contact from you."

Oh. My. God. I feel my face and throat flush hot red. We were friends. All of us were friends, well, still are in my book. Elliott and Matt go back a long, long way, I know. But we were friends. My stomach clenches and starts burning.

"I don't understand. It was a joke, that's all."

"A joke," Claudine says. "Tell me about that."

"See, Elliott and Matt had this arrangement – it was a joke." I stammer. Why do I have to explain this? It was harmless. "Elliott told Matt if Jackie ever remarried, he'd send him to Paris. I heard Jackie got married last weekend. They joked about it all the time. Why is that important?"

"Well, it sounds like it isn't. Look, I understand why you did it, but I wouldn't encourage you to contact Matt again. Things are different now for you and if he does make an appearance for Elliott, that could become an issue, if they want it to, I guess."

"Oh, okay. Well, I won't contact him again." It is puzzling to me, these lines drawn in the sand. I do not have any lines. How naïve of me.

I feel like they're all beating me, Elliott, his friends, the system. I feel foolish and small and humiliated. Elliott will win because Elliott always wins.

Outside the sky is still a pristine blue. The sun still shines brazenly but, somehow, this day doesn't seem quite so bright anymore.

CHAPTER FOURTEEN

Claudine

A letter from Elliott's attorney, Rita McAllister, hits my desk bright and early.

"On another note, Matt Lutjens just contacted me. Apparently, Mrs. Sommerfield has been text messaging him. He does not wish to have any contact with her and we advise this texting to stop."

"That's just bizarre," Leon says when I show him the letter. "Find out what that's about and tell her not to do it anymore."

I call Andrea and read her the contents of the letter. Ten minutes later, she calls me back, her voice muffled in tears.

"Claudine, I just can't believe this. I thought I straightened this out yesterday. I've been sitting here crying ever since you called – in my world, people just don't act like this. So vicious and just mean. I mean, my aunt and uncle are divorced and we still treat him the same as we ever did. I just don't understand this at all."

"I know, I know," I say, not quite sure how to fix

this situation. "Andrea, I just don't want you to cry over this. It's not worth it. Things have changed in your world. Remember, Matt and Elliott are close friends and Matt did represent him the last time around. He may have thought your contact with him was a conflict of interest. Please don't cry about it."

"In my world, Claudine, in my world, people are more civilized than this. That's why when I take Elliott his mail, I always put something a little special in his package, like his favorite candy or one day I made him his favorite beef stew. That's the right way to do things. Not like this."

"I understand. I do, but this is how things will continue to fall out until all of this is behind you. Now, it's a beautiful day. Don't let this mar it for you, okay?"

"Oh, I won't. I tell you what. Every day I'm without Elliott Sommerfield is a good day. I'm better and stronger every day."

We hang up and I take a deep breath. Why is it I feel I am failing these people every single day? I don't feel I have the right words or the talent to get them through what is undoubtedly the hardest, most painful time in their lives. I go in to tell Leon what's transpired.

He laughs. "Well, I can see why she did it and why she thought it was funny. Tell her it's not a big deal. Not a big deal at all."

I walk away.

"It's not a big deal," I tell her later on the phone. "Leon isn't concerned at all so don't worry about it anymore."

"I'm just so embarrassed," she says. "I really didn't think about it. I mean, they send a letter over something I never even thought about? That's absurd."

I agree but that is the way it goes in family law. Everybody seems to be treated as a criminal. I once worked on a case that could not be settled because a pair of water skis became an issue. Or dogs. I remember one case in particular where we had to draft a parenting plan for visitation and custody with a pair of Pomeranians. I shake my head and get back to work but the frustration persists. What about somebody like Julie Kruger? What have I offered her? Nothing except the assurance she has been heard and it has been documented, just in case her worst fears are realized. I can never tell about Leon. Sometimes I have the distinct feeling he is not listening to his clients. Sometimes I feel like he is not even in the same room with them. So I overcompensate. That is what they want, really. Somebody who listens and gives a shit. I am tired. Other people have become a burden. Thank God it is 3:30. Only an hour and a half left in my work day and I can go home.

It finally comes, that magic hour when I pull into my driveway. As I drop my car keys on the hall table, Keri meets me saying, "Dad called. He wants you to call him back."

"Is it about the shower?" I am sitting at the table pulling my shoes off.

"Probably." She looks apologetic.

"I'll get to it. Just not right now. Beth's coming over and we're making margaritas What are you doing tonight?"

"Brandy's coming to get me. A movie probably and burgers or something."

"When will you be home?"

"Mom, I'm not a baby."

I give her a big hug. "But you're my baby, remember that."

She's rolling her eyes at me again. "Okay, probably ten at the latest."

"Better be. It's a school night."

"Yes, Mother," she says and I hear her leaping the stairs two at a time, rushing to her room to primp and try on every outfit in her closet.

The house is quiet now, aside from the low hum of Keri's radio as she gets changed for her date with Brandy. It is quiet enough for me. Beth should be here momentarily. I inspect my CDs. Something to dance to... Ahh, there it is. A collection of funky disco music, appropriately titled "Funk." I shove it in, turn it up and head back to the kitchen just as "Brick House" begins. I am dancing in my kitchen, something I have not done in months, throwing my hands above my head, twirling and stomping to the music, grinding my hips down low. I don't hear Beth come in.

"Hey," she calls to me from across the living room. "Sounds like a party in here"

That's my girl, Beth. Always ready for margarita action. She is carrying a bottle of tequila, 1800 Gold, which she holds up.

"Good girl. Looks like fun," I say, laughing, dancing to her, taking the bottle and we both dance back into the kitchen. It's a night for fun. The glasses are chilled and we dip the rims, first in lime juice then salt. Together, we continue slicing limes, pouring and stirring the pitcher until our drinks are just right. Ice, triple sec, Grand Marnier, tequila, lime juice, splash of lemon, a little sugar, lime wedge. Delicious. Hamburgers are already on the grill just outside the back door. As Beth goes out to turn them, I pour us each a drink, a liberal one. We have earned it. Both of us work at the law firm and both of us are feeling a long week.

Beth comes back in. "Hey, come here. I want to show you something." She takes her margarita glass. "Umm...good."

Obediently, I walk out the back door to the deck, which sticks out past the side of the house.

"What?"

She points down the street. I see nothing, except

trees and bicycles and someone jogging. "Him," she says.

"Him who?"

She elbows me. "Now I know you're not brain dead. That guy, the one over there on the other side of the street. He's coming our way. Look."

I look but all I see is the side and then the back of his head and a pair of nice – hold it, my daughter is still in the house. Brandy happens to be pulling up just at that second.

"Bye, Mom." I hear the door slam. Keri jumps into Brandy's car. I wave and they're off, taillights disappearing into the distance.

"You missed it," Beth says and takes a deep draw from her glass. "Pretty nice ass."

"I'll take your word for it," I say, checking the grill. "I did notice a nice pair of shorts going on by."

"You need to get out more," Beth says. "You need to join the land of the living again. You know, the land where blood flows below the pelvic bone?"

Oh my God, that again. Yes, yes, of course, I would love to have a man, someone who loves me furiously, a good man, a man with humor, a man who knows how to reach a woman physically. Yes, of course.

I miss Jim.

I don't know how to let go completely. Knowing I need to let go doesn't mean I have or can quite yet.

"Well, I haven't really felt like it, you know?" I turn the burgers, even though they don't need to be turned. This is a discussion I am not comfortable with. "My pelvic bone and all areas related thereto seem a little resistant."

"You're over Jim. I can tell. You just don't want to admit it."

Beth's pretty close to the truth. I have been hanging on to heartbreak. I'm slowly easing away from the memory of Jim, the love of my life, the father of my child, the man I promised to spend the rest of my life with, no matter what. *No matter what.* Too bad he did not feel the same way. Ah well, life changes. People change. A day came when I was no longer what Jim wanted or needed and I didn't know it.

Actually, if I took it a step further, maybe I could say what I miss is the Jim I held in my mind and heart. The real Jim was a man, fallible, prone to mistakes, feet of clay. What if I've been holding onto a fantasy all this time?

There's a definite possibility I've hit on the crux of the matter but I don't feel like talking about it right now. More margaritas need to be poured and burgers devoured, after all. So instead I sidestep.

"Maybe," I say. "I guess I need a platter." I walk back through the French doors into my kitchen to retrieve the platter on the counter. All the condiments are set out, lettuce, onion and tomato sliced and assembled for us.

"Look," Beth says. "You know I'm not talking about going out to some bar and grabbing somebody at closing time and bringing him home. I'm not talking about sex. You just need to open your eyes to what's out there. I mean, this gorgeous guy runs past and you don't even see him."

"I saw him," I say. Sex. Oh, well, sex. I see Jim's fingers, long and lean. I have always liked hands. His hands I especially liked. Oh boy. Sex. It blasts into my mind in a million different colored shards. I almost gasp. What if I went to a bar and brought home a victim? A victim to my wanton lusts that have not been satisfied in – okay, not going there. Would it be so wrong to have a commitment-free one-night stand? It is a thought.

"Okay, okay, no more lecture. You're a pretty woman. You're smart, you're talented. You have a great kid. Any man worth anything would be glad to spend time with you. I'm just saying."

"You give me a lot of credit," I say, lifting the burgers off the grill. "I've been missing Jim too long, I'll admit that. I just don't know if I'm ready for the 'getting to know you' stuff again. All that anxiety and then, what if–"

"What if what? What if you meet somebody you really like? It's not the end of the world." Beth's filling both our glasses again. "And if you don't meet somebody you really want to be with, it's not like you have to marry him or anything. It's not that big a deal. Take it from me, I know."

She does know. I think Beth must be the champion of dating and marriage – and remarriage. Her husband, Lee, is currently out of town, which is why we are having a girls margaritas night. He is a great guy. She is a great girl. They are so lucky. For just a second, I wonder if I could be that lucky I was lucky. Okay, enough. Get on with it, will you?

After Beth leaves, I pour the remains of our margarita mixture into my glass and wander out to the porch. The clock says 10:05 and, while it is dark, the darkness is comfortable. It should be a cold winter night but it feels and smells like spring. Here I am, comfortable in my sweatshirt and jeans. I sit back in the old Adirondack chair and curl my legs up, Indian style, sipping my last margarita and watching the street lights. Aside from crickets singing and the occasional hum of a car as it passes, the world is quiet. A cat calls out down the street but all is well. I am feeling pleasantly inebriated and I am glad I am home and don't have to get in my car. Keri will be home soon and I will probably go in.

Beth is right when she says I need to get out more. I need to see what is out there. This woman is *stagnant*.

Nasty word. Nasty feeling.

"Hello," a soft voice says.

I am nearly asleep in my chair and the unexpected greeting makes me jump. Standing on the sidewalk is a man and not just any man. It's the jogger from before. How I know that without seeing his face before I don't know but I know it's him. Black wavy hair frames a tanned, maybe even swarthy, face where warm brown eyes gaze at me. So elegant, he stands easily, hands in his jeans pockets, wearing an oversized brown sweater with a V-neck. I think I see dark hairs at the crux of the V. He is beautiful. Not a word I would typically use to describe a man but beautiful fits this one.

He smiles at me. "I didn't mean to startle you. I am sorry." A hint of an accent, but from where?

I straighten up immediately, suddenly conscious I'm slumped. Funny, I feel no danger. He doesn't seem like a stranger. And yet he is.

"Uh, hello," I say, slightly confused. Where did he come from?

"I admire your house," he says. "Have you lived here long?" Again, where is he from? Not Springfield, Missouri, that is plain enough.

"Thank you. Twenty years, actually," I say.

He raises his hand. "Oh, don't worry. I'm not trying to get in your house. I am not a robber. I live over there—" he waves his hand to the east. "Two blocks down and then a right turn. Third house on left. I moved in last week."

"Oh, I see." I really don't.

"I am sorry. I have not introduced myself. My name is Gabriel Truvionne," he says. He looks a little sheepish and innocent, and still beautiful.

"Claudine. That's my name, Claudine." What a silly thing to say. 'That's my name.' Luckily, he doesn't seem to notice.

"Nice to meet you, Claudine," Gabriel says. Something about the way he says my name is so sensuous and gentle, yet probing. He could massage my soul with that voice. I am not kidding.

Brandy pulls up with Keri in the car. Keri leaps out and dashes up the step. "Hi, Mom." She sees Gabriel Truvionne and stops. "Oh hi," she says.

"Have a nice night?" I ask her as she beats it for the door. Gabriel is still standing on the sidewalk.

"I should go," he says. "It was nice to meet you, Claudine. I hope we meet again." He melts into the shadows. I watch him until he crosses over to the east and vanishes behind the corner house. His stride reminds me of a lion, strong, surefooted and athletic. I like the way his sweater casually drapes over his body, as if it's only purpose is to adorn him. A rag would be a rag but on him, a rag would be magnificent.

"Who was that?" Keri asks, her hand still on the door.

"A new neighbor, apparently. Gabriel Truvionne."

"Huh," she says, opening the door. "Well, I don't think we need him around here."

"He isn't around here," I say laughing. "He just stopped by and said hello, goose."

"I'm just saying," she says and then she giggles. "He's cute."

"Oh really. Well, I didn't notice," I say.

"Sure, Mom. Whatever you say."

I follow her inside.

After Keri goes to bed, I rinse my glass, setting it in the dishwasher. All the doors are locked. Before I go upstairs, I wander through the dark house to the living room and glance down the street, remembering a soft voice in my head and replaying a dark-haired, muscular man loping off into the darkness. Looking to the east, I see nothing but night and street lamps. I wonder which house is his and if I have ever seen it. I know almost all of the houses around here, like characters in a play, but I am not sure which one might be Gabriel's. I wonder if he is still awake. I wonder if there is a light on at his house. Where is that accent from?

Recounting the luxurious, sensual way he said my name, I think it's nice, it's sexy. I fluff my pillow up and drift off to sleep.

CHAPTER FIFTEEN

Andrea

Here I am, the penitent slave, sitting Indian style in the middle of my big bed, waiting on the line for Susan to come back. Finally, after what seems like an eternity, she picks up again.

"Andrea," she says. "Dr. Sommerfield is not willing to pay for the collagen injection. He's adamant. If you really want that done, you will have to fund it yourself."

Oh my God. I imagine her sitting at her desk, simply full of herself, happy to give me the glad news, gloating. Even worse, I imagine Elliott's exasperated huff when she discusses my inquiry with him. And him muttering, "All she does is spend my money."

"What? I mean why not? He's always paid for it in the past." I flop back on the bed, exasperated.

"It's just $400 for a little injection in my bottom lip, that's all. I have it done every few months or whenever I feel like a pick-me-up."

"Dr. Sommerfield is watching his finances closely. He simply will not pay for that. Now as for the garage door–"

"He will pay for that?" It's been broken for a week. What was I supposed to do? Let it go like that?

"He will pay for that. If you'll have the repairman submit the bill to me, I'll make sure it's taken care of." Good soldier, Susan. She's done her duty but she's now weary of the serf. She's ready to get off the phone. I am an interruption in her schedule, an unwanted one at that.

I feel like a beggar. The sooner I am finished with Elliott Sommerfield, the better.

"Okay. Well, thank you, Susan. And tell Elliott thank you too. Oh, Susan?"

"Yes?"

"Did he get the beef stew I sent with his mail?"

"I'm sure he did."

"Well, okay then. Thank you."

What if I took Elliott's initial offer of half a million dollars and my car? What if I did that, just to get this thing over and done? The thing that worries me the most is a big chunk of whatever I end up with going to my attorneys. Leon and his partner, Josie Weiss, are talking about hiring experts, accountants, medical people, all kinds of strategy. Depositions too. If I take the offer and walk away, I could fund the rest of my education. I could buy a modest house and, hopefully, live until I am ready to hang out my shingle and practice psychology. I should talk to Claudine about that. But before I dial the phone, it rings.

It's Claudine. I jerk into a sitting position, alert.

"Hey Andrea," she says.

"Hey Claudine, what's going on now?" I joke, even though I'm not in a joking mood. Collagen or no collagen, my life will go on, but it sure would have been great if Elliott would have okayed the procedure. I don't have the money. These days, I'm barely breaking even, something I think I need to talk to Elliott about. I wonder if he would agree to give me just a little more money per month.

"Oh, I just need to talk to you for a minute about a letter we got this morning. Dr. Sommerfield claims you've hired a personal trainer from your church and since the both of you have been using the same personal trainer, he's not willing to pay for two personal trainers."

"And you need to know what that's about," I say.

"I do. Unfortunately."

"Well, the thing is, that Ben, who has been Elliott's personal trainer and mine too actually, keeps canceling on me. I think he's probably canceled at least one session a week since last summer and I thought I would find somebody to work out with on the days Ben cancels. And this deal came up at my church, well, our church, and when you work it out, it's really a bit cheaper than what Elliott's been paying Ben, so I thought it would be a good deal. It's just for the days that Ben cancels."

"Okay. How would you feel about not using Ben at all and going with your new trainer from the church? I think your husband's deal with this is he doesn't see the need for two personal trainers."

"Oh, and I agree with that." *Be reasonable, Andrea, just be reasonable.* "Yeah, sure. I'll drop Ben if that's what you think I should do and I'll go with the church's personal trainer. I mean, Ben cancels all the time and he's not reliable for me so, yeah, I'll do that."

"Are you okay with us sending a letter back stating that?"

"Sure. There's something else though. I just can't make it on the $1,000 Elliott's been giving me per month. I thought maybe if he'll talk to me. Of course, he hangs up or ignores me altogether when I call, but I thought perhaps I would ask him if he could spare a little more money per month. Why is he only giving me $1,000 anyway?"

"Tell you what. Let me step in quickly with Leon

and ask him. I won't be long."

Half an hour later, the phone rings.

"Hi, Claudine, what've you got for me?"

"Leon says if Elliott's willing to up the ante, that would be okay but he doesn't believe Elliott will."

"So I shouldn't even ask him?"

"You can ask but be prepared to be turned down. That's what Leon's saying."

"I'll give it some thought. And I'll pray about it. That's what I'll do."

"Sounds like a plan. Well, you have a good day, Andrea."

"And you do the same."

If I could only cut loose of this whole thing. The lawsuit plagues me. I forgot to ask Claudine about the $500,000 offer and it also occurs to me I forgot to ask her how long she thinks this will go on. Months? Years, like Elliott's first divorce? A mushroom cloud of negativity sprouts in the back of my mind. It says this thing could go on for a long time and maybe Leon will fuel it to go on for a long time. He enjoyed kicking Elliott's butt the first time around. I remember when Elliott first learned I hired Leon. He said, "Why, Andrea, why did you hire that man knowing how much I hate him?" I believe Elliott is afraid of Leon Martinez. Leon insists Elliott simply hates his guts, but I think there is more to it than that. Elliott knows he's met his match.

I'm nervous. I would like to call someone but I don't know who. I have already called Claudine. She will get tired of me if I call again. I need to get to work on my paper for my psychology class but my concentration's gone with little hope of return.

I want to be fair with Elliott but I want him to be fair with me too. What is the plan? How do Leon and Josie plan on resolving my case? How long will it take?

Staring at my feet, I stalk to the kitchen, tracing and

retracing my steps, back and forth, back and forth. Maggie paces with me, staring up as I wander across the tile floor, her nails clicking and clacking on the travertine tile. I look around. This house is too much house for me. I don't want it. What would I do with four thousand square feet anyway? I'm one woman with a small dog. Sure, luxury is nice and this is a beautiful home, lavishly furnished, but I do not need all this. I don't even want it. Unless a home is furnished with love, what is it anyway?

Back to the money issue. A thousand dollars sounds like a lot of money. Well, it is a lot of money, especially when I am not responsible for the mortgage, utilities, insurance and all of the rest of it. But once I take tithes off the top, I am left with $900 for the month. Food, gas and incidentals have to come out of that. My father's birthday was last week and I could not afford to give him a gift. I felt so bad. He reassured me it didn't matter, but it mattered to me. It is just not usual of me not to gift someone on their special day. I am reduced to buying my makeup and skin care products from the grocery store.

Oh please, Heavenly Father, please guide my footsteps and provide a light for my path.

There is an answer, wobbly though it may be.

Give me strength, Lord, give me grace.

I dial Elliott, fingers shaking. Desperation calls for it. Chances are he will refuse to talk to me but I am going to try and talk to him anyway. Three rings, four – voicemail should pick up any second. I am so ashamed. I am an abandoned wife, nothing more than a beggar. Begging from my husband.

"Hello?" Elliott's voice comes on the line and I literally jump but force my stomach to stay down. I take a deep breath.

"Hello, Elliott," I say as casually as I can.

"Andrea. I guess you got the message about the garage door."

"I did and thank you, Elliott. No, that's not what I called to talk to you about." I am hesitant. I am a beggar. *Please leave me with a little dignity*, I pray.

"Oh?"

"Elliott, I'd just like to talk to you about perhaps you giving me a little more money each month. Do you think we could discuss that?"

"How much is a little more? I'm strapped the way it is." Bull crap. I don't believe that for a second. Elliott is a first-rate surgeon. His practice is huge. We never lacked for anything and we spent much more money every month without accounting for it than what I am asking for now.

"Could we double it? Do you think you could do that?"

He laughs. "No way, Andrea. Absolutely not. I'm watching the finances carefully and believe me, there's no room for doubling what I'm giving you."

I say nothing for a second.

"That half a million dollars is looking pretty good right now, isn't it?" Elliot sounds so smug.

I feel like a fool, an absolute fool. Impulse control, I have always had problems with it since, well, forever. I realize my fingers are entwined in my scruffy scalp and I tug. I take a deep breath and force myself to move my hand away. It comes away from my head with a few blond strands clutched in my fingers. The relaxation comes now, just a little bit. I can think clearly now.

"Oh Elliott, I'm sorry. Really, disregard this whole conversation. Quite honestly, I see I'm worried about my wants, not my needs, which are all covered. Just disregard this whole thing."

"Okay."

"And Elliott–"

"What?"

"I love you." I hang up.

I do love Elliott. I will always love him but I never, ever want to be with him again cn any level. Looking ahead, do I want to be with any man ever again? Someday, far into the future, when this divorce is over and I am free to date, do I want another man in my life, in my heart? I gave Elliott the gift of my virgin body, my mind, my soul, on our wedding night. Those gifts have been given, never to return to me to give again. Pollyanna me, I have always preferred older men to men my age. I like the salt and pepper in the hair, the seasoning of years. I like the intellect of an older man, one who is finished with the thoughtless partying and is stable and grounded. I thought I'd gotten lucky with Elliott.

Needing someone, I pick up the phone again and dial the only person I can talk to. Claudine.

CHAPTER SIXTEEN

Julie

A bunch of us are sitting at TGIF not doing much, just hanging out. Caroline, my manager, is here and Lisa, one of my friends, and two guys Lisa knows from an old job. One of them is named Rick. I have seen him around a few times. The other one, I think, is Dustin. Lisa says they both work at the Olive Garden. Rick is sitting across from me and he is sort of cute and I'm wondering if I could date him. I haven't dated anyone since Rodney, if you can call what Rodney and I had dating.

Angela's together with Rodney, no matter what he says. Her name is on the car title with his, on the lease, on the checking account, every place that matters. Rodney was a mistake for me, even though I got Alex out of the deal. He was a big mistake. In my mind, he's ancient history now, because I'm laughing and cutting up with Rick and even flirting a little bit. Not too much flirting. Listen, I don't want to run him off but I can tell you, I'd be into dating this one.

I excuse myself to go to the ladies' room. Checking

my hair, my face, everything looks okay. Rick is getting into me, I can tell. Caroline has been telling dirty jokes. She's a hoot.

Walking back to the table, I nearly stumble. I can't believe what I'm seeing. Rodney has pulled up a chair at our table. Where did he come from? What is he doing here? I'm tempted to turn around and run off the other way, but Lisa sees me and yells, "There she is. We thought you fell in." After that, I am so embarrassed and angry and frustrated. Why is he here? How did he even know any of us were here in the first place? I stand awkwardly at the corner of the booth, laughing with the rest of the group, trying to ignore Rodney who is staring at me intently. So much for a date with Rick. Rodney could not be more obvious. How do I get rid of him quietly?

"Oh, Julie, I'm blocking your seat," Rodney says. He gets up and scoots the chair back. "Come on, sit down."

Lisa shrugs. She and Caroline are watching me. Rick and Dustin are clearly wondering why this guy showed up. Caroline doesn't look too pleased. She's now leveled her gaze at Rodney.

"Hey, I know where I know you from," Caroline says. "You're that guy that hangs around in the restaurant. I recognize your voice. We've talked on the phone. Still impersonating a sheriff's deputy?"

Oh holy mother of God. I stand paralyzed, not ready to sit, maybe ready to bolt. I know the story. Caroline answered the phone one day and someone told her he was a sheriff's deputy looking for me to serve papers. Carolyn asked for the caller's badge number. The caller then hung up.

Rodney still has his chair pushed back waiting for me to sit. Caroline continues staring at him, eyes dark.

"Private party, pal," she says. "Got it?"

At long last, Rodney stands up. He doesn't look my way, thank God, but he's glaring at Caroline. Rick and Dustin seem poised to help him out if he decides not to go on his own. He nods at Caroline and leaves, which is a surprise because I expected a scene.

"Creep," Caroline says.

I exhale and it is painful.

Rick is staring at me as I slide into the booth.

"Everybody's got a creep in their past, including me. Surprisingly so, I know," Caroline says. "Joie de vivre," she says.

The joy of life, or at least I think that's what Caroline's saying. If I remember right, it's a reference to her days as a bartender, working for her ex-husband. It took the edge off the whole situation and everybody laughs. But the party is over now and everyone is ready to go. I figure whatever interest Rick may have had is over with the whole Rodney scenario. He is nice enough to walk to me to my car though.

"Hey, I'm sorry I ruined our little get-together," I say.

"You didn't ruin it. That guy did," Rick says. "Friend of yours?"

"No friend of mine," I say. Well, that much is true. He is no *friend* of mine. My child's father, yes, but Rick does not need to know that.

"He called you by name," Rick says.

"He must have heard it somewhere," I say.

Everyone else is taking off in their cars, waving and hollering goodbyes. Dustin is waiting for Rick over at his car. "You want me to wait, man?" he asks. Rick holds up a finger, *Just a second, asshole.*

"Can I call you sometime?" he asks.

"Sure," I say. He whips a pen out of his pocket and writes my phone number on his hand.

"Thanks, bye," he says, walking backward to

Dustin's car.

As I turn north on National, I see Angela in my rearview mirror in her Thunderbird. She trails me a few blocks from my house. When I turn onto my street, she zooms by, holding her middle finger up in my direction. *These people are never going to leave me alone*. I am afraid. More than that, I am tired, mentally and emotionally.

Renae meets me at the door, holding the phone.

"Angela called," she says. "She told me you and Rodney were together at TGIF." Mark is walking up behind her.

"Is this true?" Mark asks.

Renae is staring at me, still holding the phone.

"I was there with my friends. Rodney came in while I was in the restroom. We got rid of him. That's all that matters."

"He was there? How did he know you were there?" Renae persists. "How did he know, Julie?"

"I don't know, Mom. He just showed up. Like I said, we got rid of him."

"I tried to call you but you didn't answer your phone."

"I had it shut off so I could enjoy my friends, okay?"

Renae sets the house phone down. "May I see it please?"

Shit potatoes, she is going to check and see if any messages from Rodney are on it. Of course, there aren't because I got rid of them all, but I get it out of my purse for her anyway. I hate this. Now more rules and more checking and more house arrest will come. I know I made a mistake and I'm freaking sorry, except this time it wasn't my fault. Did I bring Rodney to the restaurant? I could scream it at them until the top of the house blows off, but they still would not hear me. Renae checks the phone and hands it back. She nods and turns around. "Alex is napping. He really wore himself out today." Mark follows her, the two of them resembling two little penguins tottering east and west.

Sometimes I wish I was dead. This is not life. This is a prison. I am only existing, a bird without wings, in this place. Mark and Renae think they will never be able to trust me and the fact is they are probably right. Then, today, me lying to Rick just so I didn't have to explain my past. I know that was bad. Mistake, mistake, mistake but, well, the truth is so much worse. Isn't it?

CHAPTER SEVENTEEN

Claudine

Dido is playing softly on the stereo. I absent-mindedly hum along as I chop a red onion and drop it into the skillet with a couple tablespoons of extra virgin olive oil. Then I roll my jalapeño over the counter to me, taking out the seeds just so and chopping and dumping it in the skillet too. I grab a red pepper and finally four cloves of garlic. Fettuccine is cooking in my pasta pot. The mix of fragrance, the spice and the sweet onion, begins to rise in my nostrils. I breathe it in, humbly experiencing the earthiness of it.

Cooking relaxes me. Cooking is where I'm in my element, creating something with my own two hands. And to think I was a disaster at chemistry in high school. They're not so different, cooking and chemicals. Recipes exist for everything. It's all come together now. I pull a bottle of tequila out of the cupboard and cream from the refrigerator. Oh yes, some parmesan for grating and a bunch of green onions, some cilantro to throw in the sauce at the last minute so it doesn't cook out.

My shoulders begin to relax, streaming warm waves of comfort down my neck and back. I feel relieved and content in my kitchen after a long hard-fought day at work. Keri has her books and iPad spread out at the table, doing homework. Watching her hunch over her books, quietly tapping on her computer keys, sucking in her lips, occasionally tossing her hair over her shoulder is a welcome sight. If I didn't have this one thing to come home to, this love between my daughter and me, I'm not sure what I might do. Drink possibly, a lot and often.

Little pings of rain rouse me from my musing. I see it smack the French doors and the patio beyond.

The orange kitten is back. He's been skulking around, mostly laying on the patio. But today in the rain I see him pressed up against the French doors to stay dry. Every once in a while, he turns and meows through the glass at me. Keri's been feeding him secretly, I'm pretty sure, or he wouldn't be coming around so often.

I hear Keri's chair scoot on the wood floor but I don't turn around. I am busy julienning two chicken breasts and dropping them into the vegetable mixture. Salt, pepper, the dish smells heavenly. Then I hear her say, "Hi Dad," and before I can fully absorb he's here or why. Jim is standing in my kitchen. I whirl around, my stomach lurching with suppressed desire and a twinge of hurt. I can't help it. I still want him as much as I ever did, but it is now bittersweet. He has moved on. So maybe have I. My heart clutches, just like my fist around the kitchen towel.

"Hey Claudine," he says. "Got a minute?"

"Sure," I say and gesture to the chairs. Keri gathers up her books and iPad and scoots to the relative safety of the living room couch. Jim pulls out a chair and sits with a weary thud.

"Work hard today?" I ask even though it's a silly

question because Jim works hard every day. The denim collar of his shirt is frayed. I notice lines around his eyes I hadn't seen before. He drums his fingers on the table for a second, a hanging second, in which I could crawl into his lap if things were the way they'd once been.

Jim nods at my inquiry about working hard. "Say, something smells good. What's in the pot?"

Amazing, we're carrying on this banal conversation as if nothing ever separated us. I wonder if other separated or rather divorced couples do this. Yes, we are divorced. He is remarried. His choice, not mine.

I find my voice, but it's scratchy. "Oh, it's nothing. Something I made up."

Jim smiles at me, the blueness of his eyes is suddenly electric. "You were always good at that. I can't say I ever had a bad meal in all our years." He didn't say "together." "All our years together" and yes, we had a lot of them. He looks away. Ah, so there it is. Homesickness. Taking note, he looks a little thinner but surely Lynn's kitchen has no dearth of cooking. Jim always appreciated good food. Good food anchored him. It anchored us.

"You know, you could refinance the house to take care of the bathroom," he says.

"We'll see," I say. The possibility has occurred to me too, but I am not sure I want the debt. "It's not crucial yet."

"I'd like to spend the weekend with Keri," he says.

"Of course. I guess you've talked to her about it?"

He says he has. Silence.

"Are you okay?" I ask. The rain's picked up a bit, slapping the French doors just a little bit harder now. Jim looks outside for a second, as do I. The orange kitten is out of sight. Rumor has it Lynn just sold another big piece of development land, just like she did when she met and snagged my husband. Times should be good in that household.

"Yeah, yeah," he says, just a little too quickly. "She doesn't cook much. Too busy, you know. I guess that's what gas grills are for." He pauses. "I guess there's no easy way to say it. I know I made a mistake. And I know I hurt you and my daughter but I guess what I want to tell you is it's hurt me too. To know I hurt you."

"You were pretty happy to do it at the time," I say.

He nods. "I know it. I do."

"You can't have it both ways, Jim," I say, astounded at the sound of my voice. "You're looking for absolution from me and I can't do that and I shouldn't. I can't tell you it's all okay. Not right now."

"I hope you'll be able to someday," he says. Are there tears in his eyes?

"Don't tell me it's not working out with you and Lynn," I say. *Not after all this. Not after you shattered my life and your daughter's life. Don't tell me that. We've rebuilt. Don't go there.*

"I know in my heart I was wrong," he says. "That's all I know."

"So, why did you do it then?" I ask.

"Because I was caught up in something I didn't really understand. I thought I did but I didn't. Because she insisted on marriage–"

"She insisted?"

Jim took a deep breath. "She thought of it as insurance for her. It would insulate her." I am staring at him. "It would insulate her against you."

So there it is. The insecurity of a woman who stole another woman's husband, a woman afraid of suffering the same fate. A woman who became a trespasser, a thief. Not that he wasn't perfectly willing to be stolen at the time. *Well, live with that, will you? Leave me out of it.*

"Now wait a minute. This isn't fair. You made that

choice," I say. All the memories, all the years, the twisted, gnarled roots of our life, are sitting between us, burrowing, burrowing downward, rumbling through the floor boards and rippling up again, spreading around table pedestal, clinging to the chair legs, wrapping its entrails around us, holding us fast. I can feel it and so can he. If we were to just reach out and take it, would it ever be the same?

He sits for a minute, staring at the table. I see his face, how his mind works, where it might be now and my mind begins screaming, shrill and high-pitched. *Please do not say it. I know we bought this table on one of our junket forays years and years ago. It was stained and nearly ruined when we brought it home. Don't say it. Don't mention how we sanded and primed and sanded and stained it. The chairs don't match. That's something I love about it. That's something you love about it. But don't say it.*

Our home was comfortable, made of the best things we could afford. I wonder what sort of furniture and furnishings Jim is living with now. Keri hints at more modern, angled furniture, not the sort of thing I ever knew him to be comfortable with. But times have changed. Maybe Jim's changed too.

I have to break the spell or one of us is going to do something incredibly stupid.

"Won't Lynn be wondering where you are?" I ask. It is not so much that I want him out of my house. It is more like I need to restore the equilibrium from before he showed up. I need him to leave. I need my fortress back.

"Okay. I better take off," he says, standing up. "I'll say a word to Keri before I go."

"Sure."

When I turn back to the stove, my hands are trembling. I'm not sure if the trembling comes from my own internal rage or if it comes from the tension of him being here, in my home, which was once our home. It's not right, it's just not right, him being here. Not the right order of things. Jim is the usurper now.

Deep breath. *Take a deep breath, Claudine.* Turn the burner on, pick up the pan, pour in the tequila. It fires up just a bit but that's okay. Let it cook down. In goes the cream, pretty white swirls. I watch my spatula blend it in. Deep breath.

I start chopping green onions. I don't turn around.

I hear two voices in the hall, my daughter and her father. I hear the front door shut. He's gone. I can relax now.

"You and Dad will be spending the weekend together?" I ask Keri over supper.

"I guess so." She is toying with her fettuccine. "Dad wants to go to Branson. I don't want to, really."

"But you like Branson." I am a little dismayed. "Is it Lynn?"

"She's trying to be my best friend. She wants to go shopping. She thinks I look good in that color or this one. She's got jewelry from her mother she wants to give to me. Sickening." She stands up and takes her plate to the sink. I know why Lynn is doing this. It is a desperate plea. *Please like me, for your Dad's sake.* Oh my–

"You don't want to disappoint your dad," I say.

"I won't. I just wish she'd let us alone, is all."

"Do you want me to talk to him?"

"No, he'd just freak out. It'll be okay."

After supper is cleared away, I venture out to the front porch, my wine glass in hand. It is warm outside, even with the rain, but then we didn't go below freezing this winter. I smell grass and wet earth and it occurs to me I have not seen Gabriel Truvionne in several days. Glancing to the east, I wonder what he's been doing, what's been taking up his time. Not my business. I only spoke with him once. It's not like we have any kind of relationship going but still, I wonder.

The orange kitten appears out of nowhere, apparently having sought shelter underneath the porch. He bounds up the step meowing as he comes and jumps up to the arm of my chair. I stroke him gently, listening to his soft purr.

My mind, fuzzy with wine, slips back to our history, Jim's and mine, our history with this house. We bought it early in our marriage for a ridiculously low price. The last inhabitant was somebody's great-grandmother, frail and unable to take care of it. The great-grandmother was elderly and somewhat feeble, so when she could no longer ascended the staircase, she had the entire upstairs closed off. Her world was the living room, kitchen, downstairs bath and a tiny bedroom. Despite the paneling covering the walls downstairs and the awful Pepto Bismol pink cabbage rose wallpaper, and despite the ugly green and black linoleum on the kitchen floor, the house held fantastic possibilities. After the old lady's death, the house sat in sad need of loving rehabilitation. Jim found it for me.

I remember the day he drove me over to look at it for the first time. My heart opened up instantly. The house completely, unequivocally, adamantly stole my breath. Jim watched me with expectant eyes, knowing what I would notice and what I would like and how I'd put it all together. Both of us saw the generous front porch, the gingerbread trim, the original wood trim, pocket doors, big windows, fireplace, the generous stair case, all the potential in the old girl. "And we can do all the work ourselves," Jim said. "Baby, I'll do it. I'll make this our home."

Buying the house was easy. The surviving children were happy to sell.

We were jubilant when the dark forbidding

paneling came down along with the rose-studded wallpaper. The shag carpeting came up exposing perfect, gleaming oak floors. The metal kitchen cabinets came out to make way for wooden white Shaker-style. The laminate countertops were replaced with granite. We built the deck ourselves, after fashioning French doors along one wall of the kitchen. We ended every day splattered with paint and plaster, tired and worn but infinitely happy.

How do you build a home and then desert it? How do you walk away from twenty years of loving and fighting and making up and cooking and paying taxes and lawn mowing and raising a child? All the love and laugher, screaming fights and cooperation, the trust, the jokes, the late night dancing in the kitchen, the remodeling, the hopes and dreams? The thought that Jim could now be unhappy in his new life doesn't please me or displease me. It was just a fact, if what he was telling me was the truth. I think about the brick house in the new subdivision, the neighborhood with no trees. I saw it once from a distance, during one of my flights of insanity, when my mind wouldn't calm down until I saw it for myself. I remember how the dark brick and the spartan look chilled me. *This is Jim's home now? Couldn't be.* No charm. No sense of history. That is one reason I like our neighborhood so much. All of the homes here have been here for generations, a comfort to me. I need comfort in my home.

It's late and drowsiness is about to claim me and send me to my bed.

"Hello, Claudine." A familiar voice pilfers my thoughts. I look up and it is him. Gabriel Truvionne is standing at the foot of my porch steps.

I smile. "You are deep in thought tonight," he says softly. "I am not intruding?"

"No, no, of course not," I say. I'm glad to see him.

"How are you?"

The kitten jumps down and retreats to the corner of the porch, green eyes watching.

"I am well. I hope I didn't scare your cat away."

"Oh, he's not really mine. He's sort of adopted us, I think."

"Ah," Gabriel says. He's carrying something, a small white plate covered with a kitchen towel. He extends it in my direction and smiles clumsily. "I have been cooking. Baking, actually. Blueberry lemon muffins. Could I offer you one?"

"Sure. I'm a sucker for a blueberry anything. Come up and have a seat." I hear myself saying it, embarrassment flooding my face. What a dopey thing to do, admitting my love of all things edible to this perfect stranger, I mean perfect in more ways than just one. The love handles poking out over the waistline of my jeans feel bigger all of a sudden. Whoever coined that phrase ought to be held accountable. I am not sure where the love comes in. I mean, really.

Gabriel's eyes seem particularly luminous tonight. Oh my, so beautiful. Deep and brown with full, thick lashes and orbs of knowing. Here he is, standing on my porch with homemade blueberry lemon muffins. How exquisite. For the first time, I see his hands. They are full and strong but not fatty. His hands, of course, are knowing hands. The nails are cut straight across and they are perfectly clean. Jim's fingers are so graceful and slender. This man's hands are built for exploration, for giving pleasure. I can sense it. A lock of brown hair falls over his forehead and he tucks it back behind his ear. He sits down beside me and I nearly gasp.

"Would you like some coffee?" I ask. "I could go make us some."

He points to my wine glass, forgotten at my elbow. "No. What I would like is some of that." Again, I nearly gasp at the closeness of him. Cinnamon curls up my nose in tiny spirals. Gabriel is wearing another V-necked sweater, but this one is the color of a ripe pumpkin straight from the field. It is erotic and arousing. Pulling myself away from him to go and fetch a glass of wine is difficult. I hurry. I want to smell more of that cinnamon aroma and feel his warmth next to me. And, of course, there are the muffins to consider. My love handles must be jiggling.

Back seated with fresh glasses of wine, Gabriel pulls the towel away. The moist aroma of freshly baked sugar, sweet blueberries and the clean smell of lemon rises up from the plate. A little heat still rises. He makes a grand flourish of handing me a muffin and, giggling, I bite into it. It is all sweet goodness, fresh fruit, rich mouthwatering tang. Sinful. Decadent, although that is a word I normally use for any chocolate concoction.

"Um, that's good," I say. "You made these?"

He laughs. "I did. I made them all by my little self."

"Oh no, I didn't mean–I–"

"Claudine, I am joking. You don't know about me yet. You see, I used to bake for a living."

He reaches across and brushes a crumb from my lip. His touch is gentle, kind and again, knowing, maybe even magical. The crumb is gone.

"Are you a pastry chef?" I ask. As much as I have wondered about this man, as much as I have made up in my own head, it had not occurred to me he could be a baker. The thought of him covered in flour and sugar is a pleasant one.

"I am or have been anyway. You're smiling. What are you thinking? You like the muffins, yes?"

"Yes, I do."

"I do not look like a baker," he says. "I look like, how you say, like a rock star."

"Well, the truth of it is, you do, sort of."

He laughs. "I have heard that before. I teach music at MSU but in my younger days..."

I laugh too. "How did you become a pastry chef?"

"My brother. He owned a shop where we lived, in Florence. Italy. He taught me everything I know and brought me to America when I was a young boy. Our parents are dead a long time. My brother, he is now dead too. He died of cancer last year. I took over the shop for him when he became very, very sick. We lived in San Francisco then. I sold the shop and I came here to start over again. Make a new life, so to speak."

"Why Springfield?" Leaving the gleaming blue bay of San Francisco for the humidity of Springfield makes no sense.

"I wanted a good, solid place to begin again. I have, you say, the Internet. I learned about Springfield. The Internet says Springfield is solid, the people here are good, friendly people. What I learned has proven itself to me. And I had other reasons to want a new beginning."

"Can I ask–?"

"No wife. No lady." He seems pensive now, remote. "I am alone."

We sit in silence for a few minutes. It is a comfortable silence though. Finally, Gabriel says, "Would you like to come by sometime and I will play some music for you?"

"I think I would like that." My heart is beating fast.

"Good. My house number is nine-two-seven, on Pickwick, just over there." He waves his arm to the right. "Can you come by next Thursday evening? I will cook for you."

"I'd like that."

He stands up. "It's been a pleasure, Claudine. I will see you Thursday." He vanishes into the darkness again, leaving me in dismay.

From any other man, the conversation would seem stilted. I am wondering how to explain to Keri, who will probably roll her eyes, and I wonder what I should tell Beth. I have not said anything about Gabriel to her yet. For now, I will keep him to myself. For now.

CHAPTER EIGHTEEN

Claudine

Of course I'm late. I'm late for the basketball game, late to watch Keri cheer. I was so proud when she made the cheerleading squad but I've hardly attended any games. So busy at the law office, preparing for this trial or that hearing.

I wheel my car into the only available parking spot and race to the gymnasium. There they are, all the girls lined up in the middle of the floor in their red and white cheerleader skirts and sweaters. I'm not too late after all.

The gym smells of sweat and tennis shoes. It's hot. It's noisy and crowded. The jazz band rips. I see Keri out in front working the routine. She's so cute, she's doing so well.

A movement just out of my vision catches my eye. Since it's standing room only, I'm shoved off to the side next to the water fountains and restrooms, which all smell putrid. I recognize Lynn stalking about in her long wool coat, talking on her cell phone. She takes several steps back for acoustics sake and beyond her, I see Jim, hands in pockets, looking less than pleased. Well, they were late too. I don't feel so bad. Lynn disappears out through the double doors, still talking on her phone. Another deal is going down. I suppose she made an appearance at Keri's game to look good, but she's all business. As if I'd signaled, Jim sees me and starts walking over.

The sheer physical presence of him is intimidating.

"She's doing great, isn't she," he says, standing beside me. He's too close. I sense his masculinity and I wish, for the thousandth time, nothing had changed.

"She's really good," I say, watching our daughter spin and pirouette, waving her pompoms in the air. The stomping in the bleachers is deafening. The jazz band has turned it up a notch and I'm almost sick from the stench and the noise.

Keri's steps are perfect. She's happy, glowing, beautiful. Her golden curls roll over her shoulders. She is lithe, accomplished. Again the best part of Jim and me.

At that moment, Lynn appears beside Jim, her cell phone nowhere to be seen. She tugs his arm, nods at me, and Jim bids me goodbye. They walk away but they don't get too far before the cell phone comes out again and once more attached to Lynn's ear.

I guess it's what he wanted. This is the life he chose, but I can't help but wonder if he wasn't truly happier in the old life with me. I also guess I'll never know.

I'm strong at this moment, but not very much.

Zipping up my jacket, I head out into the night to find my car and drive home. Alone.

CHAPTER NINETEEN

Andrea

Bending over the toilet, I wretch. Nothing comes up. Again. And again. Finally, the vanilla latte I finished off earlier surges up my throat. Straightening up, I pull the hand towel from the rack and wipe my mouth. I am sweating but I feel better. Is that all? Is that all I have consumed today? Thinking back, I confirm it was. Okay, no more.

I stare at my face in the mirror. So fat. Such a fat jawline. *Stop it, stop it, stop it, Andrea.* I replace the towel and brush my teeth. I should pray. I am so not worthy. And yet here I am. *Please Lord, hear my prayer.*

Yesterday, I visited with my pastor. He suggested a missionary trip to the Ukraine. I should pray I am worthy because the temptation to go is strong, but I should only go if I can be a blessing to those I would be ministering to. If only Elliott would agree to pay me more money. But then, if I agree to the $500,000, it would all be over. I could do as I choose.

Please Lord, give me direction for my feet and a

lamp unto my path. Bless the works of my hands and know it is all for your glory. Please forgive me of my sins, which are many and daily. Please cast me not from your sight. Please make me a worthy vessel unto you.

I recite it over and over again, on my knees in front of my bed, the bed Elliott and I once shared, rocking back and forth with the rhythm of the words, my arms locked across my chest. *Please Father God, make me an instrument. Make me worthy of your favor. Please cast me not from your sight. Please forgive me of my sins, through your son, Jesus. I only want to be an instrument for you. Please make me worthy. Open my eyes that I may see. Open my ears that I may hear you fully. I submit myself to you.*

Sweat covers my body, soaking through my sweat suit. Hot and cold at the same time. I am not worthy. I must be worthy. I should be pure. I should be completely clean before I go and tell others of God's love. How can I minister to others if I am not pleasing in His sight? My arms are unlocked and, much to my dismay, I look down on my hands. Both fists are full of the downy blonde hairs from my scalp. I didn't feel a thing. I have no memory of pulling my hair out. But at the same time, the fact that I did it brings me peace, blissful peace.

The Lord will keep me. He will guide my path.

Later, the telephone rings. The caller ID says Ted McClintock. Ted was my fiancé before I met Elliott. How interesting. After all these years, Ted is calling. I'm puzzled but intrigued.

"Andrea?" he says when I answer the phone.

"Ted, what a nice surprise." It is so nice to hear his voice again. We parted on amicable terms. Both of us realized we did not want to be married, or at least not to each other. Ted had been going through a personal ordeal, something I knew nothing about until the day we ended our relationship. We were never intimate and I eventually found out why. His inner wrestling finally caught up with him. He revealed to me, in tears, he was gay. He was so sorry. He never wanted to hurt me or mislead me in any way. I understood. Totally. What could I do but graciously bid him farewell and assure him we would always be friends?

"It's good to hear your voice, Andrea. I trust you've been well?"

Briefly, I fill him in on what's been going on. "Well," he says when I'm finished, "then I'm not surprised."

"Not surprised at what, dear heart?"

"I've been summoned to give a deposition in your divorce case," Ted says.

"You're kidding. Oh, tell me you're joking," I say but I know he's not. After not hearing from him in years, why would he call me to spring something like that as a joke? My heart is sinking. My stomach grinds and growls.

"No, I'm deadly serious. They want me to bring all messages, email or otherwise, from you to me to the deposition, along with any gifts, trinkets, photographs, etcetera, etcetera, and so on, within the last five years."

"But there aren't any. What are they trying to prove?" Appalling, the depths to which Elliott will stoop.

"It looks like they're trying to prove some sort of clandestine relationship between you and me, maybe taking place while you were married? Now you and I know that isn't true."

"No, we know that isn't true. Oh my God. How despicable."

"Oh well, I'm just too happy to give it. I mean, what are they going to do with my testimony anyway? Five minutes with me and they'll get the picture, unless they're stupid."

I laugh. Of course, he is right. "Oh Ted, I'm just so sorry they're bothering you."

"Don't think anything of it. Oh, they also want to know what I know about your drinking, drug-taking, anorexia, blah, blah, blah. What your mother said about you and all that rot."

What my mother said about me? My stomach grinds again. *My mother. My mother who did not want me but then later decided I was okay after all. She wanted my brother, yes, but she did not want me. I was female and therefore, a threat.* While our mother bestowed affection and nurturing on my brother, me, well, not so much. She demanded my father remain distant and to a degree, he did.

"Oh," I say. *Please Lord, give me strength.*

"It'll be okay, Andrea. Trust me. They won't get diddly from me and you know it. They couldn't."

"Thanks, Ted. And thanks for calling," I say.

"No problem."

I replace the phone in its cradle. My stomach is cramping and I rush to the bathroom to stand over the toilet again. Too many times I have done this. Too many times. It is enough. I slap the lid down, straighten up and adjust my wig in the mirror. *Elliott will not beat me down. All things work together for good for them who love the Lord and are called according to his purpose. All things. All things. Thou wilt keep him in perfect peace whose mind is stayed on thee.*

The sudden urge to flee grabs me. Heart thumping, I grab my car keys and jump in my car. I have no idea where I am going, where I might end up, but I am driving away. Trees whiz past, buildings appear and disappear behind me. I have no thought now but to simply drive. Rain slaps my windshield, the roads are wet but I don't slow down. I am escaping. The four-lane appears and I take the first exit. I pass a semi-truck and it sprays water over my windshield but I keep on traveling. A van from Indiana, a farmer plodding along in his pickup truck, I pass them all.

It occurs to me I could be found dead after losing control on the slick roadway. Perhaps my car would fly end over end until it reaches its final resting place somewhere off in a field. I envision Elliott arriving at the scene as the medics and firemen work to free me from my vehicle, my body like sodden putty as the paramedics pull me out. "Oh my God," Elliott would cry, throwing both hands to the side of his head, elbows akimbo. "Oh my God, the stupid bitch went and wrecked the car I paid for. My insurance rates will go sky high."

"Uh sir," the medic would say. "Your wife, she's expired."

To which Elliott would reply, "No problem. I'll cash in the life insurance policy. I'll pay down some debt."

I giggle at the macabre daydream. Too bad it would most likely be accurate.

Elliott, Ted, Rita, Leon, Josie, Claudine. All of us have been caught in a despicable web and it's choking me to death. I cannot get free. I cannot disentangle myself. It sucks to be at someone else's mercy, especially a man who has no conscience. All of my friends, my former friends, now treat me with polite coolness and just a little sarcasm. They were Elliott's friends, actually. I was a hanger-on, maybe more of a fifth wheel, because of him. So I am now just as isolated as I ever was. His children, Will and Dawn, whom I have not seen in months, are openly disrespectful. My life consists of this daily stress – the lawsuit. It is eating me alive. I look in the mirror and I no longer like the person I see. I used to think of myself as a strong person with a strong spirit but now all I see is a weak-willed, needy, pathetic beggar. I hate what I have become. I hate it. I want to be free of Elliott now and forever.

When was the last time I saw Elliott face to face? It is hard to remember. It is almost like a dream, the life I had with him. He moved out the day before my birthday. No roses, no expensive gift, no grand dinner and no love-making this year. After he left, I saw him once as I pulled into the country club for lunch. He was pulling in too. When I saw that big, black Range Rover pull into a parking spot, I decided to ask him if it would be uncomfortable for him if I were to have lunch there at the same time. Will and Dawn were with him. He laughed at my inquiry. They scoffed, quietly. I could tell they were thinking I followed him to the country club. I backed out and drove away, humiliated. Thinking about it now, I should have arranged to sit at the table next to him and pitch wet wadded up paper in his food.

I am trying to be strong. I am trying to be brave. God has never let me down one time in my whole life. Not one time. Right now, I can't see His purpose for me, can't fathom it. Won't it be grand when one day I can look with clear eyes and see all that was going on? *Thou wilt keep him in perfect peace whose mind is stayed on thee*. I slow down and look around me. A road sign is coming up – Seymour. How did I get so far from Springfield? It's only been a few minutes on the road. Looking down at the dash clock, I realize I have been driving for forty minutes. It's beginning to get dark but the rain has stopped. *Get a hold of yourself, Andrea. No wonder Elliott thinks you're a flake*. It is funny though and I laugh as I pull off into the little town to find my way back out.

My stomach is growling. It occurs to me I need to stop someplace but my stomach muscles also hurt from the dry-heaving and stress. Nevertheless, I pull into the Hardees at Rogersville and order the biggest burger they have. If it disagrees with me, I can take care of it later. In the end, I throw most of it away and head back to Springfield. What was I running from? Nothing is resolved. I am still up in the air, waiting to land.

It rains all the way back to Springfield.

When I get home, poor Maggie is dancing all around my legs. She needs to get out and do her duty. Once she's taken care of, I drag myself to the bedroom, strip off all my clothes and fall into bed. Thunder sings me a lullaby. The pitter-patter of rain on the roof sends me to sleep without thoughts of Elliott, but with more of a white serenity than I've ever seen before. My dream is full of peace and joy and I find I like it there. I like it very much.

CHAPTER TWENTY

Julie

Stretching in my bed, I feel pretty good this morning. Rick and I had our first date on St. Patrick's Day and he's called me twice since then. We had such a fun time. We did a little bit of the pub crawl but since I don't drink much, we left early and found a place to eat. Everywhere we went downtown was mayhem, but it was great. I haven't told him about Alex yet, or Rodney, but Rick hasn't asked me for more information on Rodney anyway so, for now, sleeping dogs are lying.

Only one thing troubles me today. I think I saw Angela down the block in her Thunderbird last night when I came home from work. In the darkness, it was hard to tell, but I am quite sure it was her.

My hair is up in a scrunchie and I am ready to get to work. Since it is raining, my hair isn't gonna hold a curl anyway. The restaurant will be humid, like it always is when it rains. I kiss Alex goodbye and he waves at me from the door as I get in my car. He is so precious. Renae is standing behind him and she seems a little less tense. She hasn't said much about me seeing anyone, but I suppose she is glad it is anybody but Rodney. Me too.

I get to work shortly before 11 a.m. and Caroline pulls me into the break room.

"That guy," she says. "That creepy guy is back."

"Oh God," I say. *Why won't he go away?* "What's he doing?"

"He's sitting at the bar drinking coffee. "I just wanted you to know."

"Can't we get rid of him?" Clouds pass over my day. Heavy, black clouds.

"If he starts anything, tell me and I'll send him out." *So I have to wait until he approaches me? Crap.*

"Okay," I say and clock in.

Carolyn grasps my arm.

"Sorry, babe. It's a tough deal, I know. He may not be here long. I thought I heard him say he's going to work at Ruby Tuesdays in a few. Says he's going to be a manager."

We both snicker. A manager, sure. Anything you say, Rodney.

"Hey, how's it going with you and Rick?" she asks. She is smiling as if she would like to know a secret.

"It's nice. It's good."

"Told him about your sticky little dilemma?"

"No."

"Be up front, girl. Lying ain't got you no place. And besides, he deserves better than that."

I say nothing and Caroline walks away. Watching her march off with my time card in my hand, I know she's right. I will tell Rick about Alex and Rodney and the whole thing. Soon. I'll tell him soon.

Rodney is no longer at the bar but in a booth. He is watching the waitress section for me to come out and when I do, he stands up and starts walking toward me. He blocks my way to my section.

"What do you want?" I whisper. The last thing I want is a scene at my job.

"You know what I want," he says. "I've told you and told you, Julie. It's what I deserve. I want to see my son."

"We're working on that." That much is true. The court appointed a guardian ad litem who suggested a restricted and supervised visitation schedule, probably at a neutral spot. I cannot let Rodney have Alex alone, anywhere, at any time, and not with Angela lurking in the background. And he cannot come to my house and visit, so this is the best way. I don't trust Rodney. I've got no faith whatsoever he would not take off with Alex and, I suspect, neither does the guardian. The guardian should be talking to him about this, not me. I don't want to.

"Look, get out of here," I say. "Don't you have someplace to go?"

"I'm going but remember, Julie, he's not all yours. He's part of me too."

"Go away. Leave me, leave us, alone."

"You're going to be sorry, Julie." He towers above me, looking down he seems even taller than usual. "You are going to be very sorry when this is all over."

He walks away, full of himself.

"I think he just threatened me," I say to Caroline.

"Honey, you'd better call your lawyer. Call somebody."

I call the only person I can, the only person who is listening. Claudine.

"I'm not sure but I think Rodney just threatened me," I say.

Claudine wants to know what he did and what he said. She is trying to figure out the seriousness of the situation so she can get something from Leon.

"Oh, and something else. I think Angela's been

stalking me."

"What makes you say that?"

"She's been parked at the end of my street now twice when I come home from work. She's called my mother at work. I just feel like she's following me around. I don't want Alex's safety threatened. That would not be good."

"Okay. It may be you and your folks will have to go down and apply for restraining orders. I know you've been through that before and it's old stuff, but it's all I can offer. I'll let Leon know what's going on and the next time you see Angela parked down the street, call the cops. But do get a restraining order against both of them and maybe a child order of protection while you're there. We'll let the guardian know. You've been to see him, right?"

"Not yet. I think he's coming to the house this week sometime, but I'm not sure when."

"Okay, good. Take care of yourself and your little boy."

We hang up. More restraining orders. It's part of the system, I know, but all the restraining orders in the world don't seem to have much effect, in my opinion, since none of ours against Rodney and Angela were extended last time. I don't know what good a child order of protection would do either. The system is screwed up. I cannot get help unless he kills me and what I am trying to do is prevent him from doing anything to me or to Alex.

Renae is going to have a full-blown coronary on this news, I am sure of it. Nobody is listening, except for Claudine, and what can she do? Nothing really, but to go in and talk to Leon, like usual, about all this. And what if he does nothing? Well, I will be damned if anybody is going to mess with my world and my baby without a fight. That is it. That is all. Rodney just better not come near me or mine. If the law won't help me, I will have to help myself, not that I necessarily know how to do that. I always thought the law would protect me. I thought it was on my side, but I now see things differently. If it were just me, I could handle this okay but I have Alex to consider and I don't want him threatened in any way. I hope Claudine gets a chance to talk to Leon, and then I get back to work.

Finally, I am finished for the day and it comes none too soon. Rick is working at the Olive Garden tonight so I won't be hearing from him, but I'm ready to go home and see my Alex. I toss my apron in the laundry dumpster, put my order books away and clock out. It is still raining. I wish I'd brought a rain coat.

Oh. My. God. A bouquet of roses lies on the hood of my car again. This time, I knock them to the ground and deliberately run over them on my way out of the parking lot. I hope Angela or Rodney or both of them are watching. I am finished. I am through. *You see this, you fucking maniac? Or you fucking bitch? I'm done. Done, done, done. Leave me alone.*

The *slap-slap-slap* of my wiper blades keeps me company all the way home.

Renae is singing to old Frank Sinatra songs when I walk in. Mark is working in his office. I make them both sit at the kitchen table and listen to me.

Renae's solution, as always, is Leon.

"Leon isn't listening," I say to Renae. I tell her about Rodney's visit and the flowers. She wants me to call Leon, or at the very least, she wants to call him, but I am simply tired of calling him. "He doesn't believe Rodney is a threat, remember?"

We're in the kitchen. Renae, Mark and me sitting around the Formica table from my childhood. Alex is in his high chair. It is dark outside. Thunder rolls across the roof of the house. Mark is leaning away from the table.

Renae is sitting right up to it. Alex is eating Cheerios.

"Well, we have to do something," Renae says. "We're just being terrorized by these people."

"I think we'd better go and get those restraining orders or at least the child order of protection," Mark says.

"This is so frustrating," Renae says. "We're the good guys and we can't get anywhere. All we want is to make sure Alex is safe. Why can't anybody see that?"

Mark rubs her shoulder. "Take it easy, Renae. We'll get through this. We'll go get the orders of protection in the morning. That's all we can do."

Renae rubs his hand on her shoulder. She is looking at him through tears. I am genuinely sorry for what I am putting them through and I find myself tearing up.

"I'm so sorry, you guys, for what I've done to all of us, what I've done to your lives." Sobs are coming fast, gasping, grieving sobs. Alex is curious. He drops his Cheerios and watches me. A baby sob escapes his throat and then he stops and watches me again. I have never been sorrier in my life. Grief and fear, that is what I have put my family through. We live it every day. It is all because of me and my selfishness. All because I could not keep my hands off someone else's husband. I used to think it was glamorous and exciting, being the other woman. Now I wish I would have pulled that whole chapter out of my life before it ever happened and before I hurt everyone.

Renae is holding me now, shushing me like she did when I was a little girl. She tells me she loves me. I tell her I love her too and I see a bolt of lightning across the tree tops. Family bonding feels good. Clinging to my mother, I wish I would have appreciated her more back when I should have instead of pushing her away. It doesn't seem the way I've lived my life has gotten me very far. All I can say is my life has been my own, no

excuses, and it has been purely me who has fucked it up.
It will have to be me who pulls it out of the shithole.

CHAPTER TWENTY ONE

Claudine

"Have you seen this letter from Rita?" Josie Weiss is standing outside my office, holding a letter up, beside her bulky frame. Her voice reverberates down the hallway. If she was not such a good attorney, you could imagine she might be a professional wrestler or some other occupation that requires a great deal of fanfare and noise.

I have not seen the letter. Not yet.

"What's on her mind now?"

"You will not believe this. It's just soooo shitty." Josie decides to come inside and sit, rather than bellow at me from the hallway. She throws the letter across my desk and plops down on the chair under the window. I slap my hand on the sailing letter before it escapes to some other region of my work space. "Dr. Sommerfield, who is a total and complete asshole–I always thought so–wants to sell the house. He thinks since he has to live in a rental, oh my God let me get my violin, Andrea can do that too. Like, on what money? She has no money.

And–" She holds one finger up. "And he wants Andrea out by May 15th. I mean, oh my God, who does he think he is?"

"He actually proposed that?" How cold.

"Yes, he actually proposed that. He says he wants to pay down debt with the money he gets from the house. I mean, how is this going to look to the judge if the doctor, who made all this money last year and will only make more in his career, shoves his poor wife out of the house? He's going to look like an asshole, which he is, and we win. Plain and simple." She tucks a lock of yellow hair behind her ear and stares at me. I am supposed to say something but all I can think is *we win*? Who wins in a divorce case?

"Andrea is going to cave," I say. "This could possibly do her in. I'm not sure there's much equity, if any, in that house. They've only been in it for a year."

"I know," Josie says and slaps her knee. "Call her and tell her before she gets this letter and I'm going to send a letter back to Rita that will curl her hair."

She leaves as abruptly as she came in, high heels clicking down the hall. The letter remains under my palm and I pick it up to read before I call Andrea. Josie is wrong about one thing. Dr. Sommerfield doesn't want Andrea out of the house as of May 15th. He wants her out as of May 1st. Looks as though he's trying to force her to go to work, thus negating any support from him. What is the girl expected to do?

"What an uncaring, unfeeling bastard," Andrea says when I tell her. "How do I move out? What am I supposed to do? Trade places with him at the rental and he'll be my landlord? Could he kick me out?"

"Well, I don't know what his intentions are, aside from taking over the house and selling it. But Andrea, he can't sell it without your signature anyway, so it may be a moot point, at least for now."

"What would the judge think about this?"

"I think the judge would find it pretty callous, considering you have no money and no place to go. If you agreed to move out and have the house sold, the judge would not be bothered. Dr. Sommerfield believes he's going to pay down debt with the equity he gets."

"There's no equity in this house. Neither one of us would benefit. That's why I'm so confused. I think he just wants me out and he doesn't care where I go."

Sadly, I believe what she says is true and that's not something I enjoy telling someone. I hate the way Dr. Sommerfield is treating his wife. I know every story has two sides, but this one seems skewed to the nth degree. I reassure Andrea we will do everything we can for her and then I tell Josie about the conversation. She already has a scathing letter ready to go back to Rita.

It never ceases to amaze me, the way human beings treat each other. In my career, sadly, we're talking about people who once loved one another. I bet none of them ever dreamed they'd come to the point where Andrea stands now.

Andrea shared some photographs with me, photos of their wedding and the story behind it. I remember she told me Dr. Sommerfield badgered her for days before the wedding about sleeping with him before they wed and she wanted to hold out until the wedding night. "I wanted to give him a gift I couldn't give him twice," she said. "He didn't see it that way. He rode me for days before the wedding and kept me up all night long, calling me names and finally, I took his face in my hands and I asked him to stop. It made him cry. Our wedding day was magical and beautiful. Everyone told me they'd never seen Elliott so happy and so in love." Her eyes were misty. She believed, despite her hopefulness for a beautiful wedding and a blessed life, what she really did was sell herself into some sort of slavery. To me, that seemed certain.

The wedding photographs were beautiful. Andrea showed me photo after photo of her: radiant, smiling, fitted into her white beaded gown. And Dr. Sommerfield looking handsome and smiling in his tuxedo. They seem such a happy couple. I remember thinking how much Dr. Sommerfield resembled Jim Belushi, a lovable teddy bear of a man. He looked to me like somebody who barbequed in his backyard and threw a football with his friends on Sundays. He did not look at all like a monster but then, monsters seldom do look like monsters. What darkness must be in his mind? How did someone like Andrea unleash the demons possessing him? Human nature is too complicated for me today.

Today is Thursday, *the Thursday*, my night with Gabriel. I have a splitting headache. I wander into the kitchen and find the aspirin bottle. Washing two of them down with a cup of water, I reflect on my afternoon. I spent an hour with a new client whose husband is convinced he has a blue ball of light in his stomach and that is why he doesn't have to turn on any lights when he gets up in the middle of the night for a snack. He's been terrorizing their children, telling them terrorists are falling from the sky, and now the girls are afraid to walk home from school, thinking they are going to be caught and eaten by strangers. Knowing the man is trying to get disability benefits from the Veteran's Administration, I am not surprised by his tactics.

"I want everything," the woman says, waving her finger in my face. "I want it all." *Of course you do.* Not that I blame her, necessarily. "I told him those Beanie Babies wouldn't sell. I can't even sell them on eBay."

After my new client leaves, I go back to Josie to talk to her about Andrea Sommerfield. "What about mediation?" I ask. "I'm just thinking a short-term marriage, most of the assets were his to begin with, no children?"

Josie's poring over a jewelry magazine, marking a spot with her finger. She shoots me an annoyed look. "If they want mediation, let them suggest it." She returns to her magazine and then looks up again. "Oh, I just remembered something I was going to tell you."

"What's that?"

"One of our old clients died." She mentions the name and I remember him well. He was a mechanic, a big guy, always laughing. He went for custody of his two girls, which he didn't get.

"He hung himself in his garage," Josie says. "Oh well, no skin off my nose." She flips a page. "He was a nutball anyway."

"That's too bad," I finally say. "He was a nice guy."

"Well, nice doesn't always cut it," Josie says, lost in the glossy pages of the jewelry magazine.

I take it we will not be sending flowers, I think as I walk away. *I hope I am never that jaded, that cold.*

But it's Thursday and I am looking forward to my evening, but I dread it too. How old is he? I wonder. Why would a forty-five-year-old divorced mother of one be of any interest to him? I steady my nerves by convincing myself it's just a gathering of two friends. Nothing to be nervous about, nothing to get all nutty and stuff over. Sure. So I will not get nutty already.

At home, I run through the shower, which still is not repaired, pull on my new lace panties and bra and spritz a little perfume all over. Then I pull on my jeans and sandals and a peasant blouse I bought a long time ago on one of my trips with Jim. It is a beautiful white with turquoise, black and yellow embroidery around the neckline and so comfortable. Above all things, these days, I go for comfort. Earrings. I locate my turquoise and silver ones and a bangle for my wrist. Okay. I stand back from the mirror and take a look. *Brush your hair,*

Claudine. Okay. There now. A little flushed but not bad.

Keri is with her dad tonight, which is probably a good thing, seeing as I don't feel like making any explanations for my whereabouts to anybody. I pull the front door shut behind me, making sure I have a spare key in my pocket, and walk the two and a half blocks to Gabriel's Spanish-style stucco house. It has been painted a pale salmon, which only adds to the Mediterranean look. The veranda is lined with hanging ferns and I can imagine bright red geraniums in clay pots in summer and maybe some petunias. The French doors are open in front. Wind chimes sing softly in the breeze. It is balmy and no longer raining.

I hear one of my favorite bands, the Cate Brothers, playing from within his fortress. Good old southern blues-jazz-rock. In my opinion, if this man is playing the Cate Brothers, I am in the right place. I ascend the steps to the side of the porch and knock on the doorframe.

No one answers so I step inside. His home is bathed with soft lights and beautiful colors and textures. A piano sits off to the side, a baby grand. My mother had one of those. A slate fireplace is directly in front of me and a huge painting of fields and sky hangs above it. Flowers and candles are on the mantle. A deep leather couch and chairs sit opposite one another, filled with pillows and throw blankets. The candles are lit on the coffee table.

"Hello?" I call, still looking around at the tapestries on the walls, textured to look like an old villa. This house is entrancing. I feel good here. Something spicy and exotic wafts from pocket doors, which swing open, and there he is, walking toward me, smiling. Maybe it is the white sweater. Maybe it is just him but he looks like an angel.

"Claudine, it is wonderful to see you," he says and kisses my cheek. That cardamom and cinnamon smell, distinctly masculine and oh so sexy, hits me again. He stands back and looks at me full on which makes me a hair uncomfortable, seeing as how my fat roll seems to be slipping over my waistline again and my nipples are standing firmly at attention and I am sure he can see all of it. Eroding into the floorboards seems a viable option right now and I would really like to do that. "You look beautiful," he says and takes my hand.

"Oh, well, thank you," I say, following him to the couch.

"This will be much more comfortable for you than standing over there, certainly," he says.

I sit, wondering if my fat rolls are burgeoning out and why I accepted this invitation in the first place. *Because you wanted to*, I remind myself. *Because you like him*. Okay, *okay*. Well, I am here now and so it is too late to go running down the sidewalk back to my safe haven.

"Your house is beautiful," I say. "It reminds me of a villa and summertime and a caring soul."

"Ah, I am an old soul, that is certainly true," he says settling in beside me. He retrieves two wine glasses and a bottle of pinot grigio from someplace I don't see. He pours and hands me a glass. It is crisp, cold and fruity. Delicious.

"Why do you say that?" I ask. "That you're an old soul?"

"Because when I was a boy, I was not the athletic type. In school, I was the last boy picked for any team sport. I was the boy off in the corner with a book. I wore glasses with thick lenses. Sort of a, what you say, geek. I preferred the company of my grandmother most of the time. She taught me many of the old ways until she passed away."

"But that's such a wonderful heritage," I say. "The old ways are fading away. Nobody keeps them any longer. "

He sips from his glass and his eyes meet mine. "I agree. The old ways are being lost. Not that there is anything wrong with progress, but I find I am nourished by the knowledge I gleaned from my grandmother."

"What was Florence like?" I ask him and his eyes take on a faraway look. He feels Florence in his blood, in his heart, still. I can see that.

Gabriel picks up a tray from the coffee table. His movements are elegant, entrancing.

"It is beautiful and bright and hot and dangerous. It is like this snack. These are basil-parmesan crisps. Try one."

Gabriel's treats are delicious, melting on my tongue but crisp at the same time. So enticing and flavorful. I imagine a different world now. My imagination is singing of the bustling markets of Italy, the lemons, the grapes, the olive trees, the heat, roses crawling up umber walls, my shoulders bare and warmed by the sun. Rippling laughter. Dark eyes, luminous and inviting and thick hair my hands should run through. For a moment I hear clanking silver bracelets. What my imagination and his cooking brings to my mind is beautiful, sun laden, glorious.

"Did you make these?" I ask.

He nods. "From my grandmother." He is smiling slightly.

"So good," I say.

"May I kiss you, Claudine?"

Before I can scream "yes," his lips find mine.

He is holding my back with one firm hand and his mouth is delicious, his lips firm and full. As they cover mine, I feel a rap at the very back of my brain saying, *Wait a minute, Claudine, hold it*. I ignore the cautionary rebuke. Now his tongue is playing on my teeth and as I open my mouth to let him in, a surge of terror rolls up from my chest and I nearly cry out. *What am I doing? I hardly know this man. On the other hand, grow up, Claudine. You're forty-five years old.*

Gabriel is kissing me much more intensely now and a little moan escapes his throat. His left hand begins caressing my side and I am reclining back on the couch as his mouth and tongue continue to explore my neck and throat and move back to my lips. He is gentle but firm. He is sure, that's the word, *sure*. His hand continues upward underneath my blouse and cups my left breast. Shock waves of pleasure pulse through me. My nipples swell as he takes the left one between two fingers and begins kneading it, expertly. He bends his head to kiss it through my blouse. "You have the breasts of a young woman," he says, moaning. How long has it been? I want him, I know I want him. And then, I gulp in fear and sit up straight, nearly knocking him off the couch. My chest feels cold.

"I can't," I say, stammering. "I'm sorry, I just can't." My eyes fill with tears of embarrassment. I dislodge myself from underneath him and stand up. "I'm so sorry, Gabriel. I…I…"

He is staring at me from the couch. His full lips so enticing, still swollen from kissing, his deep brown eyes looking at me with concern.

"Please sit down," he says.

"I think I should go," I whisper. I am too humiliated to stay. What will he think of me now? This gorgeous man, what will he think of me now? I've blown it. I have totally screwed up a nice evening and it occurs to me we have not even eaten. I blew it before dinner. I turn and make a stride for the door and take a hold of the door knob.

"Claudine," he says and stands up. "Wait a moment."

He walks toward me. "Please, not like this."

"Oh Gabriel, I'm just so embarrassed," I say. "I really think I should leave."

"Well," he says, putting his hands on his hips. I'm entranced by the left one that was, just minutes ago, making a pleasant journey over my breast. "Go if you must, but that is the closet door you're holding onto."

I close my eyes in embarrassment and sag against the door. I would like to laugh if I didn't feel like such a schmuck, but when I open my eyes, all I see is kindness in Gabriel's face and I have to smile.

"Uh, well, so it is." I say.

He takes my hand. "Come. I will walk you home." He leads me to the French doors, which are still open to the porch. There is an umbrella stand in the corner and he pulls one out.

"This one will do," he says as we step out. The umbrella is huge, big enough for three people.

I am simply being led along in my predicament. It is dark and raining again and I am wondering why we did not just drive, but maybe the walk will do both of us some good. I feel the need to explain but I am afraid. Explanations may make the situation worse and it is sufficient to say I have messed up my chance for a romance with an angel.

"I'm so sorry, Gabriel," I say again as we walk together underneath his umbrella.

He does not look at me. "It is fine, Claudine."

"No, let me explain." I tug his arm and he turns to me. We're standing on the corner across from my street. I can see into my windows and the little light I left on is glowing in one of them. "I was married for a long time."

"Yes, I know," he says.

"Well, that's the thing. My husband and I, we'd known each other nearly all our lives. He was the only one, you see. I never dated anyone else and now, here I am, thrown into the single world again and I don't know what the directions are. I just have no idea. I'm standing here, looking at my life, from the outside in a way and it's nothing like I imagined it would be. I don't know the rules and I don't know how I'm supposed to feel. I don't know anything."

We are walking again, crossing the street and down to my house. Comfort. Safety. My fortress.

We mount the steps together and I search for my key in my jeans pocket. I draw it out but my shaking fingers can't get it in the lock. Gabriel takes it from me.

"Let me," he says and he unlocks my door.

"This is going to seem strange," I say, "but would you like to come in?"

His eyes are dark as he gazes down at me. "Not tonight, Claudine, but soon."

"We didn't eat that lovely dinner you were preparing," I say.

"There will be other dinners, lovely ones," he says and kisses my forehead. "For now, goodnight, Claudine."

CHAPTER TWENTY TWO

Claudine

The crack in the shower is getting longer. Although I told Jim it wasn't crucial, I'm now convinced it is. I just didn't want Jim deciding to take care of it for me. I am troubled though. What if water is seeping underneath the crack and into the ceiling below? My bedroom is directly above the kitchen. I run downstairs and look up, but I don't see any water marks. I know Jim thinks a new plastic liner would be the least expensive and quickest way to deal with it, and he may be right, but I have been dreaming of something in tumbled tile, something a little bit Italian maybe? Something soothing and beautiful and all my own.

But all that costs money and I am not sure where I would get it. Nevertheless, I find myself in my car, heading to Lowe's, thanking God it's Saturday and I don't have to be anywhere at any time. I'm just going to take a look.

I feel humiliated, embarrassed and sickened over my failed evening with Gabriel. I ran away from a man like a little school girl. Stupid, stupid, stupid. It's doubtful he'd want to see me again and for that I feel a lot of regret. If only I could feel his hands on my body again, the taste of his lips, his warm cinnamon breath. I need something to get it off my mind and maybe that's why I'm driving to Lowe's. Maybe it's the diversion I'm looking for.

I love Lowe's. It has everything I could ever dream of in it. While most of my friends are shopping Kohl's for the latest sales or rushing off to Chico's to gawk at the racks, I toddle along in my home improvement store, happily inhaling the scent of wood and staring up at light fixtures.

When I finish here, I think I will stop by the grocery store and pick up something decadent for dinner tonight. Actually, frozen pizza sounds good, more convenient than decadent, since Keri is spending the weekend with Brandy and her family and I have no cooking obligations. Okay, a frozen pizza and a movie and all the space in the house I want. How luxurious will that be?

Oh my, what an array of stuff in Lowe's. I pause in front of tumbled tile, marble, ceramic and glass. How in the world does anyone choose? This one would match that one for the walls, and maybe this one for the floor, and what about – I like them all. *Pack them up, garcon. I will take it all*. Finally, I find a marbled golden mocha travertine that suits me. I pick up a sample to take home and dream over, then I am out of there and on to Price Cutter. The rain's stopped, leaving the air cool and fresh. This morning, I noticed the morning glories along my fence starting to spread out. My grandmother always kept morning glories and now, so do I.

I pull into the Price Cutter parking lot. Clusters of emerald ferns are sitting outside for sale. Another sure sign of spring. No need for a cart for what I need so I amble through the store, musing over cheeses, glancing at the deli offerings and then, as I move into fresh produce, my heart stops for a second. I am more curious than fearful though.

Jim and Lynn are quietly arguing at the fresh vegetable display. I can tell by the rigidness of Jim's back he is unhappy about something. Although they're out of my hearing, I know they're having a disagreement. I see Lynn grab a bunch of asparagus and slap it into the cart and they move on, oblivious to me. Jim has his hands stuck in his pockets. Lynn is pushing the cart. I see a case of Coca-Cola and some baking potatoes in a plastic bag, and now the asparagus.

I should leave but I can't. My feet just grew roots, and so what? This is a free country and I shop at this store all the time. Come to think of it, they're intruding on *my* territory since they live across town and they could go to the newest, sharpest Price Cutter not far from their neighborhood. I forget about leaving, but I'm not getting too close either. My hands are shaking a little but that is okay. Maybe I do need a shopping basket.

When I return to the produce, Jim and Lynn are out of sight. I pick up a bagged salad, roasted red pepper dressing, a cucumber, some cherry tomatoes and feta cheese, moving slowly. Hopefully, there's no chance of running into them. I would like some fresh flowers in the house and tulip displays are everywhere, a riot of color from bright orange to pastel pink and white. I pick out a bunch of pink ones and head over to the wine and beverage center. Maybe a nice merlot. I locate one, dropping it in the basket. I find a pinot grigio I've never tried. The label says it's got pear after-tones. Nice, pale yellow color. Gotta take it too. Finally, I need to pick out my pizza and then, I'll head home. I turn onto the frozen foods aisle and nearly run into a cart, fully laden with frozen foods. Oh happy day, it's *them*.

A small "Oh" escapes my throat as we all stop and

stare at each other. I had forgotten how Lynn's eyes slant just so, giving her an exotic air. She's wearing her dark hair shorter now, which adds to the Asian look and I see sparkles on her ear lobes. She looks attractive in a maroon silk blouse next to her dark hair and eyes. Nevertheless, she is sporting a few wrinkles around the eyes and mouth. She looks annoyed. Jim looks startled but a little pleased.

"Good morning," I muster, surprising myself. I hear my voice, and it sounds strong. I embrace it. I am strong. Better than ever, in fact. Lynn says nothing. Jim nods stiffly, hands in pockets. Maneuvering my cart around them, I manage to walk on trembling legs to the cold storage door from which I will retrieve my oh-so-delicious frozen portabella and spinach pizza. There it is. Got it. I slam the door shut.

And now I have to go. Yes, indeed, quickly, before my bravado evaporates and I am left sniveling on the floor.

As I drive home reliving the whole scene, laughter bubbles up, bursting through the surface and soon I'm cackling and it is uncontrollable and fun and I am literally high with it. Relief flows like a river, buckets of glee soar up out of my gullet, from the deepest parts, spilling over my lips and out into the atmosphere until I am cleansed and whole again.

CHAPTER TWENTY THREE

Julie

A lex is sleeping, finally. He isn't feeling well so I laid him down for a while. Mark is working at his computer in his office. Is it not weird that after all this time, I don't really know what my stepfather does for a living? Renae says he is a consultant and occasionally checks come in the mail, and he spends an inordinate amount of time on the telephone. But still, it seems sort of weird to me. Don't most white collar men go to an office? Oh well, he helps me out with Alex so I don't have to pay someone else to take care of him while I work.

The doorbell rings. And then again. *Oh crap.* Alex just fell asleep. If whoever is out there wakes him up, I am going to have one cranky baby. And in that case, I'm gonna be pissed.

"You better not wake my baby up," I say when I open the door.

A sheriff's deputy dressed in taupe and brown stands on my porch. He is young and cute and he's holding papers. Now what?

"Uh, sorry. I guess I could have knocked."

"What do you want?" I say, still listening for Alex's plaintive wail. Luckily, it does not come.

"Are you Julie Kruger?"

"Yes, why?"

He shoves some papers at me.

"I'm Deputy Sheriff Sean Nichols and I'm here to serve you with these papers."

"What are they?" I ask, taking them from him. Skimming down through, I see two orders of protection against me. One signed by Angela and one signed by Rodney. *Unbelievable.* "You've got to be kidding," I mumble.

"Sorry. Uh, what about Mark and Renae Jackson? Are they here?"

"No," I say, even though Mark is in his office.

"I guess you're over the age of eighteen," he says, which I do not find a bit funny. I glare at him and he quickly backs up. "Would you accept service on their behalf, that's what I'm asking."

"Sure," I say. He fills out a few lines, signs the stuff, hands it all to me and tips his hat. He wishes me a good day and then he's gone.

Un-fucking-believable. Rodney and Angela are frightened for their lives. They feel harm from us. For crying out loud.

"It's bullshit," I say to Mark as I hand him his documents.

"Obviously they've been served with our orders," he says dryly. "I'm not worried about it. The judge will see through them."

"But it's bullshit," I say.

"I know it's bullshit. Don't get too upset over it now. It'll be all right."

"Whatever."

I left my cell phone in the basement and when I

check it, I see one message from Rick. "Call me." I dial his number and wait.

"When were you going to tell me?" are the first words out of his mouth.

"Tell you what?"

"About your son with that guy, the one you said you didn't know and his psycho wife."

My stomach plummets. *Shit.* "How did you find out?" I say.

"Psycho wife came to my work. Told me all about it. She told me all about how you and her husband stayed out all night long, how she caught you fucking in a car, about how you chased him all over town. Just little things, Julie."

I close my eyes to keep the tears back but they slip through anyway.

"I'm so sorry," I say.

"You're sorry, all right. Yeah, well, you lied to me. And to think I was starting to like you. I thought you were something special but no, you lied. Fucking bitch." The anger in his voice pierces me. Rick's been humiliated. I wonder if Angela made a scene at the Olive Garden or if she caught him someplace alone. He hates me now and I can't blame him.

"Rick-" I want to tell him things are different now. That yes, I made a mistake and it hurt a lot of people but it is different now. I am different now. That I am operating with clear vision. That I would not put my parents or my friends or anyone through this. I want to tell him he can believe me because it is all true.

"Don't talk to me. Don't call me. And I hope you have an absolutely fucking amazing life with that asshole." *Click.*

Alex is waking up, fussy and hot. Hot tears roll down my cheeks. What a pair we are.

There seems to be no end to being called on the

carpet, paying for my mistakes, experiencing humiliation and self-loathing. Self-loathing. There it is. I hate myself. How could I have been so proud to be the diversion in a married man's life? Why did I think being the other woman gave me such control? Happy ending, really? All I feel is embarrassment and hot, putrid shame.

I hate what I've become. I can't blame it all on Rodney, although I'd like to. I was there too, a willing participant, an eager participant even. My face is hot with humiliation and the heat of holding a fussy baby.

Alex and I rock back and forth for a long time while my mind whirls.

Somehow, I have to break the cycle. I don't know if I'm strong enough or brave enough or whatever it takes, but somehow, I have to get away from Rodney and his poison. Poison coursing through my veins for so long.

Alex is finally quiet and so am I. I am quiet in my mind now.

Decisions, rock solid. I'm gonna stop lying. No more Little Queen Bitch. I'm gonna be a better person, somehow. Dammit all, I will. I have to or I see myself dying a little bit at a time, like my mother. I want love in my life. I want Alex to have the best of everything, especially a good mom. I'm gonna leave Rodney in the dust, take control of my life. That's what I'm gonna do.

That's what I'm gonna do.

CHAPTER TWENTY FOUR

Claudine

"Well, if you don't like the weather in the Queen City, just wait five minutes because it's gonna change." The TV weatherman sang it out this morning and isn't that the truth. It wasn't supposed to rain today but here we are, in the middle of a thunderstorm.

I am sloshing along down South Street looking for an antique shop Beth told me I needed to find. I would like to stop and get a giant latte for my stroll but not sure I'd be allowed to bring it in the store and so, regretfully, I don't do it. I keep moving, peering out from underneath my umbrella. It's nearly a Mary Tyler Moore moment because I'm gazing up at the old buildings as I go, which is another thing I love, old architecture.

I love the long windows and the old brick. All I need to do now is throw my hat in the air. I wonder about the people who built these places. Are their spirits still in the buildings and businesses they created? One even has a year carved into the brick, 1909. Springfield is a relatively young as towns go. But still, I love the history of it. I love that Wild Bill Hickock shot Davis Tutt on the city square, which is now just a few blocks behind me. I have tramped over Wilson's Creek so many times I could draw a map of the place. Every time I go to the library, I pour over old photographs. General Weaver's house, the Campbell legacy, the town square through the years. This town is more than Bass Pro and cashew chicken, and I have never developed an affinity for either one. Well, maybe a little bit for cashew chicken but that is food and who does not like to eat, right? At any rate, I am looking for a particular store number and it has got to be here someplace close but– *Umph.* Oh, I just ran into someone.

"Oh, I'm sorry," I gasp, looking up from underneath my umbrella. Oh. My. God.

"Claudine," he says quietly, but I think with pleasure. Red hot embarrassment flows down my body. I have not seen nor heard from Gabriel since the dinner fiasco at his house and I feel ridiculous and even a little naked in front of him now. He brushes my arm with his hand. "It's good to see you." He is not carrying an umbrella and his hair is just a little mashed from the rain but he looks heavenly. Sensual. Like the best sort of dream.

"Well, well." I look up and down the street and swallow hard. I am not smooth. In fact, I'm pretty clumsy. In the spirit of clumsy, I push my wayward hair out of my face and scrutinize him further, taking stock of the dark wool scarf around his neck. "Well, how've you been?" Again with the stupid, stupid, stupid.

He frowns a little bit at me. "I am doing well. And you?"

"Oh, good, good."

"Hmmm," he says. "Well, we are here, oddly enough, standing in front of a coffee shop. Won't you come in with me and have something?"

I hesitate just a minute, thinking of the antique shop I wanted to see but wanting to go into the coffee shop with Gabriel just as bad.

"One must learn to trust one's feelings, Claudine," he says gently. "There is no need to be afraid of me." He is bending close to my mouth under my umbrella and, once again, I am overwhelmed by the presence of him. Of course. Of course I will go in with him.

Once we enter the small, old building, I find myself entranced. The walls are exposed brick. The lighting fixtures are as close to the original as you could find. It is a clever little shop, quaint but unpretentious. I am also amazed the entire staff knows Gabriel's name and they call out to him. He waves and we take a table against the wall, close to the front window where an abundance of green plants crawl up the supports next to the glass. The aroma of coffee beans and good food permeates the space. A water fountain hangs on the old brick next to us. The water trickles and flows and I feel comfortable and not just a little languid.

A young man comes to take our order and I get a latte. Gabriel does the same and asks for a tray of cookies. Both are brought quickly.

"Are you a regular here?" I ask.

He laughs. "One might say that, yes." He looks around and then back at me and gestures toward the cookie tray.

I start to protest but he says, "American women think they are attractive when they resemble telephone poles. I, for one, do not enjoy being pierced through with someone's bones. There is nothing wrong with your body, Claudine. Nothing whatsoever."

I suddenly feel shy. My body has always been too round, too lumpy, too something wrong. Well, to be honest, *too big*.

"So what is your connection to this shop?" The

shortbread cookies are fantastic. I wish I wasn't enjoying them quite so much.

"I teach only part-time at the college. It is lucky I have no classes today and we could bump into one another. Quite literally, we bump into one another, yes?"

I laugh.

"This shop belongs to me. I am the owner."

Oh my.

"You are full of surprises, Gabriel," I say. What a pleasure, knowing I am sitting in this man's place of business. I am comfortable here. An unbidden thought shoots through my brain. *You could do this forever, Claudine.* Do what? And I realize my subconscious is telling me I could stand side by side with Gabriel for the rest of our lives. It is a nice thought, a pleasant thought and I will keep it in the back of my mind to dwell on later.

Pretty thoughts, but the man is staring at me.

"Tell me about you," he says. "Tell me about your life."

The latte is good and I am feeling sleepily sensuous. I tell him about Jim and my marriage, my daughter and my job. He tells me about his life in Florence, about his parents who died within hours of one another and were miles apart, his brother and his bakery in San Francisco and a woman he loved very much but could not keep. My life seems dull and pale next to his. He assures me it is not.

"Will you come by next week?" he asks. "I will cook again and maybe by that time, it will stop raining and we can dine al fresco."

"Looking forward to it," I say. Looking back at the coffee shop window, I see "TruBean" painted in curly yellow letters.

He walks me to my car. The antique shop is forgotten for a moment. But since I really came here to find the shop, it bounces to the foreground of my mind once again.

"Oh, can you tell me where this shop is?" I show him the name and address written on a piece of paper. He smiles.

"You are standing about two doors down from it. Would you like for me to show it to you?"

Of course. And he does. Inside, we find an antique light fixture, all antique brass and crystals. I love it but looking at the price tag, I regretfully leave it there. He is watching me. I can feel him everywhere in this place. He's wondering about what I like and what I would choose. We're dancing a tentative dance, me in that aisle, him in another, joining, parting. He walks up behind me and I sense him before he reaches me. I feel warm and pleasant and excited all at the same time. And a little flustered. My face reddens as I knock my hip against a square table and make a face. He makes one back. One step forward, one step back. Two more steps. In and out of booths, fingers pointing to this or that, a waltz of discoveries. Yes, it is a dance, which I am not sure I am much good at but I hope to not botch up too terribly.

We're finished. The dance has concluded, for now.

"Until next week, Claudine," he says as he opens my car door for me. He kisses my forehead again and my lips are burning. "I am looking forward," he says. I would love for him to take me in his arms right here on the street and press those beautiful lips against mine. Ah, maybe not. He shuts me in and I turn the key. He waves a kiss and he is back on the sidewalk. I drive away, my heart staying back, wishing I wasn't leaving, that I didn't have to go.

CHAPTER TWENTY FIVE

Julie

Raining again. Actually, it is more like storming the hell out of us. Tornado warnings are out. Lightning crackles all around me as I pull into the driveway. I've had a long day at work and I just want to go home and not be messed with. The kitchen lights are on, spreading a stream of yellow light from the windows onto the street. It makes me feel warm inside. I see Renae moving around in the kitchen. She's picking Alex up. Just for a minute, I sit and watch my little family.

Lightning flashes again and I see her in my rearview mirror. Angela is standing in the bushes across the street from my house. Instantly, I am out of the car. I do not dare get too close to her. No telling what she might do.

"Get away from us," I shout. "Leave us alone, you crazy bitch."

She isn't even looking at me. Rain is pouring down over her hair, matting it to her head. She's not wearing a jacket in this chilly rain. Surely, she is soaked to the bone. Rainwater is dripping off the bottoms of her jeans. She is watching the same thing I was watching through the kitchen windows. The crazy bitch is watching my family. She's watching my mother and my son together in our house. Angela is an intruder. She is an invader.

I take a step toward the edge of the sidewalk. "Angela!" Slowly, she turns her eyes toward me. "Listen to me, go away. Leave us alone."

Finally, she hears me. She takes a step toward me too and then stops. She turns and walks down the street in the rain.

I run for the back door and latch the screen behind me then I lock the wooden door.

"Mom." My voice is hoarse, scary.

Renae turns from scooping chicken out of Chinese to-go containers onto Alex's high chair, cutting it up for him.

"Julie, you're soaking wet." Her eyes widen. "What's wrong?"

"Angela's outside. She was out there watching you and Alex through the windows," I say. I move quickly, to pull the blinds down over the glass. Instantly, Renae is up, summoning Mark.

"Are you sure, Julie?" Renae says. "Did you see her?"

"Yes, yes. She was standing across the street, right in front of the hedge, watching. She was all spaced-out, acting like she was on something. She acted like she didn't hear me yelling at her to get away and then she turned around and walked down the street. I've seen her car parked down there a couple times when I came home. I think she's been watching us for a long time."

Mark is rummaging through one of the kitchen drawers. He pulls out a flashlight. "She's been parking where?"

"How often have you seen her?" Renae asks.

"Two or three times, I can't remember. It's that way." I point north.

"This is wrong. It's just wrong. We're being terrorized in our own home now." Renae covers her face with her hands. "Nobody will listen. I don't know what to do. Mark? Mark?"

Mark returns wearing a windbreaker. "I'll check and see if her car is still there. We should call the police."

"But she hasn't really done anything and what if she's gone? It's her word against ours," Renae says.

"I'll go with you," I say.

"No, you stay here with your mother and Alex. I'll go check it out. Renae, I think you should call just to document it."

Mark unlocks the door and vanishes out into the pounding rain. It's thundering so hard. Lightning cracks.

"Oh my God," Renae says, eyes wide. "Go get out of those wet clothes." She pulls a box down off the top of the refrigerator. "You didn't see this," she says, taking the lid off and pulling a gleaming silver pistol out. "If she comes back around, I am prepared to end this."

That can't be.

"Mom, don't you think–"

"Go get changed, Julie. You'll catch a cold."

In a few minutes, I am changed into dry clothes and Mark is back.

"The car is still there but it's empty," he says. "Did you call?"

"I did and they're sending someone over," Renae says. "Our supper is cold."

Mark sees the pistol lying on the counter. "Put it away for now, especially with the police coming."

Surreal, chilling reality cuts me to the bone. Here I stand in my kitchen, expecting the police at any moment and my mother is holding a pistol, which I assume is loaded. And Angela is still parked down the block.

Except she is not in the car. Where could she be? Is she lurking someplace else where she can peer into our house? Can she see me right now? Can she see Alex?

"Mummumum," Alex says. He wants some noodles. Renae absently spoons some lo mein on his tray. "Mummumum," he says again.

"I can't eat," I say. My stomach hurts so bad I think it might burst.

Mark shakes his head. Renae puts the gun back in the box. I shiver but not from cold.

Renae is right. We are prisoners in our own home and the jailer is Angela.

"I can't believe she's out on a night like this," Renae says.

"She's crazy," I say. "She's completely gone."

A car pulls up. The police are here. They take a statement from me and then from Mark. They check out Angela's car and run their flashlights around the street and into our yard. "If she comes around again, call us right away," one of them says.

Renae nearly comes out of her skin but Mark puts his arm around her and she says nothing.

Now the police are gone too and we are here in our home, which does not seem quite so safe or secure. It is not safe as long as Angela is allowed to roam free and nobody does anything to stop her. She must have snapped somehow, somewhere. I wonder where Rodney is and why isn't he dealing with her? I wonder if he even knows what she is up to. When will someone listen?

I bathe Alex and put him to bed. He has a full belly and he is freshly bathed and that makes him sleepy. He is such a happy baby. I do not want his world disrupted. I do not want his childhood ruined.

Mark, Renae and I are again sitting at the kitchen table. The Chinese has been reheated and picked over, but none of us have really eaten.

What about the gun in its box on top of the refrigerator. I did not even know we had a gun.

The phone rings. It's a hang-up call.

"When did you get the gun, Mom?" I ask.

Renae folds her arms on the table. "A while ago."

She looks desperate, disheveled, sort of like someone on the run.

"After the judge denied our last restraining order," Mark says. "We didn't want you to know."

"Why?" I say.

"We just thought it was better this way," Renae says. "Not sure why now."

All three of us hear it at the same time. Someone is scratching at the back door. The sound is barely discernible over the storm outside but, yes, it is there. Something or someone is scratching at the back door. Mark and Renae stare at each other and then at the door. Creeping to the back door and pulling the blinds just a bit, I can see her. Angela is crouched on her haunches on our back stoop and she is scratching at the wooden door. I turn and nod at them. Renae pinches her eyes shut for a second. Mark goes to the phone.

"Yes," I hear him say from the other room. "We need officers here, pronto."

We wait. We do nothing. We think we hear scratching and then we are not sure if we hear anything at all. The minutes tick by. Wind and rain slam into the house.

The bell rings. Mark swings the front door open but it is not the police. It is Rodney. Renae screams as he pushes the door open and marches past Mark.

"We've called the police," Mark says. "I don't know what you want but you better get out of our house."

He seems so big.

"Get out, Rodney," I say. "Get your wife away from us and get out."

He stops in the middle of the room. "Where is he?"

Oh my God. Alex. I rush for the basement door but he trips me and I fall on my hip and elbows. Pain shoots all the way to my shoulders. Struggling to get up, I see Renae also running for the basement door but Rodney grabs her arm and shoves her. She grunts and staggers against the wall. Where is Mark? I am up, trying to get to Alex. Somewhere in the background, I hear Mark on the telephone again, demanding help.

I hit the basement door before Rodney does and fall against it. He stops but only because he sees Renae. Something silver glints below the kitchen light. The pistol is out of its box, clutched in her hands. The box is on the floor, discarded. Her hands are shaking but her eyes are dark, determined.

Rodney puts his hands up. I hear sirens. Where is Angela, I wonder? But I have to get to Alex. Renae's hands are shaking as she holds the gun on Rodney. Surely it's not loaded. I hope she knows what she is doing but it makes no difference right now because I have to make sure my son is safe. Easing between Rodney and my basement door, I run down the basement stairs to Alex's bed. He is sleeping, his little chest rising and falling. Thank God there is only one way in and out of my little rabbit coop.

A door slams upstairs. Did it slam open or shut? Voices shouting, heavy footsteps, Renae's piercing scream, pounding sounds on the floor above my head. The noises are purposeful. Something falls to the floor. What is going on up there? I pick Alex up and mercifully, he stays asleep. Another roar of rain and thunder. The lights shudder.

"Did you have to summon the fucking SWAT team?" I hear Rodney complaining as I climb the stairs. The first thing I see as I get to the top step is Rodney, face down on the kitchen floor. A knee is in his back and his hands are behind him. He is being handcuffed. Lights are flashing through the window above the sink. Someone raised the blinds. Angela is half-lying, half-sitting against the cabinets next to the back door. She is dripping wet. Black streaks are running down her face from around her eyes.

"I need to see my wife. Where's Angela?" Rodney says over and over again.

The knee moves off his back and straightens up. Mark is holding Renae. The gun is nowhere in sight. I hurt. My elbows and shoulders ache.

Who else? Who else is here? What went on while I was below with Alex?

Looking around, I realize Renae is getting some medical attention for her wrist from a plumpish woman dressed in white. An ambulance is parked outside. So that's where the flashing lights are coming from. Springfield police officers seem to be everywhere. And then there is that deputy sheriff, the one who served us with the restraining orders. This is not county. Why is he here? He catches my eye and grins. Did he just wink at me? "Everything's all right," he says.

"So you say. What went on up here? Mom? Are you okay?"

Renae nods but says nothing. The medic has moved away from her now and I see her wrist is bandaged up.

"She's okay," Mark says. "She's got a sprained wrist from wrestling the gun around with me but she's going to be all right."

Someone helped Rodney up and he has hobbled over to where Angela lies, still prone by the cabinets but the medic seems to be talking softly to her. Angela is staring, uncomprehending. Finally, she says, "Shush, the baby," and points in my direction. "My baby is sleeping."

"Okay, this is just creeping me out," I say to

nobody. "What's going to happen to her? Is she gonna be taken somewhere? I mean, seriously, get her out of my house."

One of the officers stops and tells me Angela is going to be taken to the mental hospital as soon as Rodney signs off on her admission slip.

"But will he do it?" I turn to Rodney. He is crouched in front of Angela, talking soothingly to her. She can see him and only him. She grasps his arms. Rodney turns to me and nods. "It's already done," he says.

That Deputy Nichols is still standing beside me. "Let me take your son for you. I'll put him back to bed," he says and holds his hands out. Strangely enough, I let him. He bugs me but at least I'm not afraid of him. I release Alex into his arms, which seem awfully skinny to me, even with him being a pretty boy, and point to the basement door. He vanishes down the stairs.

"What about Mr. Moore?" Mark is asking. "We presume he's not going to just be let go."

"Of course not," the officer says. Apparently, Rodney is on his way to jail. "Both of them are out of your hair now for at least thirty days."

More statements. More signatures. This all promises more court appearances. I could live the rest of my life happily without any more of this. What about my mother brandishing the pistol at Rodney? I whisper my question to Mark and he shakes his head. "No charges," he says. Thank God.

Deputy Nichols returns and I thank him for taking Alex for me.

"No problem," he says and he smiles again. Pretty white teeth. Pretty blue eyes.

Hey, how did she get in here?" I ask.

"Mrs. Moore?" the deputy says.

"Yeah. How did Mrs. Moore get in our house?"

Deputy Nichols shows me the scratched up spot where Angela jimmied her way in with a small knife.

"She picked your lock," he says.

"Wow," I whisper. "It could have been a lot worse."

"Sure could have."

Finally, Angela and Rodney are gone, both taxied to their respective destinations. Only Deputy Nichols remains with us. I have questions I think we all have questions. Mark and Renae are sitting side by side on the couch. Renae seems exhausted.

"I don't know." My voice sounds like it's coming from a thousand miles away. I have no point in mind whatsoever, but it doesn't matter because the deputy seems to understand what it is I want to know.

"She flipped," he says.

"Obviously," Renae says from the couch. She does not intimidate him, the pretty officer man.

"She's been stalking us all this time then," Mark says. "She's been obsessed with the one thing she couldn't have from her husband."

"Rodney didn't come here to kidnap your boy tonight," the deputy says. "My thought is Rodney realized what danger you were in and followed her. He may have saved your lives."

Renae snorted. "We should thank him? We should thank him for all this mayhem? All this chaos? Are you crazy?"

"Why did he ask where Alex was then? He asked us that when he came in," I say.

"He may have thought she'd gotten in the house some way and she was with Alex," the deputy says. "That's the only explanation I can think of."

"He went straight to the back door after he said that," Mark says. "He heard her out there, I suppose, same as we did."

"And she had a weapon," I say. What a chilling

thought, to have Angela loose in our house with the potential of hurting us.

"A knife, the knife she jimmied the door with. Nothing fancy, just a sharp kitchen knife."

"She's in deep shit, isn't she?" I say.

"You could say that," he says. "Now look, no more worries for you all. It's all been taken care of. They're gone. They're not coming back to get you. I'll let you folks get to bed. Try and relax. It's all over now."

I walk him to the door to spare Mark and Renae the trouble. Renae is about unhinged anyway. The two of them call out their thanks and shuffle out of the living room.

It's nice looking at Deputy Sean Nichols on my porch in the clouded moonlight, pelting rain all around, flashes of lightning, trembles of thunder.

"Your son is really cute," he says.

I concur.

"What do you want, deputy, and don't play me because I know the difference."

I'm leaning half-in and half-out of the doorway, my hand on the doorframe. *I've seen liars before. I've seen players. Which are you, Deputy?*

That's when he astounds me.

He asks me if he can call me sometime and like a dope, I say yes. It'll never work out. I won't get my hopes up. Guys like Sean Nichols don't go for girls who've been around the block a few times like me. But he sure is cute. Nice butt too.

CHAPTER TWENTY SIX

Claudine

Arriving early at work, I find a voicemail from Julie Kruger. The time says 11:17 p.m. last night. She says she really needs to talk to me, that the whole thing with Rodney and Angela blew last night, big time.

"Call me on my cell," she says. "It's important."

I guess I better have some coffee. I'll get geared up and then I'll call. God only knows what she's going to tell me. God only knows when she gets up. However...

"Julie?" I say into the phone. She sounds muffled, like she has a cold. I assume she must have been crying. This must have been bad.

"Oh, Claudine, thank you for calling me back," she says.

"No problem. What's going on?"

"It's Rodney and Angela. The whole thing came to a head last night. Okay. All right. I came home from work and I found Angela lurking around in the bushes by our house and then Rodney sort of broke into the house and it was a crazy-ass mess."

Outside, the sky is clouding up again. The storm last night was hellacious. I planned on cleaning branches out of my yard this evening if the weather held but it looks as if we are in for more rain. Angela lurking in the bushes? In tornado season in Missouri? Wonderful. It just gets better and better, I guess.

"Angela was lurking in the bushes?"

"Yeah. She's been stalking me for weeks. I don't know if I told you that part but I'd see her pass through the intersection by our house or she'd be parked down the street – just stuff. And then last night, she was right across from the house and I saw her so I yelled at her to get away and she acted all crazy and stuff, like she couldn't hear me. Mark, my stepdad, he went and looked down the street because her car was down there but she wasn't in her car. So he comes back and then Rodney shows up and we called the cops and everything and he just walks into our house looking for Angela."

"Looking for Angela in your house?"

"Yeah. And, oh my God, it was so creepy, she was out on our back step, scratching at the door like a cat."

Good God. Wait until Leon hears this.

"Anyway, she had a knife and she broke the door lock with it. I didn't see her do it because I was downstairs making sure Alex was safe and the cops came and arrested Rodney and, get this, Rodney actually signed Angela into the mental hospital. She's going to be there for a long, long time. Well, I hope she will be."

"So, how did Rodney know to find Angela at your house?"

"Well, and this is really creep-o, but she was all delusional and she thought Alex was her baby and she'd come to get him. And Rodney knew what she was gonna do. I suppose she'd flipped out and all, so he came to make sure she didn't do anything."

"Oh, he's a hero now."

Julie giggles. "I guess. Except the hero is in jail. Breaking and entering, trespassing, violating the restraining order. Oh, you should have seen Renae. She held a gun on him."

"Is Renae in jail?"

"Nope. That was pretty cool. Didn't know my mom had it in her."

Didn't surprise me Renae would bare her teeth as the dominate female of the herd.

After disengaging from Julie, I go in to speak with Leon about the whole crazy event, which I suppose will provoke some sort of reaction. Well, to my surprise, not so much. He stares at me as if I am speaking Greek and then chuckles. I guess, in retrospect, it could be funny. "So, the idiot finally did something," is all he says and then he turns away from his computer screen and actually looks at me. "Here's what I want you to do. Write a letter to the guardian. Tell him everything you've told me. And then tell him we want no visitation of any sort between Rodney and Alex. Not now, not in thirty days, not in a thousand years. Okay?"

I say okay.

"How long will he be in jail?"

"Thirty days is what she tells me. She doesn't think he'll bond out. And Angela's locked up for at least thirty days anyway."

"Okay. Write that letter to the guardian. Say it nicely."

He always tells me that, say it nicely. It makes me wonder if I tend to say things un-nicely. He's abruptly turned back to his computer screen so I know it is time for me to depart. So I do, but I just can't help but wonder if we could have, should have, discussed it more, maybe done something more. Something.

CHAPTER TWENTY SEVEN

Andrea

Elliott is at it again. I will give him credit for being a full-time asshole, that's for sure.

I took the bull by the horns yesterday and went out for coffee with an old friend of Elliott's and mine, Lucy Pope. Her husband, John, happens to be a doctor and one of Elliott's oldest friends. When I called her, I wasn't sure she would accept the invitation, being on the other side of the fence, as it were, but she jumped at it. I should have known. Nobody in my old world does anything by accident.

So here I am, sitting at Starbucks with Lucy, who's dressed in white cuffed capris and a short white jacket, bangles and baubles galore. I am in my nicest sweat suit, the attire I prefer these days. She looks me over, pulling her $500 dollar sunglasses down her nose, and dismisses my appearance. She had big news, and that pre-empts my less than classy attire.

"Jackie's so mad," Lucy says over her Starbucks mug. "She's absolutely livid with you, you know."

Unfortunately, we live in a quasi-Peyton Place where everyone knows everyone else's business. It's a small town made up of doctors and doctor's wives and, of course, ex-wives.

"With me? Why?" Jackie is Elliot's first ex-wife. I have not spoken to her in at least a year.

Lucy rolls her eyes and looks out the window. "I hate this place. Is it ever going to stop raining? I swear, we're living in a marsh over there." She turns back to me. "Okay, here's the skinny. Elliott's been telling people around the community he offered you a million-dollar settlement and you laughed in his face. He says you told him you were going to go after half his personal worth."

"What? A million dollars? If he would offer me a million dollars, I'd be out of his hair so fast, he wouldn't even see me leave. A million dollars? Really?"

Lucy sipped her Starbucks delicately. "Uh-huh. Jackie didn't ask for that much. She's pissed."

"And she believes that?"

"That's what he's telling her and everybody else. Of course she believes it."

"And she was married to him for fifteen years and bore his children and she didn't ask for that. I get it. Well, he didn't offer me a million dollars. Let her and everybody else hear that. Who is everybody else, by the way?"

Lucy fluttered her hands. Her bracelets bang together. "Everybody. Oh, and he's broke."

"Sure he is." I sink back in my chair. "Ah Lucy, this makes me look like a gold-digger, doesn't it."

The subtle glint in her eyes makes me wonder if she might be perhaps a bit satisfied with Elliott's defaming of me. I wonder who my friends actually are but then, in this community, as Lucy calls it, does anyone have any real friends? How often would Lucy and I have chatted about this one and that one, dissecting their lives, laughing about their private business, casting judgment on their choices and then meeting them for lunch, kissing them on the cheek as if we knew nothing? How often had we supported one of our own, knowing every dirty detail before it was told to us? *Not too God-like, Andrea.* We were so privileged and we knew it and we wore our privilege proudly, greedily even, flashing it not only in each other's faces but in the faces of the women we knew we had authority over because their lives contrasted with ours. Some kind of authority. What kind of people were we?

Looking at my watch and feigning surprise, I tell Lucy I have another appointment. She does not seem too surprised or offended. Getting to my feet, I turn back and ask her, "Lucy, were we ever friends?"

Her eyes turn blank on me and then glaze over. No matter. I know the answer. It's understood.

"As much as we could be," she says. "Under the circumstances."

I nod and walk back out into the rain. "Goodbye Lucy," I whisper as I drive away. I see her through the big glass window, still sitting in the booth, already on her cell phone. She is pulling on her earring, most likely, I suppose, she is talking to one of our so-called group. Friendships are fleeting, if not completely opaque, in our circle. It is not difficult to bid it adieu.

Moving on to better things may be a challenge, however. My classes are nearly over until fall again. I need a reason to get up in the morning. The Ukrainian missionary trip Pastor mentioned is still wandering through my mind. Putting a little distance between me and my marriage might not be a bad thing either. Pastor says about a dozen of us will be going. I wonder if it is safe. I am a little concerned about the political climate over there.

If the divorce would be over by the time we are expected to leave, which I hear is early June, it would be perfect. If only Elliott would settle with me and I could fly off, free and clear, starting a new life. And he could do the same. Now that Jackie's remarried and he is free of that huge maintenance obligation, he should be agreeable to getting rid of both of us at one time. Just think, Elliott, you'd be rid of both of your wives. How convenient would that be? Ha. Who are we talking about here, Andrea? *Dear Elliott, Hand over a half-million dollars and I promise I will be out of your life forever. Hugs and kisses, A.* Right. Well, maybe not today but I hope soon. I really hope it will be soon. What do you think, Lord? Soon, yes, yes?

CHAPTER TWENTY EIGHT

Claudine

"Well, as it turns out they do want to mediate." Josie's standing in my office, looking pissed. She's glaring at me as if she would like me to know this mess is wholly and unequivocally my fault. Maybe since I already mentioned it, I opened a Pandora's Box and now somehow, opposing counsel and party have thought of it also. From my brain to their ears, right? Josie folds her umbrella up and props it in the corner of my office. "Rita left a voicemail for me this morning. And I'm going to have to cover it because Leon doesn't think anything will get done if he's there. Elliott Sommerfield won't cooperate if Leon shows up. So Ted McClintock's deposition is off, among other things. Things I would rather be doing."

I am not sure what to say but I get the feeling I am being blamed for something and I am not sure what it is or why. I thought mediation made sense in this case, but apparently somehow it does not. Besides that, just because I mentioned it does not mean I brought it to fruition.

"The thing is, we need to know Elliott Sommerfield's personal worth before we mediate and we don't know that for sure. We need an accounting expert and I don't know with all of Elliott's business ties in this town if we can find someone who doesn't know him or hasn't done business with him. I'll have to think on that. I'll talk to Leon." Josie gets up and then sits down again. I nod in acknowledgment. It is clear to me no matter what I might say, it will be the wrong thing so I wait and listen before I venture in.

"We've got a lot of financial information in the file—"

And would you like to review it, was what I was going to say. I have a pretty good idea of what Elliott Sommerfield is worth, but that is not the point and I know it. The financial documents are finished as well, but that is not the point either.

"I read your memo about the half-million dollar offer," Josie says. "I know she wants a letter going over to Rita, telling her we weren't aware of it but now we are so we're going to respond. I'm not sending a letter over there acknowledging it. Call Andrea and tell her to grow up. I'm tired of fighting her battles for her."

The look on my face must be causing her to retract that statement. "No, just tell her we're not going to even respond. Let them look stupid, not us."

Josie stands up, smoothing the folds in her handkerchief skirt, which, unfortunately, she is too heavy to be wearing. It resembles layers of Jell-O and pudding. "I'm leaving. I'm in need of retail therapy."

I am not sure how we got from there to here but okay.

"See ya," I say. As soon as Josie is out of earshot, Beth appears at my door.

"Did I hear her saying she needs retail therapy?

How long was she in here anyway?"

Beth and I dart a look at the clock. It's barely 10:30.

Well of course, we wish it was us, but it's not. We don't have the juris doctorate, the passport to a flimsy schedule. Both of us walk back to our desks and go back to the dirty leg-work, a little wistfully maybe.

After work, Beth and I make a run for our favorite Mexican restaurant, Maria's. It's the most wonderful little eatery, on South Street, south of the Springfield Square, wedged between an electric newspaper and a sub shop. The margaritas are wonderful and both of us feel the urge for one after our day. We're seated at a Mexican tiled table, order quickly and our waiter moves away.

"So, tell me about this guy, the one we saw that night," Beth says. I've finally let the cat out of the bag, so to speak, but so far, I have not given much detail. This is my delicious little secret and I am not sure I am ready to let anyone else feast on it. Gabriel is compartmentalized behind a door in my mind labeled "Mine, Mine, All Mine." It is, I suppose, time to share at least a little morsel with Beth though.

I grin. "He must be something," Beth says.

"Well, yes. One might say that," I say. I am still grinning stupidly.

"So, give it up, girl. We ain't getting no younger."

Our drinks arrive, along with chips and salsa. Perfect opportunity for me to stall a second or two longer while I discard the paper from my straw and give my margarita a little stir. I poke the green lime through the golden liquid, straight down to the bottom.

"He's very nice," I say.

Beth salts her chips. "He's a music professor, right? And what else?"

"And things are progressing nicely. I don't think there's anything he hasn't done. I mean, he cooks, he's musical, he's been in business, he owns a coffee shop up the street, by the way. He does remodeling–"

"Your bathroom," Beth says. She skipped right over the coffee shop part.

My bathroom. Could I? Should I ask him about that? Presuming he would even be interested in helping me? And what about the obvious – payment? Do I want someone I am interested in romantically around that much, particularly in my most private space, at least for right now? I've not only grown used to my privacy, I adore it. I am used to not having to share with anybody, except maybe Keri when she blunders in to borrow mousse or something.

"Uh, I hadn't thought about that." And I do not want to think about it. Instead, I turn my attention to my drink. Yum, this margarita is good, perfectly sweet and sour at the same time, and salty around the rim.

"I'm just saying," Beth says, but she is looking at me the way a hawk looks at a field mouse. I know she is not just saying anything.

Gabriel working on my bathroom. The idea does not really appeal to me. Seems a little bit much but I stow it away for later. What if Gabriel were to work on my shower and what if he was to kiss me the way he did the other night? And what if one thing was to lead to another? It is not like my bedroom is nine miles from my bathroom. What if? I cannot say I am opposed. Later. Thoughts for later.

Finally, we leave, running down the street in the rain to our respective vehicles. It's been storming so much, the culverts are overflowing and my street is a little flooded.

Keri is waiting for me. She has grilled cheese sandwiches and cream of tomato soup ready for the two of us. What a dear sweet girl I have. As we eat at the battered and treasured kitchen table, I wonder how many other mothers and daughters – or lovers, college roommates or other folks – are doing the same thing. As my daughter and I sit in our kitchen, lit only by the lamp on the counter, a tiny orange light pokes out into the darkness promising a safe haven.

Eventually, the dishes are washed and put away. Keri and I amble up the staircase to our bedrooms. I give her a solid kiss on the forehead before turning in.

The storm rumbles on through the night. Lightning cracks over my head and I wake up with a start. Instinctively, I put my hand out to the spot where Jim used to sleep. Not that I am afraid of storms. In fact, I rather enjoy them and, in particular, I used to enjoy making love with my husband while rain pounded on the roof. No, it is reassurance I am looking for. It is the warmth of his back, the solidness of his arm, the rhythm of his breath.

And then I remember. We are divorced. Oh yeah. *That elephant in the room, silly Claudine.* I pull his pillow close to me and wrap my arms around it. It doesn't really smell like him any longer, having been through the wash a number of times, but it is the only reassurance I am going to get. I hold it tight until I fall back to sleep.

CHAPTER TWENTY NINE

Andrea

Here we are at mediation, or everyone is here except Elliott. The mediator is a woman, Lori Lawrence, and I see Elliott will be surrounded by women, which will probably appeal to him on some level. Rita is here, checking her messages on her cell phone. She looks up and announces Dr. Sommerfield is on his way. Josie is sitting behind me. She looks annoyed. It seems to me she always looks annoyed when I see her and I am beginning to wonder if she is annoyed with me, annoyed with having to work, annoyed with my case or just annoyed period. She already told me she wouldn't say much unless I needed her, and I may. I am not sure I can hold my own with Elliott. And now Elliott is fashionably late. How nice.

I wish Claudine was here, rather than Josie. I have the feeling my case has intruded on her time. Right before we stepped into Lori Lawrence's office, I asked Josie if she liked my outfit. She looked at me as if I were speaking Greek. I explained it was the outfit I wore on my wedding day, the going away outfit, and she laughed. I thought it was appropriate to wear it to begin ending my marriage, a multi-purpose suit. I wonder if Elliott will notice.

My thoughts are tossed aside. Elliott is here. He speaks to Rita briefly and they sit down.

Before long, I realize mediation is a huge mistake and my attorney is not going to speak on my behalf.

Elliott is intent on selling the house.

"What is the house worth?" Lori, the mediator, asks.

"Roughly, four hundred twenty-five thousand," Elliott says. He is humble, soft spoken, eyes cast down. What a joke.

Lori is scribbling on her pad. "What about the debt?"

"Two hundred eighty-five thousand," he says. "I'd like to use the equity to pay down debt. I owe on my new building and equipment—"

Lori is still writing.

"You do realize, though, after realtor and commission fees and paying the mortgage, little will be left? There will be little to divide."

Yay! Someone sees it. Elliott looks sad.

"I don't mean to divide it. I think the money should go toward debt."

But wait. "Where am I expected to live?" I ask "I mean, if you're selling the house, then where do I go?"

Elliott says nothing. Lori looks at Josie. Josie says nothing. Lori looks back at me. "You don't want to sell, I take it."

"Well, no. Not until this is over. I have no place to go. I have no money. I mean, I'm barely making it on what Elliott gives me now and that's with being able to live in the house. There's just no way—"

"What I was thinking," Elliott says to Lori, "is I

would move into the house and Andrea could move into the rental I'm living in."

"And be your tenant? No, thank you. How would that be security for me?"

Elliott's face turns to stone. No one says anything for a minute.

"Well, let's come back to the house in a minute," Lori says. "Talk to me about your other assets and debts."

Rita slides a list across the table. "This is the most current list I have. What about you, Josie?"

Josie pulls the paper over and glances at it. "Looks good to me," she says and slides it back. Lori is looking at Josie as if she is a little surprised at her apparent lack of interest. I would like to see the list but it has been pulled away and Lori is reviewing it.

"What's the issue with the tax refund check?" she asks. She is looking at me, so I answer.

"My attorney has the check. We'd rather not cash it until the divorce is over. We propose Elliott and I split it equally."

"So, thirteen thousand to you and thirteen thousand to you, Dr. Sommerfield?" she says.

Elliott shakes his head. "No, I would like to take immediate possession of the check and pay some debt down."

"I see," Lori says, looking at him over the top of her glasses. "What would you apply the check to?"

Elliott explains his significant amount of debt, which is associated with building the new clinic. It is over $1 million and I am wondering how $26,000 is going to help.

"And so you're not willing to split the check with your wife?" Lori says.

Elliott says he is not.

"May I ask why not?"

"Because my wife has a spending problem, unfortunately, as well as a drinking problem, and I don't believe any amount of money would be put to good use if she were to receive it. I see it as throwing good money after bad, so to speak. I, on the other hand, have built up a practice over the years, I am an investor and I know where the money can be best spent. I have incurred substantial debt due to the purchase of the land and the construction cost, as well as equipment, as you can imagine." Elliott's face is blank. Mine is not.

Elliott is unbelievable. It is taking all of my strength not to reach across the table and slap his smug, obnoxious face.

"Well, yes, I can imagine. My husband is in construction as well," Lori says. She is taking notes. She smiles, but I think she is smiling at the thought of her prosperous husband and her own comfortable life. Elliott thinks he forged a bond here. He thinks he is winning her over.

"Here's what I think," she says. "I think the judge is going to award you some maintenance, Andrea. It won't be forever and it will be modifiable. I think if we can agree on a number and duration, we'll be one step ahead. The house will be sold. The proceeds will be split between the two of you. Elliott, you will receive the assets you brought into the marriage. That is, your retirement account, your investment accounts and your bank account. You will receive all debt incurred in your name and the clinic's name. Andrea, you will receive the property you came into the marriage with, which seems to be a bank account, the Edward Jones account and your personal property. You will receive a vehicle. It looks like there are four of them and no debt at all. Elliott will gift one over to you. You will pay your credit card debt."

"If the house is put up for sale, I want her to move out immediately," Elliott says. "I'm not happy about paying any maintenance and I don't want to split the house proceeds, either. My practice bought the house and I think I should be entitled to what it brings."

"The house is marital property," Lori says. "Granted, this is not a long-term marriage. However, the house was purchased during the marriage. Yes, your income allowed you to purchase the property. But there is case law that supports a non-working spouse in situations like this. Unless the two of you agree you will receive the proceeds from the house sale, I believe the judge will split it."

"I'm willing to give in on the house," I say. "But I do want a cash settlement."

Elliott clears his throat.

"I understand there was an offer at the beginning of this case," Lori says.

"The offer has been withdrawn," Rita says.

It seems every time I turn around, they are closing a door on me. I look to Josie for some type of reaction but there is none. In fact, she is searching through her purse for something.

"It was a good offer," Elliott says. "Much more than I'm willing to pay now. If I do end up paying maintenance, I want a monthly accounting from her down to the penny on what she's spending."

"Are you serious?" I say. "When will you just let up?" Instantly, I know it is the wrong thing to say but I am tired of this.

Lori puts her pen down. Silence. Mediation is over.

On my way out, I see Josie standing next to Lori and I hear her telling her she is on her way to purchase a labradoodle. She thinks her kids will love it. I am amazed she had nothing whatsoever to say during mediation and now she is talking up a storm about buying a designer dog. Why did Leon turn my case over to her anyway? I wonder if he would take it back. I would hate to offend Josie though.

Walking alone to my car, I wonder where Elliott is. I see him and Rita talking, standing next to his Range Rover. He looks over at me with a look that says, *don't you dare talk to me. Do not even acknowledge me*. I wave anyway and get in my car. Settlement seems so far away now. I wonder if I blew it in there. Surely not. Surely they will not throw me out of my home, not yet. I wish I knew what Josie and Leon are thinking. I would like to call Claudine. Dammit. My cell phone is messed up. I will have to take it to Cingular.

Leaving Cingular, I would like to cry. The warranty has expired. I cannot afford a new phone and I need this thing for everything from communication to address book to appointments, classes and on and on. I rely totally on it and I cannot afford to replace it. *Oh Lord, please give me strength to make it through this. Please resolve this situation. Thank you, Lord. Thank you, Lord*.

The tears are coming anyway. I keep telling myself this will not last forever but it sure seems like it has gone on that long already. I wish I could melt Elliott's heart just a little. My credit cards are due and my doctor appointments need to be paid. This is harder than it has to be. As soon as I get home, I call Claudine. She tells me she will talk to Josie and see what they can do, and she tells me to hang in there and we hang up. It is a little thing but it helps.

But not quite enough. The festering sore is erupting, spreading its gruesome, nasty discharge into my mind.

I know at least one bottle is here someplace. It is in the cabinet underneath the entertainment center. Aha, there it is. In fact, I find two. It has been a long time since I had a drink and I stare at the label for a few minutes, imagining the vinegar-grapey taste rolling down my throat and the quiet oblivion that would follow. Do I want it? Yes, I want it bad. What if? Just a taste. Just like Elliott used to try and get me to do. In fact, I think one of these bottles might be the remnants of a Christmas gift from one of his associates some time ago. Is this the bottle he wanted me to open and drink with him that year? No, no, he threw that one at me after he drank the majority of it. Bastard.

I want a drink. I need a drink. Which is worse? All the same thing, I suppose. My head is starting to reel. If only I could gain some peace somehow. Control. That is what I need in my life. Funny thing, a corkscrew is in my hand. Glass. Ah, let's use one of the nice ones. I need this. I need, I crave the sweet oblivion. Lord knows, I probably deserve it. *Oh Elliott, why did you push me to this point? I loved you. I loved you so much.*

CHAPTER THIRTY

Claudine

Another long day at work. I'd like to relax and leave it all behind but somehow I can't. It was a busy day, for sure. Fires, lots of fires. For one, Andrea Sommerfield's cell phone went out and she's unable to get it replaced and then her car broke down and she was left sitting on the side of the highway with no phone. Luckily, someone stopped to help her and she didn't end up being kidnapped, killed or any of the other grisly things that seem to be happening with regularity these days. I talked to Josie about Andrea's plight, who talked to Rita, who talked to Dr. Sommerfield, and then back to Josie and then to me.

"Well, I heard back from Rita," Josie said. "It really pissed Elliott Sommerfield off. He's refusing to pay for anything. So call her and tell her. Or wait, I'll call her."

That was the end of it. So what if Elliott Sommerfield is pissed off? Andrea is our client, not him. It seems as though Josie did the least she could do and then, since Elliott is pissed off, she is finished with it. I just don't get it.

In a few minutes, Josie comes back to my office. "Well, I couldn't get ahold of her and I'm leaving. Keep trying, will you?"

I appreciate my job, believe me, especially when so many people are without any kind of income. Leon's not a bad person. If the higher powers were more interested in what they went to law school to do for humanity, and for the rest of their lives at that, it would make my place at the firm easier.

"Nuts, just nuts," I say to no one in particular. Supper tonight is chilidogs, a particular favorite of Keri and me. We're cooking when she says, "Dad says he's taking me car shopping next weekend."

She drops the chopped onions into the hamburger sizzling on the stove while I split and brown the jumbo hotdogs in a little butter in the skillet. Scoring the outside just a bit and searing them in hot butter seems to brown them up nicely.

Car shopping? Somewhere in the back, no the front, of my mind I always imagined that would be something we would do together. Her father, her mother and her. I can't say I'm not annoyed. What trick is Jim pulling anyway? He can well afford to buy her a car. *Hold on, Claudine. Don't get mad.* Is this about me? Yes, I finally decide. I am the mother. Of course it is about me.

In other words, I'm mad.

"He is? When did he decide this?" I pull the hotdogs out of the butter, laying them in big toasted buns. Tomato sauce, some Worcestershire and chili powder in the meat mixture, stir it around a little bit. Maybe some cumin, smoky and hot. Cumin seems to make the world go around. "Want to pour the dressing over the coleslaw?" I ask her as I stir the meat.

Damn you, Jim. This should be something we do together.

It is about economics and I know it. Jim will not ask me to help pay for the car, I'm sure. But then there is Lynn and, as small as it may seem, I would rather not have her income play any part in my daughter's first car.

"I don't know. Last time we had dinner, I guess," she says. "Maybe longer."

"Oh? What are you going to get?"

"Oh, who knows," she said. "I don't want anything big."

I think of my Toyota Land Cruiser in the driveway. Jim bought it for me.

"I don't want anything too small either. Lynn said I should get a Mazda Miata."

I cock my head. *Really? A Miata? Lynn said?*

"She's so weird," Keri says. "What would I do with one of those? You can't put anything in them." She rolls her eyes and sets the coleslaw on the table. I pile chili and cheese on the hotdogs and shove the pan under the broiler.

What ridiculous bullshit.

"I'm calling your father," I say. I am tired of Lynn said this and Lynn thinks that. And I am tired of being left out of events in my daughter's life. He may have switched out one of the players but I am not leaving the field. No fucking way.

Of course, he does not answer his cell phone so I leave a message. "Jim, when were you going to tell me about buying our daughter, that's right, our daughter, a car? And please, please understand I want to be a part of that process, will you? You, me and our daughter." I am not mentioning Lynn. To hell with it. Maybe I should but I keep myself from doing it. Keri is looking at me bug-eyed.

Fifteen minutes later, he calls me back.

"Claudine, don't get all pissed off." He is annoyed with me, but I don't care. I am in the mood to fight. I feel all crackly, like a string of firecrackers lit on the sidewalk.

"When were you going to get around to letting me in on this anyway? This is our daughter we're talking about, *Jim*," I say. "This is something important in her life and I want to be there."

"I would have told you."

"When? When she rolls the car into the driveway?"

I hear him sigh heavily. "Look, it doesn't matter who's there or who's not there."

What? This is not taking the high road. He is making an excuse for being thoughtless.

"In other words, you planned on you and Lynn taking her around to car lots."

"No, no, no. I mean, she'll probably be there with us. With me." Uh-huh.

"No, Jim. I insist. This is our daughter. I want to be there." I am pacing the kitchen. Keri is outside, in the rain, feeding a bit of hot dog to the orange kitten. That annoys me too. She is avoiding the scene, crouching out in the rain, for crying out loud. Maybe I am just irritable. Maybe not.

For a minute, Jim says nothing. "All right. We'll work something out."

"Thank you," I say and hang up. I am in an uncharitable mood. The idea of involving Lynn in the car deal. What a freaking joke. It hit me all wrong, the car shopping idea, and maybe I didn't handle it well but I think I'm right. So screw them.

My whole day seemed to stem from the gates of hell so my anger could come from one of a dozen things. I met with my new client this morning, the one whose husband does not need a nightlight because a blue ball of light exists in his chest, and now she wants us to pursue his entire VA monthly benefit and half of his social security disability payment. "Leave him with nothing," she says to me. "I mean, he'll still have something like, what, $200 or $250 to make it through the month? His meds are paid. He lives with his girlfriend who's a loser too. What's he need the money for? Cigarettes, that's all. I mean, this is why I hired Leon in the first place, because he's aggressive. Know what I mean? He'll get me everything, won't he? He'll be aggressive?"

Looking into her pasty face, I can almost see a giant white pig staring back at me. What I would like to tell her is to get the hell out of this office and do not come back but, of course, I sit and take notes and reassure her Leon is aggressive and he has a good reputation, but I also tell her it is not likely she will get everything and to be prepared for that. "What? I deserve everything. I worked, I paid the bills. Well, I don't want any of the debt," she says. "I won't take it. He ran it up, he can pay for it. And what about those damn Beanie Babies?" She is getting louder. "He bought all those stupid things over the Internet and left me with them. I can't sell them. They are worth nothing. What's Leon going to do about that?"

I have to tell her I do not really know what Leon will do about that, but if she is that concerned, she could pack up the Beanie Babies and get them to her husband and let him deal with them. "Oh no," she says. "No. If I can get anything for them, I want to keep every last one of them so I can sell them. Why should he get the profit?"

Sometimes, it is the things between people that really get to me.

"Oh, and something else," she says. There's always something else. "My parents live in Arizona and they're elderly. They have a house out there and they've already said me and the girls could move out there and live in that house. I'd buy it from them and find a position at a college someplace. I've already made inquiries. How long do you think this will take? So I can move, I mean."

I have to tell her that, right now, she cannot move without permission of the court due to the two minor children. Not even across the street.

"Even if I have a job to go to?"

Even so. Permission of the court.

She guffaws at me. "Well, see, he's just messing with my life some more."

Of course.

"Well, what would Leon say if I asked him?"

The question rankles me, but I let it go. Leon is the one with the law degree, after all.

"He would tell you the same thing as I am telling you. We'd have to file a motion and ask the court's permission. We would tell the court all the reasons you want to relocate. You would have to notify your husband in writing, sixty days before you plan to leave, certified mail, return receipt requested,"

"Just so I can move and better myself?"

"Providing him with your address and telephone number and we will have a visitation schedule prepared so he can be assured you're not moving and denying him access to his kids."

"That's crazy. I don't see why he has to have visitation anyway. He's living with his girlfriend, for crying out loud. Oh well, okay. It's always the innocent ones who get screwed."

Hard day. And I understand hard days are common in family law, but who is innocent in this new situation? I wonder about it all the way back to my office, except I don't go there. Instead I take a detour and stop by Leon's office to tell him of his new client's ideas on relocating. He tells me exactly what I expect. We have to file a motion if she insists on going through with this. Sixty-day notification, certified mail, return receipt requested. Visitation schedule. I tell him about the Beanie Babies.

"Tell her to sell the damn things any way she can," he says. "But tell her they are marital property because they were purchased during the marriage. She will have to decide whether she's going to allow him part of what she gets for them or not. And tell me what she says."

"She wants his entire VA benefit and part of his social security," I say. "And none of the debt." His face darkens.

"I'll have to talk to her about that. I want you to write a memo outlining every detail of what you just told me so I know what to say to her when I meet with her. And one last thing, Claudine. Do not, *do not*, practice law without a license."

Ah, that old chestnut, the bane of every legal assistant's existence, spoken continuously but the fact is, *practice law without a license* is written in the margin of the job description. There's no way around it. Family law is fraught with high emotion and the legal assistant is the liaison between client and attorney. It's too much for the attorney to deal with hour after hour, day after day, especially an attorney with high client volume, such as Leon.

Did I speak out of line with the new client, dispense legal advice? No, but the line is so thin I can see how sometimes staff crosses over, and I can see how it would be misunderstood.

The directive is bothersome, and I wouldn't have to practice law without a license had he not put me in this position. It's not like he volunteered to meet with his own client in the first place. It has been a hell of a day, and going to bed will be just wonderful but I suppose I should make things right with my daughter first.

Keri is lying on her bed, arms akimbo behind her head. I am amazed at how beautiful she is. She is the best parts of Jim and me and, so far as I can tell, none of the unflattering parts. Sitting down beside her, I reach out to stroke her arm. Her eyes are glassy, her mascara glistens with tears.

"Hey," I say.

"Hey," she says back, staring at the ceiling.

"Look at me." I stroke her chin.

"What?"

"I'm sorry. I blew it. I ruined the whole thing."

"Not really. You didn't really ruin it anyway. I wasn't too crazy about having Lynn there. She'd just dominate the whole show. It'd be a pain."

"I'm sorry for your pain, Keri."

Her eyes fill up. "I just wish nothing had changed. I just wish it was still you and Dad and me in this house and he'd never have gone with her."

Holding my daughter, I see I was imagining she was so well-adjusted to the split. Maybe I have been giving myself too much credit as a parent. I've always known Keri suffered, that she hurt over the loss of her family. Spikey anger jabs like pin pricks under my skin. *Dammit.* I was happy too, for crying out loud. Why did anything have to change? Realizing Keri's sense of loss makes me even angrier. Angry with Jim, angry with myself, angry at the forces that brought the three of us to this fork in the road.

Jim made a decision. It left the three of us in a bad place. But for my sake and my daughter's sake, I have to go on and meet my future, whatever that may be. Strength, I crave it. Foresight, yes, that as well. Forgiveness to Jim, oh, that's the hard one. However, I have to forgive and let go in order to go on. A slow swell of warmth envelopes my insides. In this moment of release, I feel peaceful and whole. I know Keri needs comfort. She needs to feel peaceful and whole too.

"Hey, we'll get through this together, okay?" I stroke her silky hair. She nods in my shoulder and snuffles. Rain is pinging again on the windows. I hear a faint call in the house. Seconds later, the orange kitten rounds the doorway, tail held high. Padding toward the bed, he seems to think he's always belonged here. He leaps, taking hold of the edge of the comforter and drops down beside us, curling his paws underneath his chest, blinking in satisfaction.

"How did he get in here?" I ask.

"He's a sneaky bugger," Keri says.

She is quiet for a minute. "When do you see that guy again?"

"What guy?" I say even though I know she is talking about Gabriel.

"That new neighbor, the artist or whatever." Funny how nobody can put a handle on him. Not even me.

"I'm supposed to see him tomorrow night, why?"

"Promise me you won't get caught up in something?"

"Keri, your dad and me are way over–"

"Not because of Dad. I just don't know if I trust that guy. There's just something about him."

Something about him – I don't know either. And maybe that's what's eating me. I don't feel like I'm that into him. Maybe he's not on my mind that much for a reason. I like him and his stories, all the history he shared with me. It's possible I'm just being silly. Or maybe I just want to have sex again and the opportunity presented itself, which is a pretty lame reason for doing anything. The fact is I might prefer to be here with my daughter and become a recluse in my comfortable house. I sigh.

Gabriel. How can I know thee, Gabriel?

"We're just friends, that's all," I hear myself say. "Mhmm," Keri says, stroking the cat who is purring almost as loudly as we speak. "Just be careful, that's all."

It's almost as if I am looking into her father's eyes

when I promise I will. I will be careful.

CHAPTER THIRTY ONE

Julie

It's been a few weeks and I have not seen or heard from Sean, the deputy, except for a few minutes in the hallway at the courthouse. Rodney is in jail for a while, unless his mother bails him out, which is likely but I haven't heard about her actually doing it. Angela, on the other hand, is in treatment for a long time.

My parents like Sean. They're under the impression he'll keep me out of trouble. The badge doesn't hurt either. At least they approve. Twice now I have come home to find him playing with Alex in the yard. He seems to like talking to Renae, which is more than I can say. Life seems a lot lighter these days but still, I need to have that talk with him. The one I have been thinking about and dreading for some time now. If anything ever comes of this thing between us, I want to be truthful with him. I'm tired of blowing it.

I'm feeling majorly cautious though.

Shit, who am I trying kid? I'm not good enough for a guy like him. Sean deserves a girl who wouldn't put people through what I've put them through. The fact of the matter is we're just not meant to be. We're too different. He's too good. I don't deserve somebody like him.

I'm such a loser. I should probably get rid of him before I really start thinking about him, before I have myself convinced it could work.

What does a guy like Sean want with somebody like me anyway? I have the wrong kind of baggage, the kind he doesn't need.

But anyway, here he is. He stopped by out of the blue just to see me. Despite my dark thoughts, we jump in my Tracker and end up at the grocery store, running errands for Renae, who shooed us out of the house with more than a little glee. She was almost too happy about it. I'm not real comfortable with the way she rushed us out the door and volunteered to watch Alex.

Telling him goodbye is going to suck.

"Look, there's something you should know about me," I say to him as we load Renae's groceries into the back of my car. This is so hard. Never have I felt so naked in front of any man before, so vulnerable, and this one is so nice. The sun is shining off his blond hair and he is wearing a white filmy shirt that makes him look tan, which he is.

"I know all I need to know about you," Sean says and I almost love him for it. But still, he needs to know. I need to tell the truth for once.

"No, you don't. Not really. I'm not that great a bet. That's the thing. I've lied to people. I've lied to everybody, basically. I've lied when it would have been easier to tell the truth. I've caused everyone in my life pain and embarrassment. My parents, especially. I've even driven Angela crazy. The point is I'm not a real good person and if you want to jet now, here's your chance."

The sun is in my eyes, making me squint. Is what I am saying sinking in or not? *You can save yourself, dude. Maybe you should take the chance.*

"Julie," he says and takes my arms. "I meant what I said. I see a person I really like. I see someone I want to be around for a long, long time. Jet? Not a chance, darlin'. I'm afraid you're stuck with me."

I jerk my head back to look him in the eye. "Did you hear anything I said?"

"Yes, I heard it. I heard all of it. You just need to have more faith in yourself, that's all." He pulls my chin to him and kisses me gently. "I've fallen in love with that little boy of yours. I'd like to be around to see him grow up."

"Why?"

Sean just smiles and shuts the car door.

Later that day, we're eating Chinese out of boxes with chopsticks in Sean's bed. Or rather, I am eating Chinese out of a box, because he's gotten up for something. The sheets are wrapped up underneath my armpits. My hair must be a mess but I couldn't care less. Bed hair, how funny. Sean's seen me in all my bed hair glory now. I am the happiest I have been in a long, long time. It's hard to believe I'm actually here with Sean. Even more unbelievable is I want to stay. The most amazing part is after everything I've done and all the pain I've caused people, Sean sees good in me and wants me.

He leans over me, kissing me hard. He is aroused again and we are both sticky. We smell of love, never thought I'd ever say *that*. He wants me again and I am perfectly willing as I tease his tongue with mine. A small moan escapes his throat and he pushes me back down into the bed. The take-out cartons are scooted to the nightstand as he pulls the blankets down and gets in. Pulling him to me, I know there is no place else I would rather be.

CHAPTER THIRTY TWO

Andrea

Piercing light stabs my eyes. My head feels as if it's housing a marching band, and my tongue lies dormant in my mouth, swollen and…speaking of my mouth, it tastes bad. Yuck. Where am I?

Raising my head off the pillow, which brings another stabbing pain to my head, I see drab brown draperies and a plastic table with two chairs in front of a picture window. The drapes are open just enough to let light stab in. Looking down, I see I am naked. My clothes are everywhere. What did I do? How did I get here? *Shit, shit, shit*. My car. Is my car out there? Wrapping the blanket around me, I stumble over to the window and pull the drapes aside. Okay, the car is there.

Here is the bad thing. My purse. Where did I put my purse? Oh my God, I'm so confused. Where am I? There is a phone book on the bureau and it says Greater West Plains Area. West Plains? That is almost to Arkansas. What am I doing in West Plains?

An empty bottle sits on the bureau. Next to it, the

ashtray is full. *Oh my God, what have I done?* A flash of a dream, or was it, shoots across my brain behind my eyes. Lance. Lance something, a young, fresh-faced farm boy. Drinking in some bar, flirting, loud music and smoke. It was so dark in there. I sink back to the bed and bury my head in my hands. *Oh no.* I feel the bare scruff of my head.

My jeans are lying on the floor in a crumpled mess by my feet. I stick a foot out to pull them over. My cell phone is in my pocket along with $21 and some change. My purse still hasn't appeared. It's not under the bed. I didn't hang it on the door knob. It is not by the television or in the bathroom. I pull the bureau drawers open one by one. It is not in any of them. *Shit.*

My toe hits another bottle as I pull the side table drawers open. My God, I am stranded in a hotel in a town I don't know and not only that, I don't even know how I got here. Hot tears burn my eyes. The Gideon Bible is in the drawer. *Oh Lord, please forgive me. I've stumbled and I've fallen and now I'm paying dearly for it.* Where is my purse? I bet Lance stole it. If he was even in here, that is. But I know he was. I know I did something I should not have. *Weak, weak woman. Pathetic. What an idiot you are, Andrea. For God's sake.*

My head throbs. I stop and rub it but it doesn't really help. I check my phone for messages. Two are from Elliott. *Elliott?* The first one says something to the effect that he wants me out of the house so he can list it with a real estate agent. Oh right, like I believe he is going to sell it in the first place and besides that, why would my living there lessen his chances of selling the property? Claudine left a message too. She is checking in because she has not heard from me in a while and wants to know if I am okay. Oh, I'm just peachy. On top of the world. The last message from Elliott informs me we need to talk without our attorneys. The last thing I want to do is sit in a room alone with Elliott. If we were alone, Elliott would corner me and attack, and my brain would just shut down. I know I wouldn't react well. Oh God, this divorce, the process, it is so old. I collapse on my side onto the bed. It's all too much. I cannot do anything about any of it and in fact, I cannot even figure out where my purse is or where my wig is and I am stranded and friendless, basically penniless, and I don't know what to do.

People are so ugly when they cry, I think, as I sob into the mildewed blanket. I hate crying. I hate despair. Despair is what drove me here, to this hotel room in the middle of nowhere near the Arkansas state line. Well, no, I drove myself, obviously. What will I tell Elliott about where I've been? Oh no, I am not telling Elliott. This is not the first time I've driven stone drunk, oblivious to my surroundings. It is a miracle I have not been killed by now. Shame covers me.

Get up, Andrea, I tell myself. I stumble toward the shower but first, there is a half smoked cigarette in the ashtray and I grab it. I light it clumsily with the matches lying beside it and inhale deeply. *My God, my head is clearing a little bit.*

The room is a mess. An empty whiskey bottle lies on its side next to the night stand, a discarded pillow on the floor, my clothes scattered about with a wet towel mixed up with them, the dirty ashtray. My watch half hangs off the table. One of the cheap pictures of an autumn scene hangs crooked. This is my life. Scattered, lost.

Get yourself together, Andrea.

I have no clean clothes so I grab what is lying about and head for the bathroom on wobbly legs. I feel bruised on the inside. Peeing burns, hurts, feels like I was cut. Standing up, I reach for the shower knobs. Hot water will do me good. I can't think of what happened to my purse but at least I have my phone and a little cash and I can find a way to get back once I get showered and dressed.

Hot water spills down over my head and onto my back. I unwrap the complimentary soap and shake my head. Once upon a time, I though nothing of spending $200 or $300 on skin care products and specialty soaps, loofahs, and a slew of other self-pampering products. Yet here I am, standing in a plastic tub in a cheap motel – not hotel, no room service – with a piece of soap no bigger than a potato chip and it does not smell all that nice but I am happy to have it.

Pain. Hurt. Burning. *Oh Lord*

After I towel off and dress, I search the room for the rest of my belongings. My wig is tangled up in the bedding. I jam it on my head. Finally, I find my purse jammed behind the headboard. How that happened, I couldn't say. In fact, I have no idea really about what went on last night. I am not surprised. It is not the first time. It is the first time, however, someone else was involved. Who is Lance? Is he healthy? More to the point, is he disease-free? I could have gotten myself in a world of hurt. I regret my body is no longer the sacrifice I meant it to be and I wonder just how I came onto him or if he came onto me and how we ended up together in this room. It stinks like cigarettes and booze and I want to get out of here.

All of my belongings seem to be in my purse. I find my car keys, my checkbook, my wallet and other odds and ends. The money is what I am concerned about and it is all still there, along with a few more dollars in my wallet. I now have $27 to get back to Springfield. I came out lucky. This could have been so much worse.

It's bad though. Shame overtakes me. I fall to my knees in front of the bed and begin to pray. *Cast me not from your sight, precious Lord. I've committed terrible acts against you for which I am deeply sorry. Please grant me your forgiveness, oh Lord.* I am rocking back and forth, holding my middle. I am a beggar, a miserable, pitiful beggar. My life is to be a sacrifice and I only indulged my carnal self. *I am so sorry. I am not worthy.*

Finally, after what seems like hours, I stand up, weak in the knees. I feel cleansed, and now I have to deal with the reality of where I am and where I need to be. As nauseous as I am, my stomach is contracting. I need food. Not just coffee but real food, eggs and bacon and toast. I spy a small restaurant next door. That is where I'll go to regroup and then back to Springfield. I will call Elliott later. No use borrowing trouble, I suppose.

Driving down the highway, back toward my home and my prison, I call Claudine. She tells me she has a check from Elliott for me.

"How much?" I ask.

"Three hundred dollars," she says.

It is stunning the way he continually shuns me. "What? I turned in more than $1,000 in expenses to him, Claudine. Three hundred dollars?"

For heaven's sake. I hang up with her and dial Elliott's cell phone. No answer. Well, *that* is not original. I dial his office.

"Susan?" I say when she, predictably, answers the phone.

"Yes, Andrea," she says. She sounds interrupted.

"Is Elliott available? I really need to talk to him."

Silence on the other end.

"Susan?"

"Well, actually he's not available, Andrea. I'm sorry."

"No, you don't understand. This is important. Can

you get him on the line for me, please?"

"No, I really can't. He's not available. Not today, not for the rest of this week and not next week."

"Where is he?" I know my tone is sharper than I intend, but I am so tired, so sick and tired of these cat and mouse games. I am sick of being the mouse. I am just sick and tired of it.

"He's on vacation."

"*Vacation*? Where?"

"I can't say, Andrea."

My fingers would fit so well around Susan's neck right now. No, forget Susan. Why not go straight to Elliott.

"Susan, I am his wife. His *wife*. Do you hear me? Now, tell me where he is."

"You do not have the right to shout at me, Andrea. And not that it's any of your business, but he's in Brazil on a fishing trip."

"Oh? Alone?"

"Now, you know you've gone too far, Andrea. I can't answer that."

"All expenses paid, I suppose?"

"Goodbye, Andrea. This conversation is over."

Suddenly, a vision comes to me. I'm sitting in the courtroom beside Leon, who's doodling on his notepad, his head in one hand. Susan is on the stand, testifying against me. Josie is sitting on the other side of Leon, studying her boots, which somehow I know are brand new and expensive. The courtroom is polished and gleaming and our judge is red-faced. Rita is standing with one hand on her hip casually, leaning against the railing in front of where Susan is seated. Susan is wearing a cardigan. A cardigan? Oh well, it's my vision. Susan is saying, "She shouted at me. Just because Dr. Sommerfield wrote her a check for $300 and, of course, she thinks she needs more. She *always* thinks she needs more, you know, but he's just not making that much money. My heart goes out to him." At this point, she weeps into a hanky she has been carrying with her. "And I simply told her he wrote a check to her for $300 and she *demanded* to know why and where he was and just because he was on vacation in Brazil with six of his friends, expenses paid for everybody, she went ballistic. And she shouted at me."

"She shouted at you?" Rita says, feigning incredulousness. She points at me. "Her? That woman? The one in the expensive red sweater she bought at retail price? That woman shouted at you?"

"Yes, yes, yes. It was her." Susan sobs into her hand. "Mrs. Sommerfield."

"And how did this make you feel?" Rita asks, pulling a wad of Kleenex out of a box on the stand and shoving it into Susan's hand.

"It's affected my health and well-being," Susan says, gasping. "And such a good man as Dr. Sommerfield, he shouldn't have to go through this." More weeping.

"Uh-huh," Rita says and swivels on her hip staring down at Leon, twisting her lips. "Uh-huh. Nothing further, Your Honor." She sashays back to her chair like a runway model and sits. I am appalled. I assume I will have my turn to defend myself.

Leon turns to me. "Now why would we, why would we, shout at her that way?"

I could just be sick. Well, of course, that is exactly what would happen in court. Crap. Crap to the nth degree.

My daydream shatters, reality bangs the gong.

"Okay, Susan," I say. "I'm sorry." No matter. Susan already hung up.

Springfield appears over the crest of the hill and I turn on my exit, shoulder sagging.

My answering machine holds a message from my pastor. The missionary trip to the Ukraine has been scrapped in favor of a missionary trip to Mexico and would I be interested? The political climate in the Ukraine is not favorable for Americans, it seems. Oh yes, oh, heavens yes. I think it could become my reason for living, in fact. His message goes on to say the trip will not take place until mid-August, which just may work out well for me. What if I could get Elliott to settle by then? What if? My spirits are buoyed by the thought. The missionary trip is exactly what I need right now and besides being something to look forward to, I'd be doing something good for the world. It will be something outside of me, my thoughts and my sad, solitary world. I can't wait.

CHAPTER THIRTY THREE

Claudine

Gabriel and I made plans to meet at Imo's, a pizza place down the block from his house. He's already there when I arrive and a little thrill pops up in my stomach at the thought of a man waiting for me. Gabriel looks expectant and dark and gorgeous. I smile and he takes my hand.

We eat a fabulous St. Louis-style pizza, drink some wine and talk, more talking than eating. Afterward, we careen happily out into the blustery weather. There may be rain later on but for now, we have wind and thunder. Hand in hand, we rush down the street until he pins me against an old oak tree on the block and kisses me deeply. His breath smells of wine and Italian spices. I feel my thighs begin to tingle and my arms instinctively go up around his neck, my fingers twisting through his hair. His breath is hot against my neck. My need is pressing down on me as his desire swells and presses into my pelvis. A low groan escapes his throat. He breaks free and we run to his house, barely giving him time to unlock the door before we fall into one another's arms. I don't know where the orange kitten came from but he is right with us, matching our sprint.

Gabriel peels the collar of my shirt back and kisses my shoulder, tender warm lips on warm skin. His eyes are dark and hooded. His face is flushed. The desire is clear. I want to take him in, all of him, as I sag against the doorframe. His fingers are digging into my lower back just above my tailbone and I pull his shirt away from his chest. The black curly hairs are exposed, inviting me to nuzzle in, and I do, kissing and licking.

"Claudine," he whispers. "Claudine."

He pulls away and takes my hand. I look into this eyes and I see we both agree. This is it. This is the moment I have been waiting for and I can only hope he has been waiting for it too. He leads. I follow. My heart is beating fast with anticipation.

Once inside his bedroom, I barely have a chance to look around but my mind's eye sees a huge bed with an antique headboard and big pieces of furniture. This is a man's room with a suede comforter and soft pillows. Our clothes are peeling off as fast as we can make them. He whispers, "You are beautiful," and then my back meets the mattress and he is lying beside me. His fingers are deft and sure. He strokes my back and circles around to my front, bringing his fingers to my quivering clitoris. My breath is coming in little gasps now as he works inside me. Brightly colored shards of light crescendo and recede behind my eyes. These colors, these rhythms, twist and turn, pull forward and back until my entire body is alive with it. I hear him as if from a long distance saying my name and then, a quick crackle of paper, a pause while he pulls a condom on, and he is in me. He is moving as a man does when he knows a woman. I explode with pleasure, over and over again. The light is pulsating in my brain. My thighs tremble with a pleasure not felt in a long time.

When he is finished, he kisses me gently. His eyes are misty and still dark.

"Are you all right, Claudine?"

I nod. "I'm fine." My eyes fill with tears. Gabriel scoops me expertly into his arms and holds me. He's warm and oh so sensuous.

"I don't want to cry," I say. "I'm not a little kid."

He chuckles.

"No, you are not a little kid, Claudine." He raises my chin and looks into my eyes. "You are a beautiful, giving, passionate woman. I am glad if I gave you pleasure, Claudine."

"You did," I murmur. My body is still tingling. "No worries there."

He smiles. "Good. Now you rest. I will make us some tea."

Gabriel crawls out of bed and I see his entire body for the first time. Of course, it is perfect. He is perfectly sculpted, perfectly proportioned. I pull the sheet up around my middle, feeling self-conscious. He puts on a robe and leaves the room.

When I wake, he is sitting by the side of the bed, fully dressed. I smile and reach for him but he is not smiling. His hands hang by the wrists between his legs. I wonder how long he's been sitting here, watching me.

"What is it?" I say, alarmed. This doesn't feel right. Gabriel looks awful. He's staring at me. Looking down the bed, I see my clothes neatly folded at the foot of it. "What's wrong?" I ask him.

"I need for you to leave," he says. His tone is quiet. "I need you to put your clothes back on and go."

"Why? What's wrong?"

He stands up and looks away from me.

"Gabriel?" I am frightened but nonetheless, I do what I am told. I pull my clothes back on as quickly as I can. I am clueless about his change in attitude. What I imagined was a lovely interval seems to have turned cold, ugly and sinister. I do not understand and I wish he would explain.

Gabriel stands in front of me for a moment and then says, "Claudine, I am sorry. I should not have brought you here." He still has not looked at me.

He leaves the room and I hear his footsteps going down the stairs. I follow him, buttoning up my shirt as I go. I know my sandals are downstairs someplace. I think they are somewhere by the front door and by the time I reach the bottom of the stairs, he is handing them to me and I put them on.

The woman leaning against the kitchen doorframe is smoking a cigarette, looking at me nonchalantly. And I feel like a big fool, the worst kind of fool. This woman is looking me over, taking me in and finding me wanting. She is comparing herself to me. Whoever she is, she seems thoughtful yet amused. I feel mockery going through her mind, although she has not moved since I came downstairs. We stare at each other for a minute. My mouth opens and then closes. Her eye brows raise and then lower. I say nothing. Neither does she.

Gabriel's face is flushed. I wish I could think it was from love-making but I know it is not. "I've told you not to smoke in here," he says to her. She shrugs and retreats into the kitchen. I see her arm through the doorway, stubbing the cigarette out in the sink. She returns to the doorway and pulls her dark hair behind her ears before settling into her previous position.

The door is open for me, begging me to go and I walk through it. Gabriel doesn't follow me. I am numb. Nothing is coming out of my mouth and although I try to summon up speech, it is just not coming. I stumble off the porch but not before I hear the woman say, "Really, Gabriel, you can do better."

It stings. After such an intimate evening, or one I thought was intimate and exciting and new, to hear such a comment? Dumbfounded and disappointed, I run home to find Keri and Brandy watching a movie and doing homework. How teenagers can multi-task like that, I will never know. Keri's eyes meet mine and the look on her face tells me she knows all. There is nothing for me to say. Nothing I want to say. The cold howl in my stomach is coming up. Excusing myself, I go upstairs and take a long shower in my cracked shower stall, staring at my humiliation as it washes down the drain. The one good thing to come out of this is I have a business card of someone who might be able to fix the damn thing. Gabriel, and I do not particularly want to say his name, gave it to me at the pizza place. At the time, I took the gesture to be gallant and maybe it was. I guess I'll never know. "He does good work," Gabriel said at the time. Maybe it was not sex. Obviously, I made a mistake, an error in judgment. Maybe this card is the favor Gabriel did for me.

Memories of the languid dark-haired woman remain. Who is she? Who is she to Gabriel? Is she a sister? Doubtful. She seems pretty sure of herself in that house, Gabriel's house. She has been there before, obviously, if he forbade her smoking there. Is she an ex-wife, ex-lover? Even worse, present wife, present lover? How did she get in the house? If she has a key, it seems to be self-explanatory. How does he know her?

Why did he invite me there, knowing she would be a part of the picture? Why?

I get out of the shower, dry off and put on my robe. The business card is lying on my dresser. Emmanuel Withers is printed across the top in big block letters. I'll think about this. I don't want to tell Mr. Withers who referred me, or that anybody did. Maybe this is too complicated. I should find somebody else. No, I will call him. The work has to be done and aside from throwing myself on Jim's mercy, another thing I abhor, I have nobody else. Emmanuel Withers will have to do. We just will not have any conversation. I snort at the absurdity and crawl into bed. *It will be fine.* My mother used to tell me when I was little, "Things will look different in the morning. Tomorrow you won't even remember this." Will things really look different in the morning?

I groan and roll over, punching my pillow. The thing is I think I will remember this tomorrow, whether I want to or not. And then I remember the car shopping. We are going car shopping tomorrow, Jim, Keri and me. Facing Jim right now, I'm not real wild about it. Somehow, I almost feel as if I cheated on him with Gabriel. What a joke. I hope I never see Gabriel again. However, if I do, then what? I could stand across his path and demand an explanation and an apology. I could reach out and slap him across his beautiful face and accuse him of taking advantage of me in my pathetic, love-starved state. But I am forgetting something. I was there too. And yes, while it may be true I am pathetic and I may be starved for love and I allowed myself to be humiliated because of it, he led me somewhere. I thought he was honest. I thought he was honorable.

I really missed romance. I didn't know how much.

Nobody will really ever compare with Jim Coulter, I suppose. My opinion might be unhealthy. Then again, maybe it's the wise choice. Who am I to say? I am just a single woman trying to get through every day. I wish I was a better person but, well, I am not. I am just me. And that has to be good enough.

Morning comes and my mother was right. Things do look better. I am still sad though. I am still feeling forlorn and dejected. Rejection is an ugly, lonely feeling. Maybe there is an explanation and maybe it is not so bad. Maybe. Well, anyway, this is a day for my daughter, so I will put on a happy face and we will do what needs to be done.

It seems somewhat strange to be going on this excursion with my daughter and her father and, with all the bridges between Jim and me, it feels a bit uncomfortable. *This is what being divorced with children is about, Claudine. Other people do it every day. It's your turn.*

A little more lipstick and I'm ready. Keri's already thumping around. She wants me to hurry, so I do.

It turns out to be a long day. Figures, Lynn comes rolling into the first car lot we go to. She makes a huge scene about hugging my daughter and laughing and pulling Keri's hair out of her eyes. Turning my back, I roll my eyes, knowing Keri is not so crazy about all that. Lynn finally leaves so she can tend to yet another huge – and we are talking huge from the sounds of things – real estate deal. I smile. I nod. Oh, how nice. More money into Jim's pockets which will empower her to brag about being able to contribute to the acquisition of Keri's first car. Yuck. I am unable to do what they do.

At the end of the day, Keri, Jim and I have test-driven five different cars and Keri is the proud owner of a brand new gleaming white Honda Accord.

After Keri and Jim drop me off at home, driving off to dinner without me, the world seems different. All the noise is gone, and so is all the excitement, all the electric brightness that is my daughter. I feel blah and I know exactly why. Since I do not have to put on a good face anymore, I just let it sag, frown, whatever it wants to do. It is nice to be sitting here on my porch, again in my Adirondack chair, listening to the radio inside the house. Truth be told, I pled off more festivities with Jim and Keri, claiming I had a headache. Not exactly true but any excuse will do. I have a glass of pinot noir at hand and I am fine. Yes, well, almost fine, that is.

There's no reason to cry. I barely knew Gabriel. It wasn't like we were long-time connected or something like that. No, I think I just saw him as a beginning to an end. The end of being alone. The end of feeling humiliated while Jim lives his own life with someone else. The end of this uncomfortable celibacy. The low feeling in my stomach isn't going away. The heavy steel ring circling my heart is grief for an expectation lost and I know it. But I also know this will pass.

I've had a full and busy day and I have not thought of Gabriel once until now.

Not until Gabriel is standing at the bottom of my porch once again like he did that first night he came by. Why is he here? No idea what I should say. I also don't know why but I'm glad to see him, at least on some level. I want to know. I want to know why and what.

As it turns out, I don't have to say anything. At least, not at first.

"I'm sorry, Claudine," he says. "You don't know how sorry."

"I should believe you?"

He looks down the street for one long minute and then looks back at me. His shoulders are hunched. Defensive? Could be. Contrite? I don't know. His hands are in his pockets, which I have always been told is a sign that a person is hiding the truth. Is he hiding the truth? Will he tell it to me now? Or is whatever he has to say another lie?

"Claudine," he says.

"What? What can you possibly say to me to make this right?"

"There is nothing I can do to make it right. I know this. I would like to tell you about my situation, if you will hear me." He seems humble enough. "Please know, Claudine, I did not use you."

I snort. "Well, tell me what you came here to say

then."

"Anna is my wife–"

I groan. "I knew it. You said you had no wife."

"No, really, you only know a little bit. I only said no wife was with me. She is my wife and she has been away for a long time. We have been separated for years. She came here to convince me to move back to San Francisco with her. She did not come announced, Claudine. Your surprise was mine as well."

"So she's your wife and she wants you to move back to San Francisco? How nice for you." I have a little buzz going and I know from experience I am likely to say anything.

"Yes, I suppose," Gabriel says. He looks puzzled. "But what I came to tell you is I did not, I repeat, I did not use you, Claudine. I sincerely enjoyed every minute we spent together, all of it."

"Fine. Great." I am feeling cavalier. "Listen, those are pretty words, no substance. I don't think that works for me, Gabriel."

"What do you want from me?" He seems genuinely troubled, as am I, because I do not know the answer to his question. What do I want from him? What did I ever want from him? Maybe I got it, that thing I wanted. Maybe. Or maybe, I just wanted someone I could count on. Maybe I wanted someone who would not leave when he found someone more beautiful or skinnier or interesting or whatever it is that men want. What is it humans want from one another? Is it comfort, confidence, trust, a feeling of being accepted, warts and all? Whatever it was Jim wanted and then I catch my breath. Whatever Jim wanted was what I wanted to be.

Gabriel reads my mind. "I cannot speak for your husband, Claudine," he says. "But I think you are beautiful. And I think what happened between us was beautiful. I will always think of it that way."

My eyes fill with unbidden tears, knowing what will happen next. "Please go," I whisper. "Please go now." How ironic I am voicing the same thing he did only twenty-four hours ago. "You need to go now."

"Goodbye, Claudine," he says. He blows me a kiss. He seems genuinely sad. Can I trust that? "But I would like to know the answer to my question."

"Okay, here it is. Honesty, Gabriel, integrity."

He does not seem too taken aback. "I am sorry, Claudine, that I did not give that to you. I am perfectly capable of it. My only hope is you will not judge me too harshly."

He is gone, swallowed up by the darkness.

Judge him too harshly? In my mind, I know I used all that up. I did not set out to be the other woman. I did not even know I was the other woman. As usual, it all goes back to Jim. I cannot have Jim back. Part of me would not even want him any longer. Oh yes, the memories are there. Of the love I carried for him, day in and day out, for twenty years. I recognize those things. Do I want him back? No. I may not know what I do want right now, but I know I will not go backward. I will not take one step backward. That is the way of a woman, yes? I down the last of my wine and go inside.

It's not that I really want to tell Beth about all this, but I dial her number anyway. Of course, she is livid. "That snake," she says. "What a bastard."

"Yup," I say, not knowing what to say. I knew she would go berserk and I probably called before I was ready to take that. But, well, here I am on the phone and she is full blown ape-shit.

"I mean, the least he could have done is, I don't know, sort of *mention* he had a wife even if he was separated. I tell you what, if Lee would have done that to me, I'd have his penis on a platter."

I am nodding on the other end of the phone. Yes,

yes, you would. Anyway, this is me here, not you.

"I mean, what kind of person does this?"

"I don't know, Beth. I don't know."

"I'll tell you what kind of person does this. A sneaky, lying son of a bitch, that's who."

I am still nodding. "Well, unfortunately I was there too, and I'm sort of responsible for something, I suppose."

"For what? For liking a man who lied? Give me a break."

"Well, I sent him away so that part of it is done. I'll be okay, Beth. I'm a big girl."

"Well, I wouldn't let that happen to me. That's for sure."

"I'm tired, girlfriend. I'll talk to you later." I hang up. People who have led perfect lives seem to forget sometimes that other people do not. I can't think of any misstep Beth's ever made. Not one mistake in her life. As wonderful as she is, sometimes Beth in her superior mode gets on my nerves, along with the rest of the world. I break up a few pieces of kindling left by the fireplace. After laying it in the grate, I strike a match and eventually I see a sputter to a small flame. It is nice to see a little fire in the fireplace. The house feels dampish tonight. Old houses have their quirks. *I love it here*, I think as I look around. *I can always count on home.* A couple of logs are left in the wood basket and I gently lay them atop the not so confident fire and fan the flame.

I turn the stereo on and listen to Lucinda Williams softly as I rummage through the fridge for more wine and a bit of Havarti cheese. While Lucinda sings about car wheels on a gravel road, I see brown eyes burrowing into my soul. *Stop that. Be a big girl.*

I am so glad I am not absolutely heartbroken and heartsick over this betrayal. I feel like I've crossed a bridge somewhere along the way and then I remember.

Gabriel is not Jim. I did not spend a lifetime with Gabriel. I did spend a lifetime with Jim. Gabriel made me no promises in front of God, all my relatives and friends.

Settling back into the couch, I sigh deeply. I can be pragmatic. I suppose I could say I got out of the gate. I had a fling and it is over and for now. I think it's enough.

CHAPTER THIRTY FOUR

Julie

Sequiota Park is beautiful today. Purple redbuds, pink and white dogwoods and giant hosta lilies greet us as we walk the trail by the lake, feeding the geese. It's Sean, Alex and me. Life could not be better. Somehow, things have started going my way and I didn't even have to force it.

Claudine called me the other day. A letter came via the guardian ad litem. Rodney has been talking to him and wants to settle. He wants to be done with all of this. What a surprise, a total and complete turnaround. His mother bailed him out of jail. I heard he lost his job at Ruby Tuesday's and then went back and asked to be hired again on a probationary-type deal. Whatever. It makes no difference to me so long as the child support checks keep coming. It is not much, but at least Alex is getting something.

We've been meeting at Common Ground, the family resolution center, for an hour each week for Rodney and Alex to have visitation. Alex does not even know who Rodney is. He thinks he is some uncle or cousin or somebody he is just now getting to play with. Alex does not mind. He really does not even notice. Rodney never makes him say "Daddy" or anything like that. That was the deal we made and he seems to be sticking to it. It seems to be going well.

Then there is Angela. She will be away for a long time, apparently. My parents have decided not to press charges against either one of them. I think they just want to forget. They want to forget and to heal. Who could blame them? They're happy now. I think, for the first time in a long time, they may actually be proud of me. The worry lines around Renae's mouth seem to have eased up anyway. It is a relief, a genuine relief, to know life can be good and uncomplicated and real.

As for me, well, things have changed quite a bit. I find I am spending a lot of time with Sean, something I would never have imagined myself doing a year ago. I didn't realize back then I could break away from Rodney. I didn't realize I could be happy, that it was possible. Sean really loves Alex, I can tell. Here we are, walking the trail in Sequiota Park. Sean is actually carrying Alex around. We feed the geese. Alex is laughing.

A little bench sits further up the trail surrounded by evergreens. Sean heads for it.

"Hey buddy," he says to Alex and stands him up on the sidewalk. "Gotta stop for a minute, okay?"

"Stop, okay?" Alex says. "Stop, okay?"

Sean laughs. "Stop, okay, buddy."

"Buddy," Alex says, clapping his hands. "Buddy." He laughs.

"What are we stopping for?" I ask. "Are you tired already?"

"Nah, not really," he says, as I sit on the bench. "I just wanted to ask you a question."

"Oh yeah? What?"

He is squatting now, holding Alex between his legs. He bends his head around to Alex's and says, "You gotta help me now, okay?"

"Kay," Alex shouts. He titters as if some big thing is about to be revealed.

"Are you ready?" Sean asks him.

"Yeah, ready," Alex says. He is watching the geese on the pond. Whatever is going on, he does not really appear to be ready.

"Ready?" Sean says again, pulling something out of his jean pocket. I realize he is down on one knee now, holding something gray. It is a square box.

"Yeah," Alex says, looking up at the evergreen tops behind me.

"Julie," Sean says, opening the box, looking me straight in the eye. Sean's eyes are so blue. He is so handsome today, so earnest. "Julie, I love you. I love you with all of my heart and all of my being and all of my soul. I can't imagine a day in my life, for the rest of my life, that you wouldn't be a part of. You are the woman–" Alex mumbles "woman." "That I want to spend the rest of my life with. What I'm asking is will you do me the honor of marrying me?"

Sean extends his hand, the hand with the ring in it. The ring is perfect and bright and gold. It is just a little filigree with a diamond in the middle. Feminine. Dainty. But oh, so strong. I gasp because it is so pretty. And because I cannot believe I just heard a proposal of marriage, something I never thought I would hear from anyone else but Rodney. What was I thinking?

My hand is on my heart. I can feel my heart shaping a soft O in wonder and happiness.

"It's beautiful, Sean," I say, taking it from him and admiring it.

"Well, what do you say? I want to marry you, Julie.

I hope you want to marry me too."

I look into his blue, blue eyes which are full of love. Finally, I can see love, real love, and it brings me a wave of joy I'd never imagined before. Unbelievable, this sensation and how new. I see Sean's love for me through tears forming in my own eyes.

"Yes, yes, I will. I will be proud to marry you."

He seems so relieved.

"Did you think I'd say no?"

"Well, I don't know," he says and then he climbs up on the bench with me and takes me in his arms. "Thank you, Julie. You've made me very happy."

"Uh," Alex says from below us. "Duck, duck."

Alex is pointing to several geese on the other side of the lake.

"I love you, Sean," I say, cupping his face in my hands. He has already slipped the ring on my finger. "I really do love you."

"Duck," Alex says again, oblivious to our scene on the bench. "Uh-oh, duck."

The rest of my life is before me. I would like to tell someone. I should tell my best friend, Lisa, but I don't. For some reason, I would rather tell Claudine. Not sure why.

CHAPTER THIRTY FIVE

Claudine

TruBean is closed. The windows of the Pickwick house Gabriel lived in are dark and empty. A for sale sign squats awkwardly in the yard.

Beth, Keri and I are standing on the sidewalk in front of Gabriel's former coffee shop, the one I had the odd premonition in. *You could do this.* We are staring at the big window still bearing the bright yellow letters, TruBean, and none of us utters a word. The little shop has been abandoned. In the corner of the window is a blue sign with white letters: For Lease.

I remember Gabriel's dark eyes, the lips that caressed my flesh, the smooth touch of his hands, a lock of brown hair falling over his forehead. So lovely. So treacherous. Could I take this spot, the one he worked in? Could I erase his memory from these walls and make it my own?

You could do this. I remember the smells, the aroma of sweet yeasty baked goods and the coffee beans. The plant that lazed across the window is still there but a little worse for wear. Nobody has watered it in a while. I step a little closer and peer through the door. The space is so dark and lonely. Then I jump back. Someone is staring out the door at me from the inside.

The door opens by a husky woman in a suit. She introduces herself as the leasing agent. "Would you like to have a look at the place?" she asks.

I look back at Keri and Beth and they shrug. Why not? *You could do this*. I need to know whether it is a fleeting fantasy or something tangible. Could I really do this? Could I operate a little shop like this? The kitchen area is small and compact but well-organized and the appliances seem decent. I am thinking of a specialty food shop, like the one Jim and I visited once in the Hamptons, something comfortable and homey with some elegance thrown in. I am seeing salmon spread and crusty breads and blueberry muffins, jams, spinach quiches and shortbread cookies. What about being my own boss? What about keeping my own hours and making people feel good with gifts of my own specialties? What if? My heart beat speeds up just a bit.

"The equipment can stay if you need it," the woman says. Her name is Janice. "Could serve as a deli or a small restaurant, something simple, you know. If you need more than that, an investment would need to be made on that end. Terms are simple. Good location, as you can see. Downtown is thriving. Tell me, what would you use the space for?"

"Uh, well, I've been interested for a long time in a specialty food store. Or maybe a bakery."

"Ah," Janice says and I cannot tell if she is impressed or not. She waves her arm around. "Well, you certainly have all or at least most of what you would need here. Needs a little elbow grease, but what down here doesn't? It hasn't been empty that long but it'll need some work. If you're interested, here's my card.

Let me write the terms on the back."

She pulls the card out of her bag and writes. "I've got another appointment in a few minutes but you think this over and if you think there's something you can do, give me a call. I'd like to get this space leased again, obviously." She hands the card to me and shows us the door.

Outside, Keri and Beth are over my shoulder to see what Janice had written on the back of her card. The lease isn't too high, workable actually. I wonder what I could do with that.

"Mom," Keri's saying. "Are you really–"

"I don't know, Claudine," Beth says. She is the voice of reason. "It's a gamble and what about your job?"

What about my job? "No kidding," I say. "But this just dropped out of nowhere, like I should give it a try, you know?"

"Sounds like impulse to me," Beth says. "You could lose everything. I don't know if I'd do it."

"Well, I won't know until I do it," I say, shoving the card into my pocket. I know Beth does not understand. She has no stomach for risks. Well, generally speaking, neither do I. But still. Still. Wistfully, I turn away from the window.

"Come on, girls, let's have lunch. My treat." I link their arms with mine. "Mexican anyone?"

Of course. How did I know?

Obviously, that other thing is hanging in the air like mist. *What if?*

What if I opened a shop and called it my own? And even wilder yet, what if I was a success at it? And wilder still, what if I loosened my dependence on a regular job and became my own boss? Janice's card is carefully stowed away in my pocket. What if I lit some candles tonight and put some good music on and drank a nice wine and really thought it over?

What if?

"I'm telling you, I wouldn't do it," the Beth in my mind says.

"Why not?" my alter ego asks.

"Why take a risk?" the ugly Beth in my mind says.

"Why not? I'm not stupid and I work hard," my alter ego says, puffing up a bit.

"You don't even know if you'd be good at it," the ugly, pessimistic Beth in my mind says.

That does it. I will have to do it. She has pissed me off sufficiently now. The glove is down, slapped into the mucked mud as it were.

Fuck you, Sir Pessimism and Mistress of Unused Chances. I am ordering a hot, steaming plate of change of life carnitas and I am planning a coup.

Get out of my way.

CHAPTER THIRTY SIX

Julie

The wedding date is set for August 1st and it can't come fast enough. Every time I think of it, my heart starts beating out of my chest. Holy shit, just the thought of it.

I'm hanging in the lobby of the law office, waiting for Claudine to finish with a client. Somehow, Claudine's approval about the way I'm living my life is important to me. It seems just as important as my family and friends' opinions. Claudine has seen me through a lot, and although I really didn't like her at first, I like her a whole lot now. I hope she will be proud of me. *There it is.* I hope she will admire how much I've grown up since she and I met. Finally, being over and past Rodney means a lot to me. Having a man like Sean in my life means the world. Claudine would understand all that.

A blonde woman in a pink sweat suit brushes past me. She's reed thin, reminds me more of an adolescent boy than a full grown woman, but she's beautiful and well-kept. Her hair seems odd – is that a wig? She smiles and excuses herself for running into me (she didn't) and then says, "Do you know where the ladies' room is?" I point down the hall, still wondering about that hair. She says, "thank you," with a broad white smile. "I bet you're waiting for Claudine. Isn't she wonderful?" Without waiting for an answer, she lunges down the hall. Then she turns and rushes back to me.

"I'm sorry, we haven't met. I'm Andrea." She pumps my hand.

"Hi. I'm Julie."

"Nice to meet you, Julie. Well, you're probably here doing what I've been doing, that would be crying on Claudine's shoulder. That's what I do. She's probably sick of me by now. Good luck to you." She smiles another perfectly white smile, turns again and rushes back toward the ladies' room.

Before I can say anything, Claudine is standing in front of me, smiling. She calls to the other woman and wishes her a good day. I find myself impatient to get her attention and when she finally turns to me, it is a relief.

"Hello, Julie," she says. "What can I do for you today?" She shows me to a conference room and shuts the door behind us.

Now that I'm here, shyness takes over. The wedding invitation is heavy in my hand, reminding me of why I came. "I wanted to give you something. This."

Claudine breaks the seal and pulls out the invitation. A smile crosses her face. "Why, Julie, this is wonderful. Congratulations."

She pulls me to her in an embrace and I feel like crying. "I wanted to give it to you personally. It's just – it's like how far I've come, how much I've been through, how much I've put my parents through and you've been such a big part of that. I just wanted to share this with you personally." Now I am crying, but I'm crying for joy, relief. I'm crying for just the knowing of it.

Claudine knows it too. She knew a little bit about Sean but I hadn't told her we were serious or about the proposal. Impulsively, I shove my left hand toward her. The stone sparkles impressively.

"This is the best news, Julie. I am so happy for you. And what a beautiful ring." She hugs me again. "It's been a long road for you, I know. I wish you all the happiness in the world."

I pull back. "But will you come? Will you come to the wedding?"

"Absolutely. I'll be there with bells on."

Somehow, this makes me happier than nearly anything else associated with my wedding. Except marrying Sean, Claudine sharing my wedding with me makes me happier than I could have ever thought.

CHAPTER THIRTY SEVEN

Andrea

All my bags are packed. I am ready to go. Was that a song once? Claudine is being gracious and taking my dog, Maggie in for the next twenty-one days. Her bag is packed too with everything she should need for the next three weeks. I am so excited. Mexico. Ministry. Praise God.

"We'll be working out of an abandoned schoolhouse," I say to Claudine. She seems excited for me, although I have a feeling she is not quite with the missionary thing. I want to reassure her. "My grandparents were missionaries in the West Indies," I say. Claudine and I are standing in her kitchen and this is the first time I've been to her house. She is leaning against the counter, drinking a cup of really good coffee, and she's given me her best coffee mug, full of fresh pressed. "I just feel like I'm following in their footsteps, sort of."

"I can understand that," she says. "I wish you all the best."

"But what happens in the meantime?" I ask, with more than a little hope.

"In the meantime, we'll send your documents to the judge and they'll be entered by the time you get back." Claudine smiles. Done deal then. It seems a lifetime ago Elliott walked out of our house, leaving me to face the world alone. Stranger things have happened but Elliott decided he was willing to settle at last. He called me. We met at a restaurant and worked it out. We went back to the half a million, my car, my personal possessions and he agreed to pay $3,000 per month in maintenance for one year. I would have liked a longer period for the maintenance, but everyone I've talked to about it tells me I got a good deal. I guess I did. Right now, I feel pretty good about it but besides that, I have a chance to do something meaningful with my life, a chance to touch others with the love of Christ. And I am getting divorced at nearly the same time. Truly, I am blessed.

Maggie is wandering. I will miss her for the next three weeks. Claudine will be good for her, I can tell. Her daughter is delightful. So pretty and charming. Maggie will be happy here.

Maggie will be happy here. Where did that come from? No time to think about that because time is wasting and I need to get to the airport. Grabbing Maggie up for one last kiss on the nose, I have to go before I start crying. I will be back. Nothing will change. That creepy-crawly feeling sliding up my spine is just my imagination.

Maggie will be happy here. Shake that off.

"Thank you, Claudine," I say and I mean it. "Thank you for all your hard work on my case."

She laughs and I see how totally unpretentious she is. "Not a problem," she says.

I give her a hug and a little squeeze. She seems surprised but not offended. Then, I am off. One phone call before I get on the plane and I am gone to minister in Mexico. Praise the Lord.

CHAPTER THIRTY EIGHT

Claudine

Emmanuel Withers is measuring, poking, inspecting, squinting and grunting in my bathroom. I am glad I called him. I can already see how perfectly in tune he is with this old house.

"It's a grand old lady," he says in broken English. He is Mexican. But with that name – Withers? I have to ask. He shrugs. "Makes it easier sometimes. It was my stepfather's last name. He thought it would make my life easier. Look at me." He spreads his arms wide. "Do you think I'm fooling anybody?"

I tell him what I want done but he seems to have a better vision for the space than me. Maybe it's clearer to him. Certainly, Emmanuel Withers doesn't have to argue with the disorganized, foggy bathroom list charging through my mind at four o'clock in the morning. At any rate, he is ready to take on the challenge. For a price. And I already made arrangements for that, saving a set amount out of each paycheck. It's all good. When Emmanuel is finished, I'll have a brand new, luxurious bathroom. In the meantime, I don't even mind sharing Keri's cramped bathroom with pink with zebra print border. We'll make it, we will.

"You see here," Emmanuel says to me, shoving a sketch of what he has in mind for the space under my nose. He points a brown finger at the page. "You see the walk-in shower, here." Yes, I see, or try to. "Here is the tub you want, tucked under the eaves. All good, Jacuzzi style. Nice sinks, yes?" Yes. "All the fixtures will be burnished brass." And we will tuck the toilet away into its own little alcove. I like it. I like it very much. I think Maggie likes it too. She is wiggling her stubby tail, looking back and forth at the both of us as if to say, "Well done. Good job."

"One of my guys should be here any minute. He's finishing up another job," Emmanuel says and slaps his sketch book shut. "You will be happy with our work. This is a grand old lady, this house. You are very lucky."

He tells me he is married with six daughters. No sons to leave his business to. That makes him sad, but he loves his six daughters. He lives on a little farm outside of town. Emmanuel's wife is beautiful. Her name is Juanita. She grows all their vegetables. He takes the time to show me her picture in his wallet. He is proud of her. "She makes the best tamales."

"Oh, I love tamales. She could show me how?" I feel brash but I would like to know.

"She could show you," Emmanuel says. "I'll ask her to make you some." He nods and goes back to the bathroom. He hums. I like him. He is a nice man.

Below, the doorbell rings and I dash down the stairs. This must be the worker Emmanuel has been waiting for.

Before I hit the bottom of the stairs, I feel as if I am being bathed in a destiny of sorts, pushing me forward. I feel as if I am gliding along in golden light and it is beautiful. Opening the door, I see him.

Can a person fall in love, true love, twice in one life time? Is it even possible? All those years with Jim – since we were seven years old, for crying out loud, all that love – could it happen twice? Poised in the moment, my hand on the solid wood door, the warm security of my home at my back, the rush of moist spring air in my face, I feel as if this is what I have been waiting for. As if he was on a parallel course with Jim and me, and now Jim's gone. It is just me so he and I collide. Never mind, the man is introducing himself.

"Jake," he says. "My name's Jake. I work with Emmanuel. Is he here?"

"Sure," I say, stepping back to let him in. I am locked in his gaze. Those are the bluest eyes I have ever seen and such a clear blue, like the ocean. I am staring. I wonder if he notices. My face is hot. "He's upstairs, in my bathroom."

The man, Jake, starts up the stairs but he is looking back at me. He sees a lunatic, I just know it. It could not be stronger, this gilded sensation, if I had been knocked against the newel post my hand is resting on. "Thanks," he says and keeps going. My breath has stopped. I know this man. I have known him all my life. Even without Jim, who I knew better than anyone. Until recently, that is. Anyway, this Jake, well, he has captured my imagination and maybe my heart as well.

"Do I know you?" he asks me, abruptly.

Oops, maybe too much staring.

"Uh, well, I..."

"No wait, I do know you. Parkcrest High School?"

"Yeah, that's right."

"Nineteen eighty, right?"

"Yes, did we graduate together?"

He comes back down the stairs, nodding. "You're Claudine. Jim Coulter? You married Jim, right?"

"Right," I say, feeling a little surprised and put off by the mention of my ex-husband's name.

"So, how is Jim these days?"

"Uh, well, he's fine, actually." Instinctively, protectively, I put one hand over my mouth for a second and then say, "We're divorced." I splay my hand outward.

Jake nods. "I see." He looks up the stairs where he hears Emmanuel grunting and heaving. Things are being knocked around up there and I wonder what things that might entail. "Well, it was nice to see you again," he says. "I better get a look up here and see what he's doing." Back up the stairs he goes. I am left with an awesome vision of a rear end in blue jeans.

Problem is I do not remember him from high school. I cannot even think of what his last name might be, but I did enjoy the blue eyes and the blue jeans. I will dig out my high school yearbooks later. Right now, I have Maggie to feed and I have plans to make. I have plans to make, Jake. Move out of my way, Jake. Right.

CHAPTER THIRTY NINE

Julie

Today's a big day and I'm scared out of my bleeping mind. How did I get into this? How did I get to the point of meeting his parents? Oh. My. God. Not that I am opposed necessarily, but what if they hate me? What if I make a gigantic fool of myself? What if Sean decides I'm not worth marrying after all because I am such a pathetic loser? What if, goddammit, what if? He's so sure of himself and sure of me as he drives us down the highway to the point of my complete undoing.

I'm staring at him so much, he says, "What?"

I say, "Nothing."

He says, "Gotta be something."

I say, "You are just so beautiful today," and he takes my hand and kisses it and tells me he loves me.

I should have refused to get in the car.

We just keep on zooming on down I-44.

Okay, I have to admit I'm getting a little nutty. Just nervous, that's all. Nerves. Plain and simple. Nobody has ever asked me to marry them before, not seriously anyway. I always thought eventually Rodney and I would marry but I thought it would be because we eloped to Miami or Oklahoma or something. After he divorced Angela, of course. Nobody's ever said, "Hey, let's have a church wedding and all of our family and friends will be there and this will be an honorable day and it's all I ever wanted." Nobody. I would have married Rodney once, but it would have been on the sly, an elopement for sure. Not quite as romantic as what I'm doing now. Not that eloping couldn't be romantic. I think with Rodney, it would have been cheap and maybe just a little on the sleazy side. Let's face it. It would have been a lot on the sleazy side. We won't think about that now because I am on my way to Fair Grove to meet Sean's parents. Something I never thought would happen in my life. Nope. Not today anyway. And here we are, in his parents' driveway, and I am here and I'm fine.

Something else is nagging at the back of my brain. Something I never cared about before, never thought about anyway, has been whirling around in my brain for some time.

I. Cannot. Cook. I cannot cook. True story. I never cared to learn and what's worse (maybe) is I never asked Renae to teach me. She's not much of a cook either. And my grannie, who can cook, is in a nursing home and none of my friends cook and even if I had ever wanted to learn and I didn't, no one can teach me.

See, the philosophy is as long as drive-thru and delivery are available, why bother? That may have been Renae's philosophy as well because I cannot remember the last time she cooked. Maybe it was spaghetti or something like that. The home ec gene definitely missed me. Anyway, I am here, about to meet Sean's downhome family-orientated parents, and I have this fatal flaw written in huge letters across my forehead. *Be advised: This woman cannot cook. Your son will starve.*

What if his mother asks me if I cook? Well, the answer, the real one, would be "hell no, what for?" Okay, I will have to re-think that and come up with a halfway sensible answer.

I love Sean. Of this much, I am certain. With that said, I will be okay.

The house is huge. It seems like it runs on forever. White clapboard, long windows, porches. I think it is beautiful and I say so.

"This is the house I've lived in all my life," Sean says. I smile at him because I know he wants me to be impressed. I am.

There is life after Rodney. Oh yes, there is life after screwing up your life so badly you don't know the way out. Can I get an Amen?

But seriously, I am impressed.

Sean seems happy today. If I can make him happy this day, I will be happy.

Her name is Iris, Sean's mother. She's alone in the house when we get there. Jerry, Sean's stepfather, is outside somewhere. The sisters, April and Amy, are at their respective homes for the time being but they will arrive any minute. Sean knows where to find Jerry, probably at his shop in back, and excuses himself. So here we are, just me and Iris. Pretty name, Iris. Something I would not have thought of. Strong. Simple. Beautiful. Iris.

This Iris is not willowy and delicate. This Iris is short and heavy-set. This Iris wears glasses. She is not garden-variety Iris. I like that. She intrigues me. I see her strength but I don't know the story behind it. What will she tell me someday?

"Can I ask you a question?" I say once Sean goes in search of his stepfather.

"Of course you can," she says. She is turning fine dough onto a baking sheet. I see a bowl of what I think is apples and raisins nearby. Now she coats the dough with melted butter. "You can ask me anything you want to."

"What are Sean's favorite dishes? What does he like the best?"

To my utter surprise, she throws her head back and laughs. "Somehow, I thought it might be a more difficult question than that. Child, he will eat anything that doesn't eat him first," she says, still laughing. So here I am, sitting in this huge country kitchen with a woman who is laughing either at me or with me (I'm not sure which), and I wonder if the joke is on me.

She stops messing with the dough for a minute and leans in.

"Sean loves you. I can see that. And I mean it when I say he'll eat anything that doesn't eat him first. I can tell you I have firsthand knowledge about that. But here's one thing and it's not that he's a chauvinist. Mercy no," she says, still leaning over the counter toward me. "No, Sean's no chauvinist, but girl, he takes pride in being able to support those he loves. If you make any effort whatsoever for him, and I see you will, he will love you for it." She shrugs. "I'm his mama. I've known him all his life and I can tell you that much is true. Now, come on over around here and help me with this strudel. Come on."

And with that, I get up off the counter stool and start spooning the apples, raisins, brown sugar, nutmeg, cinnamon and butter onto the pastry dough. Iris shows me how to roll it up and then helps me brush more butter on top.

"My husband, Jerry, he loves the strudel. I make it all the time, just for him. Now listen to me," she says. "There was nothing going on between Jerry and me while our spouses were alive. Nothing." She crosses her heart. "I know people in this community want to think there was something going on beforehand, but there was not. I swear on my life." Again, another cross. "Jerry and me, we were always friends, from a longtime back. And then my husband died and Jerry's wife got struck with the cancer and from then on, we was a suspicious pair. But I tell you, there was nothing between us until both our spouses were in the ground and respectably buried. Nothing."

She stares off in the distance for a minute. "Oh now, I can't tell you I didn't have feelings for him either, or he for me for that matter. But I will tell you, everything was above board until my husband, Sean's father, God rest his soul, and Jerry's wife, God rest her soul, were decently buried in the ground. That was the deal."

Awkward. Too much information, or not. So I say, "Well, it doesn't really matter to me so long as you're happy now."

She seems to come back to Earth, somehow. "Right," she says, "of course. Now let's see about getting this strudel in the oven. We'll just bake the hell out of those apples."

A copy of *In Our Time* by Ernest Hemingway sits on the counter next to where we were working the strudel. She sees me eyeing it.

"Ah yes," she says. "Could he not be famous? I mean, if your father had blown a horn to announce your birth, would you not assume you are destined for great things?"

"Well, I don't know. So far as I know, no one blew a horn anywhere when I was born."

Iris smiles. "You just don't quite know yourself yet, my dear. You don't know your possibilities."

"What do you know about me?"

I am not sure whether she antagonizes me or sparks me, or whether she just old-fashioned pisses me off, but she certainly has piqued my interest. She smiles at me.

She just smiles.

"Julie, I am so happy my son found you." She's still smiling. "I am happy to know you and someday, you will know exactly what I'm talking about."

"No, no, I don't know."

Tell me. I'm thirsty and she knows it. This is me at the river and I want a drink, a long, lusty, deep drink. Will she show me? Will she show me how to drink it all up?

Iris puts her arms around me and, for once, I don't mind that kind of familiarity from someone I hardly know. Once upon a time, I would have resisted but with this woman, it is the absolute right thing. I feel strength surging through her. I feel a force before unknown to me and I recognize it as strength, but it is more than that. It is a resolve. It is being the person you really are and loving that person within and honoring that person. That is it, a feeling of honor. What in the hell does that mean? I have no experience with honor. What a revelation that is, to realize how low I went with Rodney. Sean is real. He is.

A refreshing breeze slices all the way through me during Iris's embrace. Renae doesn't have that kind of presence. Too much worry with her, I suspect. This woman is a different breed, however. She is earthy, sensual like the Earth itself. She carries love with her. I wonder if I could be like that. I would like to be like her, in fact. I'll have to stick close and learn what she knows. That'll make Sean happy and making Sean happy makes me happy.

CHAPTER FORTY

Andrea

Ten of us are in the company, our band of ministers to the starving souls in Mexico. It's a lucky thing the village has been gracious to donate an old schoolhouse to us for our ministry. Our lodging, an old cabin, is next door. Pastor leads worship services every day, sometimes three times a day, when the villagers stumble in, curious or maybe looking for something. A balm for their hard existence. Every day, I see their eyes glow with curiosity, a will for salvation. I long to give them what they come here to find. Maybe it's simply love they crave.

Two days ago, a girl came to me. Our interpreter, Juan, told me she was fifteen years old. She had been married since she was thirteen. She couldn't give her husband children and he didn't want her any longer. The husband cast her out. The girl had nowhere to go. She cannot go home to her mother. She's too old. All I could do was hold her while she sobbed. I pray for her constantly. There must be someone who will take her in.

She is afraid all she can do now is become a prostitute. She has nothing. No one wants her. When I looked at her and heard her story, I could see myself. I could envision Elliott throwing me aside.

It is hot here and humid. This place smells of unwashed bodies and dust, and some kind of oily stink that may come from cooking pots in the community. I'm not sure. I see insects the size of mice. Everywhere I look, the surroundings are primitive and dirty. We live in part-jungle, part-desert. Our cabin is next to a stream where I often see chocolate colored women and children scrubbing brightly colored cloths. I don't know what they do with the fabric because they don't seem to sew them for clothing, but they certainly keep them scrubbed.

Nine days we've been here now. Has it really been that long? Huh. Juan, my interpreter, took a group photograph of us. It was my camera they used. When I get back home, I'll have a print made and send everyone in our group a copy. I took some photos of the village children here too. They are curious. They stare at my wig. Could it be they've never seen golden blonde hair before? Somehow, I am at home here. I am at peace. There are rumors it is dangerous for white people, for Americans, to be here. But I feel safe. God will protect us.

It's noon (I think) and hot. The sky is blue and cloudless but wind is stirring the dust around.

All the days roll seamlessly into the next. In the end, it seems to be one continuous day. It's been a wonderful experience so far. The villagers seem to accept our presence and are eager to be hear our ministering. They bring their children too for Bible school.

None of the villagers have come by today for church or Bible school. It is strangely quiet and empty around the compound. The flies are buzzing, but the flies are always buzzing here in a grand cacophony of humming vibration. They're attracted to the dampness underneath our arms and between our legs. We smell. My fingernails are black. I would never have thought this would be me. Not in a million years. Where are my designer soaps, powders, expensive makeup? I was a doctor's wife at one time, used to a world of expensive comfort. I was pampered, spoiled. How incredible to be here, doing the most rigorous of work. How incredible it is I am not complaining. No, in spite of the rigors here, in spite of the deprivation, I am content. Some members of our company are napping in the cabin. Others, like me, are organizing our materials for our next service. Something is hanging in the air. What is it?

The colored pictures from the village children hang inside our makeshift church and school. The children love the crayons. They love the bright colors, the brighter the better, and they draw all kinds of wonderful pictures. But most of all, they seem to like to draw the likeness of Jesus, who they sing about. He's beautiful in their pictures, mostly brown with darker black hair and eyes, dressed in a white robe with a gold halo circling his head. The children from the village were here yesterday. Today, no one comes.

Lost in my reverie, I continue to organize our materials for the next service. I am enraptured in the glory of the Lord. Music, the music we play and sing at our services, fills my mind. The Glory of the Lord. God is in His firmament. How beautiful a firmament must be. How splendid and bright and totally blinding in its beauty. We all must praise Him for His many blessings. I want to praise Him more. I want to be more of a blessing and less of a burden. No more episodes like that last one in the motel. No more. I've forgiven myself. Jesus has forgiven me. I am totally free. Free in Jesus.

Something in the brush cracks. The attack is swift and sudden. How many? Twelve? Ten? No, only five. Five olive-skinned men rush from the bush, screaming and waving automatic weapons at us. Someone, probably Carmen who I have grown close to, shrieks and the air is filled with a whirring sound. It is the sound of chaos. I am stunned. My legs are not working. Those of us outside are instantly herded into a circle. Somehow, I am stumbling into the circle with everyone else. Carmen grabs my hand. These strange men are shouting, waving guns at us. Carmen's fear wears heavy on my nostrils, weaving around my legs and arms, paralyzing me. It is hard to breathe. My own fear is rising. What do they want? Where did they come from? Have they been watching us? How did we not know? So this is why the villagers have not been by. They knew. They had to have known.

Pastor and Juan are in the middle of us. Pastor is saying something to Juan. Juan shouts to the invaders. They stop momentarily, staring at Juan. Pastor says something else. Juan speaks it.

"We do not bring trouble. Tell us what you want."

One of the men pulls the pastor out of the midst of us. I see this man has a gun tucked into his waist band. He stares. He turns and gives a command and the rest of them close in, pushing us in a single line toward our cabin. The leader forces us into our building. I do not understand their language. Every so often, I think I hear an English word thrown in but I can't tell.

It seems as if I am watching this from a long ways away, yet I am in the middle of it. "Please, Jesus," I whisper. "Let them go without hurting us." The leader hears me and turns toward our little huddle. He does not know who spoke but he is not pleased. He spits something out to Juan and Juan tells us to remain still and quiet. Juan does not seem afraid. I wonder if he is.

Then something inexplicable happens. Juan and the leader begin bargaining for our lives. Juan laughs and the leader pushes the pastor out the door. Juan follows. We move as a group to the window. They are in the yard in front of our cabin. Pastor is on his knees. They are tying his hands behind his back. His wife, Connie, stares in horror out the window and pushes her fist in her mouth to keep from screaming. Carmen grabs my hand and holds it hard. And then a shot rings out. I reach for Connie, who evades my grasp and bolts for the door. Someone, one of the men, grabs and holds her. She is shouting, "Let me go. He's my husband." She is not let go. Pastor falls sideways, kicking his legs up and then he is still. Juan smirks at the leader and turns as if to walk away. He thinks they made a deal. He thinks they are friends. The leader shoots him in the back of the head. His knees buckle and swing sideways. His head flops forward and then back as he falls to the ground. I see blood spraying out of the back of his head. The leader kicks at him and then turns back to the cabin. The rest of his group falls in behind him as he darkens our doorway and comes inside.

Oh my God. Please Jesus, don't let them hurt us.

The leader barks something at his men and two of them pull us into a line so he can inspect us. The leader stares. He looks us over, his black eyes showing no emotion, and then he points at me.

"You."

I am weak in the knees, whether from the realization he speaks and understands English or from being singled out. Someone gasps. Someone else is throwing up. Connie is sobbing quietly. The renegades pay no attention to her. I swallow hard and say nothing. Someone pushes me from behind and I stumble in front of him.

"Your camera," he says. I had forgotten it was

around my neck. "You take picture." He beckons his minions and they rush to his side to pose. "Take picture," he says once everyone is lined up and ready.

My hands are shaking so bad, I am not sure the picture will be any good but I go ahead and shoot it. One, two, three. He wants as many as I can shoot. He smiles for the camera. They all do. It's like a celebration. Outside, inside, by the well. Over the bodies of our fallen comrades. My stomach is oily sick. "You," he keeps saying. "Take picture." As long as I take pictures of them, he is congenial. Finally, he is tired of having his picture taken and he begins shouting at his men. They line us up single file again and we begin to march. It had not occurred to me we could be kidnapped. I pray silently as we march, realizing now we could be killed before sundown. I wish I could leave a clue as to our whereabouts. The camera. The photos. Surely someone will find my camera and know what happened to us. What if no one ever finds us? Out here, in these remotest of places. *Don't kid yourself, Andrea.* What will they do with us? What if we die out here? Where are we going? *Help us, Father, protect us.*

I quickly pull the camera card out of my camera and drop it discreetly on the side of the road and keep marching. No one notices. Surely someone will find it.

Can we escape? Can we overtake them? What is wrong with this group that we are so docile? We move like cows being led to a slaughter. I wonder if I can signal one of my comrades to do something, anything, but no one is paying attention. Everyone is absorbed in their own misery. I smell fear like the stench of so much sweat. Oh God, I am frightened, too frightened to pray. I cannot string the words together.

We do not even know where we are. *We do not even know where we are. What do they want? Why us?*

We stop. The men are shouting at us, gesturing with

their guns. What do they want? They shout some more. Women are crying. One of the men jabs one of them in the side with his gun. She crumples to the ground, still weeping. We don't know what to do. We don't understand what they want. Are we supposed to go, stop, what? Where are we? They march down the line, shouting in our faces, their white teeth gleaming out of their dirty faces. They look like the devil.

We are all confused and tired. The leader looks bored. Finally, he shouts something and they stop yelling at us. He says something else and they begin pushing at us. They want us to line up again. I see a wooden fence running behind us and up the dirt road. They want us to line up against the fence. They are grabbing some of us and rearranging our order, shoving people here and there, where they think each should go. One of them took my camera. What if he opens it up and discovers the missing camera card? He doesn't seem interested in the camera right now. What if no one ever finds the card and see the pictures? No one will know what happened to us and who did it, except our corpses will be lying here or somewhere. They are still yelling. I know we are going to die.

The leader walks down the row, looking each one of us in the eye. He comes to me and stops. "Thank you for the pictures," he says and keeps going. My back is pressed against the fence. One of the other men shoves my shoulders back so I smash against the fence. Bugs are crawling up from the stalks of the weeds we're standing in onto our calves. We're sticky, grimy, hot. The leader claps his hands together and his men line up in front of us. All my brain will utter is *Jesus*. They draw their guns, leveling their sights on us. There is no one to save us. All my life, all my thoughts, my hopes, my dreams, my wishes, they all end here on this dusty, hot road in Mexico. I hear weeping somewhere in the background but I do not cry. I look the man across from me in the eye. I look at him and I pity him. What a waste. I have few scant seconds to think. What have I not done with my life? Who did I not love enough? Who will care if I end right here, in a country not even mine? My parents, my brother, they will care. Elliott? No. Maggie? She will miss me only briefly. My friends, yes. Claudine, yes.

All of this is moving fast-forward now, skidding ahead at the sound of light. Hot sun bears down on us. Dust swells up around our ankles. The leader shouts again and I hear several loud cracks and then nothing.

Ah, here I come, sweet Jesus. Here I come to be nestled into your arms, precious Lord. Take me in, oh Lord, my Savior, the keeper of my soul.

CHAPTER FORTY ONE

Claudine

For the love of God, my bathroom bears a marked resemblance to a dust bowl. It's been gutted and stripped. I will be so pleased when the project is finished. I can already tell my bathroom is in good hands with Emmanuel and Jake. Of course, I cannot forget Jake.

I just got my coffeepot started, while I wait for Emmanuel and Jake so I can set off for work. I wish they'd hurry up. Keri has already gone to pick up Brandy so they can ride together to school. A new boyfriend may be in her future, but I am not sure. All I've heard so far are giggly whispers and hints. I wait for the proclamation. Why she's being so secretive about this one I have no idea but that is the way of a girl growing up, I suppose.

The little television in the kitchen is on. Maggie is outside to do her morning ritual. I see her through the French doors, flopping down on the deck to survey her domain. It is going to be a soft, sunny day. It is going to be one of those spring days I love so much, carrying just a hint of moisture in the air, with the smell of damp earth wafting up and the promise of rebirth all around. I am toying with the idea of a garden, albeit a patio garden. How wonderful it would be to pick my own peppers and tomatoes and maybe some spinach. The time is past to cultivate spinach this year, but I would like to do more than flowers and herbs. Maybe even a lemon tree by the back door. I chuckle to myself, listening to the gurgle of the coffeemaker. I think I will become a vegetable gardener this year. I will have to put the majority of it in pots and put netting up to keep the birds out – what about some strawberries? Sweet. Strawberry jam, strawberry shortcake, the old-fashioned kind with the sweetbread biscuit and real whipped cream. But my favorite is plain, old strawberries on homemade vanilla ice cream. Simple. Plain. So good, so good, so good. Ah, I am salivating.

The television news man interrupts my sweet thoughts. "Twelve members of a United States missionary group were found executed today outside the tiny village of Oaxaca City, in the Mexican state of Oaxaca." Grainy images of a mud building with shutters on the windows and a low-slung cabin come into view. I see a body lying in the mud and debris. Thankfully, I do not recognize it. "Pastor Joseph Wiemens of Springfield, Missouri, was apparently killed, execution style, as his missionary team watched," the announcer says. "What we know now is the interpreter, Juan Ortiz, was also killed in front of the shelter the group was living in and the rest of the group was led away into the brush where they were executed at the side of a dirt road by a militant unit. We know little about this militant band and the Americans may simply have been in the wrong place at the wrong time." Pictures of the members of the unit rambled across the screen. Only one face I know for certain. In an ironic twist, I see Andrea looking sweetly into the camera, in her wedding gown. I've seen this photo before. She showed me all of her wedding photos and this one I thought was particularly beautiful. Radiant, tanned Andrea, waiting to become a doctor's wife, gazing up into the camera, diamonds around her throat. She was so beautiful.

My knees buckle. I pull one of the kitchen chairs out and plunk down on it. The newscast has knocked the wind out of me. Andrea, dead. Andrea, executed and left to die in the dirt like an animal. No longer radiant. Cold, lifeless and still. *Oh my God.* Could it be a mistake?

The newsman is still talking. He is pointing out various faces and giving little stories about them, but nothing about Andrea.

"Terrible tragedy," his co-anchor says, then they switch to a story about a twelve-year old entrepreneur in South Dakota.

I cannot believe what I just saw and heard. My own blood roars through my head. I cannot speak. Thinking is beyond me. Maggie is nosing about my grape arbor across from the French doors, oblivious. Her mistress is dead. I cannot believe it. My client is dead. This cannot be true. How long since she was executed? Two days? There must be a mistake. I know there is no mistake though. I know it. Oh my God, how horrible. I'm trying to absorb it, get my head around it and my stomach wretches in self-defense. I put my hand over my mouth and sob. My mind hears me, the sharp, loud cry of women mourning as in Hebrew times. Rocking back and forth, I can only think I must be in shock. Although I know it is not professional to feel so much for a client, it doesn't matter. Andrea, beautiful, radiant Andrea, had become a friend of sorts.

The telephone is ringing. It is Beth.

"Did you see the news? About your client?"

"Yeah, I did." I sniffle.

"It's just so sad," Beth says. She talks for a minute about what a terrible tragedy this is and we hang up.

Terrible. Unbelievable. Here, in my town, we live such a sheltered life. Things like this do not happen here among us, except they do. And when they do, they hit with such alarming speed and velocity, it leaves those of us behind astonished and questioning. I am somewhat comforted in the fact that, at the end, Andrea was involved in something she believed in. I am comforted if she had to die, she died making a difference to a people she didn't even know. I think of how unselfish that idea is, how noble it is. I can take comfort in that. Andrea was good. Andrea's heart was where it should have been.

But now, as I weep, my mind wonders *Is this fair? Is this the way God intended for Andrea to live and perish?* I will never know the answer to that question and the not knowing is hard. It's unfathomable for me to think it is acceptable to a heavenly deity someone who loved it so much would have been taken out of this life in this awful way. *Is this God's will?*

Oh Andrea, I am so very, very sorry.

CHAPTER FORTY TWO

Claudine

Unbelievable, the number of people who've come out for Andrea's funeral. Andrea never knew how loved she really was.

Standing in the back of the church, because I arrived late and all the seats are taken, I'm amazed at the sheer number of flower arrangements surrounding the mourners and the casket. It's at the front of the church, draped in purple velvet and topped with a huge bouquet of white roses and lilies. A photograph of Andrea rests on an easel next to her remains. I feel myself tearing up again. How could this happen? How could this incomprehensible, terrible thing happen to Andrea?

I recognize her parents, Dr. and Mrs. Whitely, at the front of the church, and her brother. Unbelievably, Elliott is here as well, sitting a few rows back from the Whitelys, dressed in a black suit. All I can see is the back of his head and his broad shoulders. I never imagined I would see him here, in this place, honoring his dead ex-wife.

The air is dense with the scent of stargazer lilies and peonies. "Dear Lord and Father of Mankind" is playing. Seems a strange song for a funeral but at least we have music.

"Our Father, who art in Heaven," the associate pastor is saying. "Hallowed be thy name." I remember. I prayed this prayer every night after my father died of a heart attack when I was thirteen, and I prayed it every night until my mother – drunk with a broken heart and whiskey – stumbled into my bedroom one night, and caught me praying. She slapped my face and told me never to pray that prayer again in her presence. She said God took my father and God takes everything. I prayed it anyway, just not out loud. Once it sustained me. Today, it fortifies me.

I came here alone, even though Keri offered and Jake half-way insisted on accompanying me. But I didn't want anyone with me on this journey of sorts. This part of my life is sealed off, private, from them. It is part of my work, yes, but it's also a private part of me mourning for a dear friend, someone who I should have kept at arm's length for professional reasons but didn't. Missing Andrea will not go away easily. My throat constricts. How often I wished this was a bad dream. How horribly sad for Andrea to be lying under that coffin lid, motionless, still, her vibrancy silenced. Her mother is sobbing quietly. I look at Elliot, wondering what he is feeling. Surely he is not so heartless that he would not grieve.

Julie tugs at my elbow. This is a surprise. She is wearing a sleeveless pink dress, gathered around the waist in Grecian folds, with a full skirt and sandals. Next to her, I feel rather matronly and conservative in a black skirt, black hose and a white blouse with black piping on the collar. I guess I could have shown a little leg or something but it didn't seem quite right. Julie looks pretty and I tell her so. She smiles shyly.

"Did you know Andrea?" I whisper.

"I met her once at your office. When I saw her picture in the paper, I just wanted to come and be supportive, you know what I mean? I thought you might be here."

How sweet. I slip her arm through mine and pat it. "I wonder if Leon is here," Julie says, twisting to look around.

"I doubt it. He doesn't go to funerals," I say, which is true.

"He just doesn't like to remember he's old," Julie says and giggles.

Maybe, but I nod and say nothing. I know if Leon can avoid the inevitable, his own mortality, he certainly will. He doesn't watch movies that don't have happy endings. I'm confident he wouldn't approve of my presence here, much less being here with another client.

"Thy Kingdom come. Thy will be done, on Earth as it is in Heaven. Amen."

"Amen," I whisper, hoping Andrea is at peace, wherever she is. I offer up a little prayer, a practice I seldom utilize, that Andrea finally find the peace that evaded her in life. I pray she is comforted. I pray she is loved.

Andrea's father and brother stand with their arms around Mrs. Whitely. They're standing strong but they must be crushed. Leon, who seems to know everybody and is acquainted with them, told me it took three weeks to get the body back to the United States. The family made the journey themselves to identify her. Her father and brother went to the spot of her death but her mother refused, staying behind in the hotel. Andrea had been frozen in the interim to prevent decay and once she was thawed out for embalming, she began to putrefy rather quickly. Hence all the fragrant flowers, I suppose. Leon also mentioned Andrea would be buried in a plain white gown.

"We have come to honor a life cut short and sent back to the Father, the life of Andrea Whitely Sommerfield," the minister says. "A lovely young woman taken from us all too soon. We are here to honor her life. We are here to honor those who brought her into this world, Clyde and Annette Whitely, and those who loved her. We are here because God has called us to be here."

I smooth my skirt and give a sideways glance to Julie. She sits perfectly upright, her mouth open in a tiny O, taking in every word.

A soloist sings. Candles are lit. Another prayer is said. Andrea's brother reads the twenty-third psalm. A short eulogy is followed by another prayer.

"We commit into our hands. Oh Lord, our sister and loved one, Andrea Whitely Sommerfield. Amen."

Strangely enough, fog set in while we were in the church. All of us look like ghosts drifting through the fog to our cars. Julie whispers she has to get home to Alex and leaves. I stay and watch as the pearl-white casket is loaded into the long white hearse. The family is guided by the gentle hands of the funeral director to their vehicle. Elliott Sommerfield follows behind, expressionless. We travel the short distance to the cemetery, swathed in damp mist. Another short service and the first clumps of earth hit Andrea's casket, which is now lowered into the ground. Elliott steps forward and drops one white rose into the grave before turning and walking away, disappearing into the mist. Mrs. Whitely gasps audibly.

My heart goes out to Mrs. Whitely. She must have had dreams and wishes for her daughter, dreams and wishes never realized, in part thanks to Elliott. She must have known all the indignities Elliott put Andrea through. She must have known of the cruelty. How did she stand for his presence here, I wonder? At least he didn't cause a scene. At least he didn't laugh out loud. I'm glad he is gone and I wonder what brought him here to begin with. He is left with no one to spar with now that Jackie's remarried and Andrea is gone. What will he do, I wonder, besides practice medicine and travel all the time? Poor, sad, evil man.

CHAPTER FORTY THREE

Claudine

Jake is at the door, camouflaged by a huge bouquet of apricot tulips. Since I'm not sure what do to but laugh, I go ahead with it and open the door to let him in. It always amazes me how handsome he is. A few nights ago when sleep eluded me, I unearthed my old high school yearbooks, piled them up on the bed, climbed in and poured through the old photos. There he was. Well, it took me some time to get to him but, nevertheless, there he was.

It was a black and white photograph of a basketball game, an old timey kind of photo compared to today's standards of color and motion. I love black and white. Jim and Jake are dressed out in their Parkview uniforms. Jim was at the free throw line and as he aimed and threw, his mouth hung open in concentration. The photographer caught him as the ball left his fingers, erupting into the air. It is a beautiful photograph. Just to Jim's right, crouching at the line, is Jake O'Rourke. His mouth is hanging open too and his arms are coming up from his sides and he is watching this beautiful, awesome throw and he can't help himself because he knows it is going in. It is going in and they're going to win the game. I love that photograph. Running my fingers over it lovingly, I revel in those high school memories. Jim's basketball games and my cheering him on. Cheering on the boy I loved, that was my duty. I remember the sweat and the plastered hair and the locker room smell. It was so long ago. Joie de vivre. Where have I heard that? It must be a little high school French. Well, that was a few nights ago when I'd had a little too much wine and I was reliving my youth.

This guy, Jake, is here in my house, carrying the biggest bouquet of tulips I have ever seen. How did he know I love those? I may have told him but I don't think so.

"Hey lady," the voice behind the tulips says. "Got milk?"

Keri, thank the heavens above, is with her father tonight. I am cooking and maybe, with a little luck, I'll stir up more than food. On the menu are New York strips and mushrooms. I love this gorgeous bunch of tulips and I tell him so. He is already putting them in a vase. The flowers are placed immediately in the middle of the kitchen table and I give Jake a kiss. It is a little kiss but a kiss, all the same.

"You're teasing me, lass," he says and grins. That is one thing I really like about him, his smile. It just seems to light up the room.

"Maybe. But if you know what's good for you, you'll come over here and help me finish this," I say with more than a little swagger as I strut to the stove. "How about a beer or some wine?"

"I'll take you up on that," he says and helps himself to a Guinness from the refrigerator. I like that too, his sure way of helping himself. I like everything about him and I like it more and more every time I see him.

Oh yes, the bathroom is finished. Finally. Emmanuel was proud on that last day. He even brought me some tamales wrapped in wax paper. His wife cooked them and promised she would teach me how to make them if I ever wanted to learn. I was thrilled. When all was said and done, Emmanuel took me on a tour of my new space. Not just any tour but an Emmanuel Withers tour of my own bathroom, crafted with his hands.

Every detail was exactly the way I dreamed it. Everything was the way I asked. It was nothing less than perfect. The walk-in shower with the rustic ceramic tile, the new toilet in its own compartment under an eave and the huge jacuzzi tub under the window in the alcove surrounded by more rustic tile. He even found the exact same light fixture I admired that day on the hunt with Gabriel. And here it is, hanging above the tub, bright and glitteringly beautiful. I don't know how he knew.

Gabriel seems such a long time ago now. No residue is left. Or maybe there is. *Thoughtus interruptus.* What about your dream, Claudine? What about that notion you have to be your own boss and do your own thing in your own space? What about that, Claudine? *What about that?* Indeed. I decide this is not the time, not with this man here with a humungous bouquet of tulips and my heart all aflutter. Not to mention my lower regions are vibrating. Oh my God, let us get on with things, shall we?

He is not much help in the kitchen, but he tries.

We laugh together, a lot, such a delicious treasure. It's been so long since I have laughed with a man. Surely Jim and I laughed during our years together? Yes, we did. There was no laughing with Gabriel, but we didn't really have a relationship anyway. Not like I hoped and maybe secretly longed for. It was all a mirage. This man, Jake, is real. And every time I catch a glimpse of his long eye lashes, every time I see another freckle on his cheek, I realize just how real he is.

I feel so alive at this moment, it defies description. I am just living in the now, the present and I realize if I just step out and claim it, just claim this newfound fortune, I can have it. I can have it all for myself and nobody else can ever touch it. I can feel him breathing. It is like nothing I ever felt before, not even with Jim. I loved Jim, I did, but maybe, just maybe, I am beginning to grow up or grow outward. Jake, here and now, is wearing a denim shirt and jeans, which I would love to peel off him. Come on, universe, grant me this one wish.

Sitting at my well-worn kitchen table, chairs pulled close together, I am feeding him brandied mushrooms and we are laughing. I drink wine while he drinks beer. We are laughing in my kitchen, in my home, and I cannot think of anything better in the whole wide world. Laughing has been in short supply. A hint of Andrea crosses my mind and then it leaves me with a little pain. I cannot even remember what in the world we talked about, except he does not care for little dogs, like Maggie. I like Maggie and I see I am stuck with her now. Keri loves her and vice versa. It is probably too late for Maggie to find another home since we are both so enamored with her. But no matter, I stuff another mushroom between his lips and he sucks with more than a hint of abandon.

It is time. And we didn't even get to the steaks.

CHAPTER FORTY FOUR

Julie

Oh. My. God. I am shopping with Renae, if that can be believed. We are looking for my wedding dress. So far, I have found the most beautiful dresses for the maid of honor and bridesmaids. Thin straps, tight bodice, sequins, the color is umber. I think these are the most beautiful dresses I have ever seen. Mine is proving a little bit stickier though. It must be perfect. This is my one and only.

"What about this one?" Renae says, holding the sea of gowns back to show me something. It is not for me, I can see that. The bouffant sleeves are just too much.

"Too much like a tea party," I say and keep looking. I look up just in time to glance out the window. I see Angela. A gasp which nearly becomes a scream comes out.

"What?" Renae says.

"It couldn't be. Never mind," I say, rifling through dresses at breakneck speed.

"No, really, what?"

"Mom, I could have sworn I saw Angela, just for a second. Outside the window."

Renae stares out the window dumbfounded but I can see she is faking her incredulousness. "Mom, you better tell me, what do you know?"

"We didn't want to spoil things for you. We didn't want you to worry," Renae says.

"That was Angela, wasn't it? And you knew?"

Renae puts a hand on my arm. "Keep it down, Julie. We made an appointment to come here, remember?" There is movement beyond us.

"What gives, Mom?"

"We didn't want you to worry," she says again. The saleslady hovers nearby.

"Is there anything I can help you with?" she asks. Renae apologizes and sends her away.

"Mom?"

"Angela called me a couple weeks ago at work. She's been home for a while. I told her not to bother us and that's all." Renae goes back to the clothing racks, nervously shoving and shifting garments around, not really looking at anything.

"Why didn't anyone tell me?" I ask. "Why didn't anyone tell me?"

"Come on," she says and she rushes me out of the store, calling back apologies as she goes. The saleslady looks more than a little perturbed.

"Mom, stop it. Stop treating me like a baby." When will they understand, anyway? We are on the sidewalk, walking furiously to nowhere.

"Julie, listen," Renae says. I am walking ahead and she is rushing to catch up. Finally, she does and she grabs my arm. Her hair is blowing in her face. She pushes it away.

"What Mom, what?"

"Julie, we didn't tell you because we didn't want

you to get upset. We didn't want you to worry."

"I can handle it, Mom. I should have been told. Who is 'we' anyway? How long have you known?"

She sighs and shrugs. "She called me two weeks ago. Mark and Sean and I thought—"

"You thought? Sean knew too and nobody told me? Not you, not even the man I'm supposed to marry? I should have been told. This is my life, mine and Alex's, and what if she would have done something to him, to us? Then what? What would you have told me then?"

Here's the car. "Where is she now?"

"They're living with Rodney's mother. That's all I know, really. She said she meant no harm to any of us and I believe her."

I stare at her over the top of the car. "You do?"

Renae shrugs again. "I do."

"I don't," I say as I open the door and slide in. Renae turns the key in the ignition. "And you shouldn't either. You know what she did to us. Have you forgotten what she did to us?"

Renae turns to me. "No Julie. I haven't forgotten anything. You have a good man in Sean. He's not going to let anything happen to you or Alex. Leon seems to think—"

"Leon knows too?"

"I called immediately after she called me. He doesn't think there is anything to worry about. We're supposed to keep track of anything unusual, that's all."

"Well, of course he doesn't think there's anything to worry about, Mom. Leon isn't even listening. He doesn't care what you say or what I say or what anybody says. Haven't you noticed he tunes you out completely? The only person listening in that office is Claudine. Does she know too?"

"I don't know. I suppose he may have told her. I don't know. Now Leon is our attorney and he's a good attorney and you have Sean, who is capable."

I had forgotten Sean for a moment. I groan. "I can't marry him, Mom. Not when he kept this from me. Don't you understand? This is my whole life – running and hiding and trying to recover from what I did and from those people. And he kept a secret from me."

"He did it to protect you, Julie. We all did it to protect you."

"What's wrong with you? He kept this from me, Mom. I can't marry someone who would do that."

"You know in your heart you want to spend the rest of your life with this man. If you let him go, your heart will chase after him the rest of your life, do you understand me? It will drain you." Her voice is taking on a harsh tone. "Don't make him go away on a technicality. You'll never get over it."

She puts the car in gear and pulls away from the sidewalk. "Now, which one of those gowns did you like best?"

Later, I leave a message for Sean but he doesn't respond. "Why didn't you tell me? And don't act like you don't know who I'm talking about." Of course, he is on patrol tonight and I should not expect he would pick up anyway. "You should have told me," I say into the phone.

Why? Why did no one tell me that the one person, the most dangerous person I can think of, is roaming the streets unfettered? Why? Why did no one think I had a right to know?

My mind and my heart know I want no part of a future without Sean in it. I am not weak, nor am I dependent on a man. This just happens to be the man I should have waited for all of my days. This is his mistake. Sean should have told me. At least that way we could have faced it together, but he chose to treat me like a child. Had I not seen Angela downtown, in person, I would never have known she was out on the streets again. He is not my father. He is my future husband, my soul-mate, my lover. He is everything to me. I want to marry him but I want to be able to trust him. I have to be able to trust him or it all amounts to nothing.

I cannot sleep. Listening to Alex's rhythmic breathing is soothing but irritating at the same time. Finally, I get out of bed, wrapping my robe around me, and head upstairs.

Renae is standing in front of the kitchen sink, staring out the window. She is rinsing out coffee cups and putting them in the dishwasher.

"Mom?" I say.

"Hey," she says and shuts the dishwasher door.

"Mom, who is it?"

"Who is who?" She looks irritated somehow.

"Who is it your heart chases after?" I know I should not ask this question. She will not answer me truthfully, I can already tell. She may even get mad.

She exhales heavily, folding a towel and hanging it up. "I shouldn't have said that. I was trying to illustrate a point, that's all. You'll be unhappy without Sean."

"Don't lie to me, Mom. Not after what we've been through today."

Luckily, Mark is not here at the moment. She tells me she sent him to the store for a few things. He won't be privy to any of this.

"Mark is a good husband to me, more than I could have wished for," she says quietly. "I would never hurt him, not in a million years."

I wait.

"But I never would have divorced your father, never, if he had not asked for it."

"How did he ask for it? You mean, he seriously asked?"

Tears fill her eyes. "He came to me and he told me

about Miriam. He asked me to divorce him. And I did it because he asked me to."

"Miriam left him, didn't she?"

Renae snorted. "Yes, she left him. It didn't take her long either."

"But you still love him."

"I think you can love more than one person at one time. Maybe in different ways too. I love Mark. I will never leave him. But I'll never forget being asked to move aside. Your father was so polite about it too."

"Are you unhappy, Mom?"

"No, I'm not unhappy. Mark is wonderful. It's just I know what it is to love someone ferociously and lose them like a dry cleaning ticket, maybe even less casually than that."

"You're comparing keeping a serious secret from me. It's not like losing a dry cleaning ticket, Mom."

"It's who can stand you at the end of the day, Julie. It's who can put up with your shit when they've taken all they can take themselves. Nothing is guaranteed in this life, not even tomorrow. Take what you're given and give thanks for it."

I nod and move back toward the stairs.

"Mom?'

"What, Julie?" She turns halfway from the sink.

"I love you."

Her face relaxes. "I love you too. He's a good man, Julie."

"I know. Goodnight, Mom."

"Goodnight, Julie."

Sometime later, I hear Renae quietly singing upstairs in the dark. I never knew my mother was so sad. I didn't know she lost someone she loved. Maybe sometimes compassion is a good thing.

CHAPTER FORTY FIVE

Julie

Sean is at the door. He does not look happy but then, neither am I. I have not slept, or at least not much in the four days since I saw him last. I missed him.

I step out onto the porch for privacy's sake.

"I guess you got my message, huh," I say.

"Julie, I worked all night. In fact, I worked the last five nights. I'm tired and all I want is to go to bed. Let's straighten this out so I can do that, okay?"

"Why didn't anyone tell me? *Why didn't you tell me?*"

His eyes are intense green. He is angry with me, I know it.

"We all thought what we did was in your best interests. You were happy and we wanted you to stay that way."

"Look, you're not my father, Sean. I could have handled it."

He turns to the porch rail and leans both hands on it, looking sideways at me. "Julie, when are you going to realize you're with someone who wants to treat you right, someone who wants you to be happy and would do anything, anything at all, to make it and keep it that way? When? I mean, what've I gotta do?"

"I just wanted the truth, that's all."

"Well, you got it. You got the truth. I'm sorry we didn't tell you. In retrospect, we should have but we didn't and – forget it." He stands up and turns toward the stairs. I reach out.

"Sean?"

But he already has his foot on the step and he is going down, leaving.

"Sean? Come back, please?"

He turns and looks at me before getting into the Jeep. The window is rolled down. "I'm going home and I'm going to bed. You gotta quit trying to make me leave. I'm tired of it. I'll call you later."

The white Jeep Cherokee backs out of the driveway.

Going back in the house, Renae sees my ashen face.

"Oh my," she says. "Is it off or on?"

"I don't know," I say and wander into the kitchen. I cannot stay still. Breakfast dishes need to be washed and I begin slapping them into the sink, spraying hot water and dish soap all over them. Alex is in his highchair.

"Mama," he says. "Mama, ball. Mama, mama."

Sean thinks the world of Alex. What if they never saw each other again? He said he would call. If he said it, he will do it. I will simply wash these dishes, despite the fact that Renae is staring a hole in me. I will then tidy up things and maybe take Alex to the park. I will do that. Sean said he would call.

But he doesn't call. I would like to call Iris, but how silly is that? What kind of ninny would she think I am? All I would accomplish is to show my insecurity and ignorance. So I do not call Iris. I do not call my friends. I do not talk to Renae. I am silent. I will stay busy.

We have not really talked about the matter at hand. We have not discussed how crazed Angela makes me feel, sort of like a hunted rabbit. I have not told him how, after all this time, it frightened me to know she is out there somewhere, watching, maybe waiting for a chance to kidnap Alex. We have not talked about how I would want to know if this woman was in the vicinity anywhere, not that I could really do anything about it, but at least I would know. Renae cannot be with me always, neither can Sean. I should have known so I could protect myself and Alex if I had to. This is my life. Angela has been a part of it and I should have known what potential was shaping in my own life.

By the time 5:30 rolls around, I have cleaned the kitchen, taken Alex to the swings in the park, dust mopped all the wood floors in the house, vacuumed the rugs and dusted every wooden thing in sight. Renae has wisely left me alone. Mark is working and is not paying any attention anyway. Sean has not called. It was about 7:30 a.m. when I last saw him. If he slept today, he would have gotten up around 2 or 3 this afternoon. I am not going to obsess about this. I am not.

I am not trying to drive him away. Do I deserve someone like Sean? No, I can honestly say I do not. Finding Sean was the biggest surprise of my life. Plenty of Rodneys are out there and I never aspired to anything greater. Tunnel vision, that's been my affliction, not seeing the big picture. Geez, what an idiot I am. I do not deserve Sean. Maybe I was trying to do the right thing and let him know he could take off if he wanted to because I probably deserved it. He is right. I have been punishing myself, trying to deprive myself of something that mattered to me to compensate for my past sins. I smack myself in the head. Now, dammit, why is he always right?

At 6, he calls.

"Hey," he says.

I say the same.

"I've got to go back on duty in an hour. I just wanted you to know my mom beat me up about this whole thing. She says, and I believe her now, you should have been told about Angela being out. Iris is mad as hell at me, Julie. She read me the riot act here just a little bit ago and now I'm pretty mad at me too. And then she got Jerry in on it and I was chastised in the proper Baptist way. I thought it was the right thing to do. I didn't want you panicked. I know, I know, you're not fragile. I made a mistake is all I'm saying. We all made a mistake. I hope you can forgive me."

"What's the proper Baptist way?"

"I was forced to confess my sins and then red-faced yelled at continuously for probably a half-hour until I repented of same, which I did readily."

"So they did a good job?"

"An excellent job. I am washed clean, even as we speak. White as snow, I am."

"And so, what do you think it will take to get back in my good graces?"

"I'm on my knees right now. Please forgive me, Julie. I am sorry beyond sorry."

"Okay. And you'll never keep anything from me again, even if it might hurt me? Especially if it might hurt me? We will talk about it like adults?"

"Girl, you know how to hit a man good. I promise. I will never keep anything from you again so long as we both shall live, amen and amen."

"You know I'm Catholic and we believe in penance."

"Okay."

"I think your penance shall be the biggest, brightest sunflower you can find, on my front porch, tomorrow morning. This is your penance."

"You got it."

"Fine. We'll see how you fare. Tomorrow, then. Goodnight."

My eyes are barely open the next morning when I hear Renae say, "My goodness, what is all that?"

Oh no, I think. *Oh shit, is it something else that's my fault?*

Mark mumbles something while I race up the stairs to see.

Renae is holding the front door wide open. She turns to me, eyes wide.

The scene on the front porch stops me dead in my tracks. I look around, dumbfounded but giggly. Sunflowers of every shape, size and color are everywhere – everywhere – in pots and vases on the front porch.

"I told you he was a keeper," Renae says while I gape. "I told you so."

CHAPTER FORTY SIX

Claudine

My visitation starts out like a bump in the night, like somebody is pushing me over, nudging me to the other side of the bed. It's kind of like when Keri used to crawl in bed with Jim and me – first, I would hear her little padded feet in her footed jammies (she was so cute) approaching. She would grab onto the sheets and hoist herself over me and dive in between us and snore contentedly until daybreak. This thing is like that but at the same time, it is not. I hear no padded footsteps to the bed. No childish tugs are pulling the covers.

It's a bump in the night all right, but it is not a warm child shoving herself between her father and me for security and comfort. This thing here is a wake-up call.

Some people call it sleep paralysis. Some folk claim it comes from a bad witch sitting on your chest. I could not say, but it is starting to frighten the bejesus out of me.

And here it is again. The familiar bump and not so

subtle either. Despite the fact that I have been a living train wreck the last several months, I can figure this one out. I know without knowing.

She is here, pushing and nudging me to attention. If I could say hello to Andrea, I would. But I'm unable to. I lie paralyzed, turned to stone.

Moonlight streaking through the window lights her hair on one side. My God, she is unblemished. I wonder if this is what we all look like when we cross over to the other side. Do we remain beautiful, youthful, sweet? No, I suppose not since quite a lot of us die of old age in our sleep, without youthful beauty on our side. Andrea's lips are moving but I can't hear her, except in my mind. "You can do it, you have the tools," she says.

"Do what? What tools?" I say out loud but she is already gone, already back to rest in her white gown and eternal blonde hair beyond my sight. "What tools?" I say again as I lay back down, pulling the covers up to my chin. "What tools?"

Sleep is out of the question. Tossing and turning only makes me feel more frustrated. I don't understand what she means by tools and what she thinks I can do. Swinging my legs over the side of the bed, shoving my feet into my slippers, I stumble to the bathroom Emmanuel created for me. We're so different, he and me. Emmanuel is a craftsman. I am a legal assistant. Emmanuel is self-employed. I am reliant on an employer. Emmanuel knows what he wants from life. I am indecisive, confused. Confused for the sake of confusion, perhaps. Confusion masking the need to make a decision. *Are you happy, Claudine?* I ask myself. *Happy can be so many things*, I say and the voice comes back. *No, Claudine, are you happy? Stop avoiding the issue.*

Beth's voice rings in my ears. "I wouldn't do it." Keri's eyes shine at the possibility but she looks a little scared at the same time. Risk, adventure, daring to live a different kind of life. Could I survive without Leon? Do I want to leave the relative security of my job for the unknown? The longing in my heart intensifies. I do. I do want to leave it all behind. I want to be my own person, stand on my own two feet. I want to flourish. My job drains me, keeps me from enjoying life. Is this how I want to live, slaving away until I can maybe retire at an older age than what I'd like? And then, the final act, death? Okay then. My brain is moving into overdrive. What do I know how to do? What are my talents? All I really know outside of my work is feeding people. I can feed people. It's failure I'm afraid of. Jim never worked for anyone else. He never worked in the corporate rat race. Jim is successful. Lynn is successful, wildly so. Sitting on the closed toilet seat in the dark, forehead in hand, it comes to me. I am just as afraid of success as I am of failure, maybe even more so. This is a revelation. It is big, bigger than I am.

The tools. I do not know what the tools are. I wish Andrea would come back and tell me exactly what the freaking tools are. Money? I have no money for entrepreneurship. Money is now an issue for me. Talent? I have some talent. Talent only goes so far. What about business sense? I have only a little of that. Would it be enough to get me by? *You can learn, can't you, Claudine?* Oh, that voice, Andrea's voice is forcing me to make a decision, snap out of the mold and become my real self. *Get up, Claudine. Get up off your ass and go to it.*

Andrea's unrelenting but the fact of the matter is she's right. I know she's right. I have to put it all in perspective, to quit running away from how I really feel deep inside.

We each hold our own potential. Have I been running away from mine?

To shine a light in a dark place, I am not happy in that unenlightened, technical world of the law office. In fact, it's a burden to me with all the unhappiness and strife I deal with every day. We deal in dirty laundry and we take money for it. I mean lots of money too. Do we really help anybody? I wish I could say we do but in my heart, I don't believe it. My head is in my hands. *You are talking about a big risk here*, I say to myself. *If you leave, Leon will never hire you back should you fail.*

In that case, I cannot fail. I won't fail. My gumption is rising. Now I have to find the tools.

CHAPTER FORTY SEVEN

Julie

Oh. My. God. I am in *hell*. This has got to be one of the hottest days of the year, one of the hottest days *ever* in my entire life. I'm standing in Iris's kitchen with her, completely mystified, watching eggs boil while she peels potatoes. She has celery and onion already chopped and once the potatoes are cooked, she says we're gonna make potato salad for a cookout later. I don't know what any of this is but it's not take-out, that's for sure. I don't know what I'm doing and I feel like an idiot. And I'm sweating. The AC doesn't seem to be much help.

Sean's very pregnant sister, April, is sitting up to the counter, eating carrot sticks. The radio is on, country music of course. This is Iris's kitchen after all.

"I feel like I could pop," April says. She's due in two weeks with her third child. April's distended belly nearly reaches her knees as she perches on her barstool, her elbows on the counter. Her two boys are outside, playing in the back yard. "I mean, my God, is this kid ever coming out or what?"

I laugh. "I know how you feel. I was beginning to wonder if Alex just wanted to stay in there." Of the two sisters, April is easier for me to deal with. Amy still leaves me a little nervous.

"Neither one of the other two plagued me like this one. I am tired of being pregnant."

"Not to mention barefoot," Iris said. They laugh, why? I act like I get it, and I resume staring over the boiling eggs. For whatever reason I'm watching them. I can only assume Iris will explain all this in time. Sheesh.

Sean and Jerry walk in to get beer. Sean beckons me outside. He wants to show me the new deck he and Jerry built on the back of the house.

"I've got something to tell you too," he says once I have admired the deck.

"What's that?"

"I have heard from a good source – your mother – that Angela left Rodney."

"My mother said that? How does she know?"

"Per her usual telephone antics, Angela called her up and told her all about it. She left him, she's enrolled in college and she says she's putting her life back together. Your mom wanted me to tell you. Think about that, Julie. Without Rodney, Angela has no reason to pursue you anymore."

"She really left him?"

"She says she did. Says she is making a new life for herself, without him in it."

"I'm free. I'm free of her?"

Sean nods and takes a pull from the bottle of Bud he carried out with him.

"I'd say so. Good news, eh?"

If I can believe it.

"Oh yeah, baby, the best news."

"I love you, Sean."

"I love you, Julie."

As Sean pulls me into his arms, I hear Amanda open up the screen door and say, "Ahhh, you guys, quit being disgustingly happy, will you? You're giving the rest of us a bad rap."

CHAPTER FORTY EIGHT

Claudine

Leon leans against the doorframe to my office. He looks terrible, greyish and weak. Ordinarily, I would jump up to help him, to find out what's wrong or if he's okay but something keeps me in my seat.

Leon takes a deep breath.

"I have to let you go." Leon looks like hell bit him. "There are just things—"

"What things?" I say, not knowing what is going on.

"It doesn't matter. I have to let you go. It's just not working out." He is standing, leaning against my office doorway. My first thought is he may fall down. Leon has heart problems. He could be having a heart attack. My second thought is he would deserve it.

I am fired. I am terminated from the position I have held for seventeen years. After seventeen years, it is not working out? What kind of bullshit is this?

"I'm sorry," Leon says. "You will be paid for the next three pay periods. I will see to it. And if anyone calls me, I will give you an excellent reference. This I promise you. *I promise you.*"

"But why?" Finally, I stand up and face him. He looks so bad, I'm afraid he might die right here, right now, in front of me.

"Claudine, you have until the end of the day to have your office cleared out and turn your keys in. That's all I will say."

Leon pulls on his tie.

Although I don't know why I am saying this, I do. "Thank you, Leon. I appreciate your concern."

What I would like to say is, "You son of a bitch, if you were half the lawyer everyone – including you – thinks you are, you would pay more attention to your clients and manage your cases and stop leaving it to me, a person without a bar license. And why in the hell should I care about you in the first place? And *you're* firing me? I should be firing you."

Of course, I say none of that, but I'm dazed. Humility stands in to remind me. I am a little fish swimming in a big tank –of sharks. And so I tell him I will clear out my office as soon as possible and return my key of course. It is stunning, this course of events. It is so surreal.

"I am sorry, Claudine," he says and turns on his heel.

"I'm sorry too," I whisper but he does not hear. In a minute, I hear him exhale in the kitchen or maybe he is choking. I don't know. It is no longer for me to know. All these years, my mouth being at Leon's ear and vice versa, what has it come to?

Our bookkeeper brings me a record of my pay package. Leon's severance package is generous. It is, quite honestly, unheard of. Three pay periods? I will be receiving a paycheck for six weeks? My God. He must have quite a lot of guilt associated with this. I will never know the reason why I'm fired because employers are not required to tell an employee. It could have been the color of my shoes for all I know.

It has nothing to do with the color of my shoes, or something equally as silly, and I know it. I was good with my clients and I worked hard. No, there's something else going on, something beyond my knowing and control. Seventeen years here and it's all over today.

My hands are numb as I pull my pictures down from the walls and fold up my belongings, my books, my plant, my photos of Keri. How will I tell her? My stomach spasms. I clear out my emails and delete every personal item on my computer. I take a deep breath. *One. Two.* No one comes near me, not even Beth. I am now the pariah, the outcast. I must be shunned and then forgotten as I make my miserable journey into the outside world, friendless, completely alone. *Three.* It is time for me to carry my box of office possessions out and take my leave.

I hurt. My clients, what will they think? What will they be told? My work – what will happen to that? My mind is a blur as I pack the last few things in my box. No one speaks to me. Leon's door remains open but Josie's door is closed. The office manager's door is closed. Everyone seems to have their doors closed. Will I seek Leon out? Cry and beg forgiveness, demand to know the exact reason I am being terminated? No. I refuse to lower myself. I am stunned and hurt, no doubt about that, but I will not grovel. *Let me keep a little dignity, please.* I will walk out of here but I will not beg.

What options do I have? I wish I knew and, frankly, it is probably too soon to talk about options anyway. I need to recover from the blow. I need to regain my strength and my perspective. I load the last box into my truck and return to the building. I knock on the office manager's door so I can return my key. She grabs me in a bear hug. She is so sorry. She cannot believe it. She hopes I will find something better. "When one door closes, another door opens," she says.

Sure. Those silly proverbs seem appropriate to everyone in these situations, like a Hallmark card. Who knows what to say in the first place? Certainly not Hallmark. Have we become so shallow we allow the dictates of a card factory to tell us how to feel? Get off my back, will you? I am not subject to a Hallmark interpretation of my life.

There is nothing more to say. It is time for me to leave. Goodbye.

Beth appears and hugs me. She's been crying and it makes me cry too. "You'll find something else. I know you will," she says. Her face dissolves like a watercolor in front of my eyes, shifting, blurring, washing down the front of the canvas. I have nothing more to say, so I walk out the front door.

Internal terror is setting in. Leon's severance package was generous but it will not last forever and I need work. I am not a person with options. I have a daughter to support and I no longer have the support of a husband. Jim finding out about this bothers me. What will he say? Will he blame me? What will Jake say? I suppose if this is the time for him to get out, he will. I will know what he is made of shortly.

Was I burnt out? Did I make mistakes? Was I a liability? How would I even know? I worked hard. I was on time, didn't take excessive time off, followed the rules, bled for my clients. Did they just not like me – the color of my hair, my shoes, what?

Turning into my driveway, I sit for a minute in my car looking up at the house. I have a few minutes before Keri is home and a few hours before Jake comes by. I am overwhelmed by grief. The sobs come, erupting from deep within me, spasmodic, rising to the surface. I cannot believe what happened.

The future. What is the future now? Will anyone hire me after being fired, and not just fired but fired by Leon Martinez? Everyone in the legal community respects Leon. He said he would give me a good reference. I wish I knew what I had done wrong.

In the house now, I wash my face and pour a glass of red. The future looms but I can't think about that now. Keri is here.

"Mom? What are you doing home? Are you sick?"

She is glowing and tanned. Her hair is streaked with gold again, just like every year when she spends more time outdoors. She has a part-time job for the summer working at a children's play park and she loves it.

I take a gulp of my wine. She is watching me, curious and concerned.

"What's up, Mom?"

"Can we talk?" I say, feeling helpless, vulnerable, lost.

"Sure," she says and I once again love the pleasure of just being with her, of just loving her. But will she love me in a second, when I reveal what has happened to me, to our lives? Will she feel the same terror? The same betrayal? The same uncertainty of the future? Will she worry about the house, the bills, as I do? Or will she blow it all off in typical teenager fashion – *this stuff doesn't happen to US*, – and keep going, oblivious? Will she be oblivious to the pain I feel? Oblivious to the possibility of a life change for her? A serious life change, not just a barely perceptible downsizing?

"I lost my job today, just a few minutes ago. Leon fired me."

"He fired you? You're joking, right? Leon would never fire you."

I shake my head. "Well, he did."

"Did he give you a reason?"

"No, he just said it's not working out. I asked why but he elected not to tell me." I set my glass on the counter. The sobs are coming again. Keri puts her arms around me.

"Oh, Mom, I'm sorry. It will work out. You know it will."

I have to pull it together for her.

"I know," I say, although I do not know any such thing.

I wish I did not have to face Jake with this news. But he shows up promptly, of course, and I blurt it out.

"You have many more choices than you think, Claudine," Jake says. His initial shock at what Leon did turns into pragmatism. We were supposed to cook dinner together tonight but, given my awful news, he decided to cook dinner for me. A comfort feature I'm sure, and the man's become quite good at roasting a chicken. In light of all of that went on today, I let him.

"I was so afraid to tell you," I say. I drink his face in, now so familiar and so wanted.

"Why?" He carves a piece of breast meat off and puts it on my plate beside tiny red potatoes with onion and garlic and fresh green beans.

I stare at him, not moving toward my plate. "I was afraid of what you would think of me."

He shrugs.

"Everybody gets fired at least once," he says. "And besides that, why would I think less of you because some disingenuous old fart wasn't loyal?"

"You shouldn't call him that," I say, smiling. "I stood next to him for seventeen years but somehow, right now, I do not feel as if I ever knew him at all. I did not see this coming, Jake. I didn't know a problem existed or that he was unhappy with me."

"I call them as I see them. Look, you worked for him for a long time, Claudine. From what I hear you say about your work, I believe you did well for him and your clients loved you. That says a lot right there. He made a mistake. He did, *not you.*"

"Well, mistake or not, it's done and now I don't know what to do." I toy with my food, which is really good, and I want to eat it all but it is hard to put anything in my mouth. My stomach may send it back up. "It's all I've ever done. I'm no great brain."

"In the first place, that is not so. What I started to say was you have options. You're a talented, warm, funny and beautiful person."

I laugh. "Well, I thank you but what job prospects are there out there for a talented, warm, funny and lovely person, pray tell?"

"I was getting to that. What do you really love, more than anything? What do you really love to do?"

I lay my fork down, considering his volley. "I was thinking about this the other night. All I know how to do is feed people. I love to cook. This is really good, by the way."

"Bingo. You see, your heart already knows." He winks at me.

"Oh, right. Me? I have no credentials, I have no training. I have no money."

Jack ignores this. "At the very least, do a cookbook. Self-publish if you have to. I will help you. But if you want my honest opinion, I think you can do more."

I can do more. Is that so?

Later, after making blissful love with Jake and falling into a deep slumber, Andrea comes to me again. "Believe in yourself. You can do anything if you believe in yourself," she says, without moving her lips at all.

The phone is ringing downstairs. Somehow, I know it will be Jim on the other end of the line. Since it's so late, I really don't want to deal with Jim right now.

"Claudine, are you all right?" he says to me.

"What are you talking about?"

"If you need anything, just holler."

"Jim, what are you talking about?"

"Your job, Claudine."

I close my eyes briefly. "How did you know?"

"Lynn heard it from someone. Nobody can believe it, least of all me. Leon firing you just doesn't make any sense."

Oh, for God's sake. This again. Lynn beat me to the punch. I cannot even blame my dear daughter for telling.

"Well, it's not your concern, Jim. I mean, thanks but I've got to deal with this myself."

"I understand. Just know if you ever need to talk, I'm here."

"Sure."

I hang up. Sure, I will talk to you, Jim. When pigs float in pink punch, I will talk to you. The nerve. And for Lynn to have been the one to tell him. I almost forgot, he said she heard it someplace. I forgot to ask him where she heard it. *Shit.*

I am pacing in the kitchen and I turn abruptly and find Jake leaning against the doorway. He looks so strong. I want to be strong too but I am not. *Dammit.* I dissolve against his chest, sobbing.

He puts his arms around me and kisses the top of my head.

"You're going to be all right, Claudine. You will."

This pain, it is like being left again. It is cold, stabbing rejection. It is having everything, even my dignity, stripped from me. It is like having Lynn in a thousand places at once and knowing I can never escape the knowing gleam in her eyes.

"You're taking this too seriously," he whispers.

I pull away. "Don't you understand? It was my livelihood."

"So you'll find a new livelihood, Claudine. This is

bad but it is not the end of the world."

I understand. We are back to the tools again, the fucking tools. I'm willing to work. I'm ready. But this is all fuzzy to me. I'm confused. Not sure where to start.

Would somebody kindly point me in the direction of the tools?

CHAPTER FORTY NINE

Julie

I need to call Claudine. All the weirdness with Angela and Rodney ought to be reported and if she knows anything about it, I want to know what she knows. Rodney hasn't been exercising his visitation privileges like he said he would. I do not know if that is good or bad, maybe it is a good thing in a way. I do not want to press the issue, but at least Claudine would know. She sort of predicted Rodney would just fade away anyway, given enough time, and now it looks as though he has.

"I'm sorry, Claudine no longer works here." Kelly's voice comes back bright and chipper on the phone.

"What did you say?" *What did she say?*

"Claudine is no longer with this firm. I'm sorry." Kelly is about to hang up.

"No, no, wait a minute. Why is she no longer with your firm?"

"I am sorry, I cannot discuss that."

"Is Leon in?"

"One moment please."

Leon's voice comes on the line. He sounds as if he is in no mood but then, neither am I. The bedrock of my entire case has gone missing and I would like to know why.

"Leon, they're telling me Claudine is gone. What's going on?"

He hesitates. "Well, Julie, we've had a little bit of a staff shakeup around here and Claudine is no longer with us."

"You mean you fired her?"

He says nothing.

"Leon, you fired her? How could you do that?"

"Julie, I am sorry you're overwrought about this but I do not have to discuss my staff with you or any other client."

"Leon, this is just wrong. She is the only person in that office who ever gave a shit for me or for anybody else. I relied on her. This is just wrong."

"This conversation is over," Leon says and hangs up.

My God. What a mess. Claudine, fired? How does that work? Who do I talk to now? Who in that office is going to give a rat's ass about my life? What kind of craziness is this? I hope Claudine is okay. If she is not, I can't do anything about it but I wish I could. I sure wish I could.

CHAPTER FIFTY

Claudine

My mail holds something odd today. Rifling through the Walgreens and JC Penney ads and offers for credit cards, my eyes light on a bone-colored envelope. Taylor and Whiteaker PC. I know who they are, or at least I know they are attorneys. Am I being sued? That would certainly be pleasant, now wouldn't it? Suing the unemployed, how nice. Surely it is not anything like that. I've not been served with anything. Yet.

I quickly slice the envelope open and pull out the correspondence. Pretty letterhead, nice paper.

> *In re: The Estate of Andrea Whitely Sommerfield*
> *Dear Ms. Coulter:*
> *Our firm represented Andrea Sommerfield in her estate planning interests prior to her unfortunate passing on or about May 20, 2010. One of Ms. Sommerfield's requests in connection with her estate planning was that she be able to divide her estate in any manner whatsoever she desired. We are writing to*

advise you that you have been included within the framework of Ms. Sommerfield's estate planning provisions.

Enclosed you will find a check drawn from our trust account in the amount of Two Hundred Fifty-Thousand Dollars ($250,000), made payable to you on behalf of Andrea Sommerfield. This sum represents one-half of her entire estate and it was her wish that you inherit these funds. We strongly advise you to retain an accountant to assist you in managing this amount of money and advising you as to the tax consequences thereof. Please contact us with any questions, comments or concerns you may have.

Sincerely yours,
Richard T. Whiteaker, Esq.

This is not a joke. Turning the bond paper over and over again, I want to pinch myself. I am holding a check made payable to me in the amount of a quarter of a million dollars. How did she do this? More importantly, why did she do this?

Richard Whiteaker's telephone number is on the letterhead. I dial it with shaking fingers. In my mind is a vision of a toolbox. In my mind, I see the tools. I need to verify first. What is it that keeps my hopes down? How ridiculous. *Be a grown-up, Claudine.* But if this is all a dream, I need to know that too.

Richard Whiteaker's secretary puts me through.

"I thought you might be calling," Mr. Whiteaker says.

I tell him I am holding a check for a quarter of a million dollars and he chuckles.

"Yes, Claudine, you are. Let me tell you, your friend, my client, asked me specifically to be sure the money was transferred to you. This is no mistake, Claudine. The money is yours. Don't spend it all in one place."

After being counseled once again to hire an accountant to take care of such funds and advise me on tax issues, I put the phone down and take a deep breath. It's real. This money means a big change for Keri and me.

The month since I was fired has not been easy. In my mind, Leon's endorsement should have opened up all kinds of opportunities, but I found it not to be true. Doors have been shut in my face. Interviews have been canceled at the last minute. Interviewers, incredulous Leon would have let me go for no reason I could give them, questioned me over and over again. I am so tired of trying to explain to their suspicious faces what happened. One interviewer even told me, "I am going to get to the bottom of this. How did you say this happened?" I have been unable to find any kind of employment whatsoever. My severance from Leon is dwindling and pulling from savings is the next option. Aside from Jim's betrayal and our divorce, I can't say I've felt so low in my life.

After I was let go, I hid in the house, except for the interviews I did get, which were few. Call backs were even fewer. Humiliation kept me isolated. Venturing out to the grocery store became an exercise in terror. Every time I got in the car, I had an anxiety attack. What if I wrecked the car? Everything I owned became precious. It could not be replaced. Just the terror of being seen by others, other employed people outside of my work environment, kept me inside. What if someone I knew saw me and asked me why I was at the Price Cutter in the middle of the day?

To add insult to injury, Beth is out of touch. When she didn't return my calls in the beginning, I stopped calling her. The reality is I am tainted goods. I know Beth would not want to absorb any kind of taint whatsoever. It hurts to know my dearest friend sees me in that light. There's nothing I can do nothing about it though.

Jake has been patient. Keri has been quiet. Jim offered to raise his child support for a while but I turned him down. I couldn't see baiting Lynn that way. But now, I have my own tools. The tool box landed solidly in my mailbox.

"Keri," I shout, running up the stairs.

"What, Mom?" She meets me in the hallway, looking frightened. I show her the check.

"It's for real. I just checked on it."

"Oh my God, Mom. You know what you can do with this money?"

We are hugging and jumping up and down, laughing and shrieking.

"The shop. I can do the shop."

Her eyes are huge.

"Mom, you've got to do this. You know you want to."

My God, the possibilities.

"Find out, Mom. Find out right now if that space is still open. Go. Do it now."

"Right, right." I am in a daze.

I give her a look and she takes my hand and we careen down the stairs together. I have the card from that leasing agent, what's her name, in my purse somewhere. I rifle through my wallet. There it is. Janice Corvella.

I dial the number listed on the card. She answers immediately. Fate. This must be fate.

"Hello," I say and give her my name. "You might not remember me but we talked one day on South Street at the TruBean coffee shop? You talked about getting the space leased?"

"Yes," she says.

"Well, could you tell me whether the space is still

available?"

"As a matter of fact, it is not. I just leased it thirty days or so ago."

My heart sinks.

"However," Janice says. "I do have another space not far from that one and it's a little newer and in a little better shape. I seem to remember you talking about opening up a specialty shop, if memory serves. I think the space I've still got would be a better location and a better all-around space for that type of venture. If you are interested, I could show it to you."

My heart rises.

"Certainly. I would appreciate that."

She tells me she has appointments the rest of the afternoon but she has an opening in the morning and I tell her I will meet her there.

Now for the work. I have to come up with a business plan. My brain is reeling. My stomach is doing flip-flops. This money could be my salvation. Something I thought was just a dream, just something I mused about, could actually become a reality now.

"My God, Keri. This could change our entire lives."

"Mom, you have to do this. You just have to, for your own sanity. Besides, I think you would be good at it."

I am out of breath. My brain feels as if it is floating away from the rest of me. Andrea brought me the answer to a prayer. I cannot believe she would be so generous, and with me, someone who, but for her divorce, would have remained a complete stranger. My heart swells with gratitude. I will make this work, not only for my sake but out of a sense of responsibility for having been given so much.

But first things first. I need to hire an accountant and possibly one who knows a little bit about a business plan. I need someone to help me manage the money. I will meet with Janice tomorrow. I will find out what kind of work the place needs and what kind of equipment I need to purchase. Once I get my plan together, I'll apply for a business license and insurance. Somewhere in all of that, I will sit down and organize my recipes and roll my sleeves up and get to the work.

Oh my God, I am so excited. I whisper another thank you to the air, to Andrea, before falling asleep. She does not come to me but I'm certain she heard it.

CHAPTER FIFTY ONE

Julie

"Are you ready?" Renae asks me in the basement of the church. Everything is in place, my veil, my flowers, my dress. But not my stomach. My stomach is doing the hoochie-coochie, and having much more fun than I am at this moment. My face is flushed. All that aside, I am definitely ready.

I nod, nearly ready to cry. This is my day, the day I waited for all my life. These are my last few moments as Julie Kruger. Not too long from now, I will become Julie Nichols. I say that name in my mind over and over again. Julie Nichols. Mrs. Sean Nichols. Sean and Julie Nichols. Oh. My. God. I am so blessed.

"Thank you, Mom," I say and turn to hug her. She pats me, aware we do not want my hair or my veil to come off and she is smiling.

"T'weren't nothin'," she says.

One more turn in the mirror. My dress is fabulous and since I lost those last ten pounds, it fits the way it should. I am strapless today. The shimmering white bodice is nearly plain, except for a small patch of sequins and pearls right above the tulle waistband. My skirt is layered in tulle, decorated with more sequins and pearls and more shimmering silk is underneath. I am wearing the diamond studs Renae lent me, something borrowed. I have a spray of white roses with one blue delphinium in the center, something blue. The prayer book buried in my bouquet is old. My garter is new.

"You are so beautiful, Julie," Renae says. She is really happy today in her new apricot suit. "You're stunning."

I know it is true.

"Mom." I start but I'm not sure how to finish.

Renae looks over my shoulder into the mirror. Our two faces reflect, mother and daughter, young woman and older woman. I have Renae's eyes, her facial shape but not all her features. She is holding my shoulders.

"What, dear?"

"Thank you for hanging tight with me."

The organ sounds upstairs. Renae lets go of my shoulders.

"It's time to go, dear." Renae steps away from the mirror, away from our telling grasp. "This is your day, Julie, and you look like a dream. I'm so proud of you, of the woman you've become."

I wish I could pry the information out of her, but someone calls down that it's time and she helps me up the stairs with my skirt before she is led away to her seat as mother of the bride. Mark will take me down the aisle. He smiles and offers his arm. The bridesmaids have already gone in and it is my turn. The heavy organ announces my arrival, the entrance of the bride, the jewel of the party, the absolute center of gravity.

The heavy double-doors slowly open and I stand ready to take my steps down the aisle to my groom, who is standing by the priest with his hands folded in front of him. Tears fill my eyes when I see Sean. What will we remember about this day when we are old? What will be the one thing we will always remember exactly right?

Blood red rose petals on the carpet. So many glowing faces, to the left and right. Everyone is standing up. The candles are lit. I see Lisa, my maid of honor, smiling. I look at Sean. He is looking at me. My eyes are glued on him. He looks pale. All the way down the aisle, my eyes lock in on him. This is who I am coming for. No one else, forever and ever. Amen.

Alex, our ring bearer, is standing by Sean. When I come close, I hear him say, "Ooh Mama. Pretty." The church titters.

It is almost like a dream, although we rehearsed all this just last night. We have the pronunciation and scripture and then a soprano solo. The sacraments and more scripture. We stand up and then we kneel. We stand up again. Another song and then the vows. I look deep into Sean's eyes. He looks deep into mine. We do not falter. Another prayer. Another solo. It seems like we've been standing here a thousand years. The rings slide on. We are finally introduced to the parishioners as husband and wife.

I am his. He is mine. Forever and ever, and I'll make it forever and ever. Amen.

CHAPTER FIFTY TWO

Claudine

Providence, luck, divine guidance, whatever you want to call it has been with me. I found a wonderful accountant, Bob Bender, who knows a thing or two about business and banking and has good connections. I met with Janice at the new spot and found it to be everything I wished for and more. The real lucky thing is the space was once a deli and a lot of the equipment and fixtures can stay. Everything is in working order. All it needs is a good cleaning and some sprucing up. Keri, Jake and I tackle it with all the gusto of three hair-brained entrepreneurs on crack, out for their first ride in the world. We clean, paint, polish and decorate for days and days and nights and nights.

Finally, we're finished. The new place is beautiful.

"I love these walls," Keri says, running her fingers along one. They're textured to look like an old Tuscan villa and color washed a gentle shade of apricot. The light fixtures are black, which contrasts beautifully with the walls. The deli case and bakery case gleam silver beside the black granite counter. We sanded and refinished the wood floor, which also gleams. Pots of green plants and herbs sit in front of the window and colorful prints line the walls. It is not big, but it is big enough for me. My business license hangs in a frame on the wall beside the cash register. Inside the kitchen, a huge stainless refrigerator, ovens, a prep space and a sink take up nearly all the room. Storage and a small bathroom is in the back. Supplies will begin coming in a week.

"My God," I say. And then we are jumping up and down, hugging each other. I can see the muffins, scones, coffee cakes, jams and spreads lining the shelves of the cases already. I can see baskets of baguettes on the counter and cheesecakes in the cooler. My mind's eye sees cookies, dozens of cookies, in the bakery case.

It hits me then. This is real, no turning back, nowhere to run. Here we are and this is the real deal. So many things to think about, like fourteen hour days and being on my feet for nearly all of them. Of course I'll need employees before this is all over. Keri volunteered to help me. My God, this will be a journey. I am up for it.

That is right. I am up for it. In fact, I am looking forward to it with anticipation. Whether I succeed or fail, and I am banking on success, at least I will have put all my effort, all my soul, into creating this new life. I'll do this because I want to do it and because someone trusted me enough to enable me to do it. A tiny picture of Andrea in a silver frame sits on the counter. I cut her obituary out of the newspaper.

"Look, you guys," I say and I rearrange her photo on the counter beside the cash register. "She made this all possible. I think she needs to be here and be a part of it."

Jake puts his arms around me and holds me tight.

"I'm so proud of you," he says. "You've found yourself, Claudine. I believe you really have. I'll tell you something else. I am behind you all the way. All the way."

He kisses the top of my head.

My heart is overflowing with gratitude, love and the knowledge I have support from people who care for me. It's almost too much but I can work with it.

I feel Andrea's presence here. Her approval and support rolls through me.

"Thanks for your patience with me, you guys, and all your hard work," I say. Tears of gratitude well up. They too have sacrificed so much in an effort to help me realize a dream.

"I appreciate it more than you can imagine. This is going to be a whole new life. I mean, really, what a departure from working in an office. I can hardly believe it."

"Oh Mom, you're going to make it. I like that you put her photo up," Keri says, looking at the tiny photo. "Good job, Mom."

Jake and I are holding each other close. I can see our reflection in the glass. He is tall, I am not. He's lean and fit. Something else I'm not. Still, we fit together. I am beginning to feel less self-conscious of this lumpy body. Even though I lost twenty-two pounds during the divorce, my body carries a rounded look. I have to remember I am no longer twenty-one. Gravity has staked its claim on me after all, but it is not all bad. Instead of the jagged angles of a young woman, I have curves bestowed on me through years of seasoning. Jake is happy with it so I should be too. I am.

"Let's get out of here," he says. "Let's get some supper."

When we finally leave the building, we stare at the window for a long time in the darkness. Next week, the workers will paint "South Street Bakery" in the center of the window and "Claudine Coulter, Proprietress" in the lower right corner. Here we are, standing there on the sidewalk, staring at the imaginary future letters. And someone touches my shoulder.

It's Beth. We have not spoken since I was let go from Leon's office. I knew she was avoiding me for whatever reason and it hurt. Without saying a word, she takes me in her arms and hugs me.

"I am sorry," she whispers.

I hug her back. "Me too," I say.

"Can you forgive me?"

I must forgive her. I cannot live with a grudge on my heart. Of course I can forgive her and I tell her. She is my best friend, after all. She says she will call me and then she gets into her car, parked at the curb, and Lee is driving. Looks like they're going out to dinner. She just thought she would take a chance on finding me. From the passenger window, she tells me she loves me as the car pulls away from the curb.

I watch them drive away but somehow, even though my heart is with her, I know I must begin my work. I must realize my dream. Smiling to myself, I turn and look at my bakery, my spot, my new life, my new man. I realize *I am happy*.

CHAPTER FIFTY THREE

Julie

Sean and I have been back from our honeymoon in Colorado for two days now. We had a great time, so much fun. We went rock climbing, hiking up around Colorado Springs on the old trails, played around in the hotel pool. Good, good time. I've never been so happy in all my life. Colorado's a beautiful place, the sky seems bluer than here, no haze, and the greens really are green. Even the yellow flowers planted in the medians seem to sparkle. Or maybe it all seemed so special because I was with the love of my life. Either way, I was entranced.

Two days after we got home, Sean fell off a ladder cleaning the gutters on the house and broke his arm. So now I have a crippled husband for a while but it doesn't seem to slow him down. Sean's the perfect husband. He mows grass, takes the trash out, makes love with me as much as I want. He's perfect with Alex too. So patient, so kind.

Today he surprised Alex with a red wagon. He's been pulling Alex around the yard in it all morning.

I've been decorating his house to make it our home. I bought a new rug, brown, beige and orange, for the living room and some candles and knick-knacks to set around. It was pretty bare when it was a bachelor's house but it's a family home now. Sean's bed was once adorned with a boring green blanket, now it wears a fluffy yellow comforter and decorative pillows. I even bought new dishes – they're red. Red is a good color. It makes me happy.

When I pull up to the house after work and I see the lamps shining out the window and flowers on the porch, I see what my life was meant to be all along.

CHAPTER FIFTY FOUR

Claudine

The grand opening of South Street Bakery proves to be a phenomenal success. We have been open for just one week and I am exhilarated, thrilled. I could not be happier. Now I will tell you, I am busy beyond belief. The days are long. My nights are short. My feet hurt all the time, but yes, busy beyond busy and doing well. I hired two girls, Desiree and Robin, to help me. Then I found a young man named Miguel who has proven to be a fantastic baker, and he's beautiful besides, chocolate brown, tall, muscular. He wants to become an attorney someday and, while I wish him well, inside I cringe at the thought of him disappearing into that caustic void, the legal world. That world is distant and foreign to me now and somewhat distasteful at that. I try not to think about it. I try to think about only what is now. I am no longer disappointed I missed out on the space that was once Gabriel's. This space seems so much more mine and no remnants of failed love are here. Every day, I smile at the photo of Andrea sitting by the cash register.

Gone are the nocturnal visits to get me moving. Perhaps her job with me is finished.

Jim and Lynn came to the ribbon cutting ceremony. All of us were there in our pristine white smocks, even Jake who showed up for moral support. I saw Jim cast Jake an odd look, but he said nothing, or at least not to me. I gather Keri has not mentioned Jake to Jim at all.

Jake, now a mainstay in my life, a rock, a shoulder, is the voice of reason during all this turmoil. He makes it clear he believes in me and that is a treasure in my heart. Some days that is all I have to keep me going. I believe I have come a long way. But it will be up to the community as to whether that is true.

I am setting yet another batch of lemon curd tarts into the bakery case when I look up and see Leon. He is standing in the doorway looking at me. My heart stops momentarily. Conscious of my white bakers smock and the flour that must be on my nose, I watch him move toward the case in front, straight to me. *Some things never change*, I think. His pants are baggy and his tie is blown over his shoulder. His shirt matches nothing else he has on. For an instant, I am angry. How dare he intrude into the sanctity of my life, my shop. How dare he sully this refuge I built. For an instant, I want to throw my tray down and march up to him with all the venom I can muster and demand he get the hell out. Sadness takes over, however, and I don't do any marching or demanding. I am still. We are not enemies. I am not sure what we are, but we're not enemies. We are more like that divorced couple who always wishes it could have been different somehow. Well, he cannot fire me again, that is for sure.

"Congratulations," he says. "I always knew you had it in you."

I don't know what to say. "Thanks" doesn't seem adequate. I finally settle on, "It's good."

His eye catches the framed photo of Andrea and he simply nods and says nothing.

"Why, Leon?" I say.

He's walking to the door so I slam the till shut and follow him out to the sidewalk.

"Leon, you owe me an answer. Seventeen years? And you can't tell me why? Seriously?"

His back is straight, his tie blowing over his shoulder in the wind again, but still I follow him, my own apron billowing around me.

"Leon." I'm finally furious and he hears it.

"Claudine," he says, turning ever so slightly toward me.

"What? What is it?" I can't believe I'm beleaguering him this way, but at the same time I'm jubilant I am asking him the hard question. Finally. I should have asked him why a long time ago but I didn't have the guts, and I was grieving Jim. My heart wasn't strong enough to take on another blow.

"You were the best legal assistant I ever had, believe me." The lines on his face are so deep now, they're crevices.

"I worked hard for you. My clients loved me. I didn't make major mistakes. Why did you fire me? Tell me why, just tell me why."

Suddenly, Leon seems to loom close.

"You cannot practice law without a license, Claudine."

He turns toward a car, a gleaming Mercedes parked along the sidewalk.

"Practice law without a license? Are you crazy? Because that's what all of us did for you and that's what your girls do for you now. That's crap, Leon. *Crap.* You're a coward, that's what you are. Don't admit it, I don't care. If that was the problem with me, then fire them all. All of them."

Leon sags against the car for one brief moment.

"None of them matter, Claudine. None of them are as strong as you were."

"What?"

Leon looks tired. He opens his mouth and closes it again.

"We outgrew each other, Claudine. You overtook me."

"You make no sense, Leon. That's not the answer."

Leon pulls his keys from his pocket and points to his car. The fob squeals. "Good to see you," he says, climbs in and turns the engine.

Tears choke me as I watch him pull out into traffic. I shake my head and, wiping my hands on my apron, turn back to my store.

Leon would never know, or never care for that matter, how he wounded me. After spending seventeen years by his side, he would have no more understanding of what he did to me than if he would have sneezed in my direction. We spent so much time together, he and I. I knew so much about how his mind worked, except for one time. One time I did not see it coming. No matter what anybody says, I did not see that coming. My face heats up and I struggle to banish the feeling of betrayal.

Leon Martinez exasperated me. He frustrated me with his non-responsiveness and lack of instruction. He angered me with his secret ways, but at the same time, he fascinated me. I admired how his mind worked. I would have stayed with him forever had he not forced me out. If I had not been pushed out, I wouldn't be here now in this moment doing something I truly love. *Oh Leon, I miss you so much, but at the same time, I really don't.* It is still hard for me to allow that realization to seep through. I feel disloyal somehow and I reprimand myself for that. Leon wasn't loyal to me. Why should I take that burden on?

I check on my rustic Italian boule, browning in the oven prettily around the X slashes, and I feel a momentary stir of listlessness and a wish nothing had changed. I think about the law office and how it is going on without me, something I never dreamed of, and I wonder if it is better for my absence. I cannot call back the past, and why would I want to anyway when the present is so much better? Leon's visit set me on edge. I almost wish he would never have stopped by. What in the world did it prove anyway? Did he hope to vindicate himself? Did he think by seeing my success he somehow could erase the past? Or was he simply curious?

I haul the bread loaves out of the ovens and turn them out on boards. My spirit is exasperated and hurt. Miguel is watching me with concerned dark eyes. He knows when I am upset but he also knows it has nothing to do with my present circumstances. He can only guess about Leon. He goes back to work, washing up baking sheets and muffin tins. I admire his strong back for a minute and his black pony tail. I like him. I admire his work ethic and his drive. I like his sense of humor and his quiet intelligence. He is good looking, always a plus.

Keri likes him too. He likes her. When she helps me in the store, she gravitates to him and him to her. I see them smile at one another, so unashamed of their mutual attraction. I marvel at her goldenness and his darkness, blended together like the most exquisite café mocha. They have established a bond. I cannot say I disapprove but I am somewhat concerned about the age difference, although I doubt Miguel would say or do anything that would frighten her or bother me. Keri is just beginning her senior year in high school. Miguel is a college man of twenty-four. They are both responsible. They have goals. I shouldn't worry about this so much. It will be their life, after all, not mine.

Robin is a quiet girl but hard-working. She is a

single mom with a son. I hope she will stay with me for a long time, but I could not blame her if she opted for more pay somewhere else. I do the best I can but I know better positions are out there.

Desiree brings her partner, Jayne, to meet me. Strange how Desiree bounces around the shop with unbounded enthusiasm, but when she brings Jayne in, she is unabashedly shy and gentle. She introduces Jayne, who shakes my hand vigorously. They are affectionate with one another without being showy. I like Jayne. I admire them for the difficult choice they have made, and for having made that choice in this town. I wish them well.

Jayne is studying to be an architect. Desiree still does not know what her life's vocation might be. At this point in time, she is happy to be mixing dough and making pastries for me. Later, she tells me how disappointed and shocked her devoutly religious parents were when she told them about her orientation. "They're over it now," she says. "They just want me to be happy."

"That's what I want for you too," I tell her and I mean it. She seems genuinely pleased with receiving immediate and unconditional approval. We are, I suppose, a family here in this tiny bakery on South Street. We are in every way bonded to one another. And then I think, what is family anyway? It is those who you cherish and who cherish you, who gather around your table or at least around your life. Those who you laugh with and cry with and hope and dream with. I look around at my daughter's face and each of my employees. This is my family. Only Jake is missing and I will be seeing him soon. The thought of his comfortable hairy chest and open arms cheers me.

I toss my apron aside and walk to the doorway of my shop. Leaning against the comfortable old brick, absorbing the street life around me, I wonder whether things have come full circle. I feel a sense of contentment I never felt working at the law office. I feel fulfilled. Even with the initial terror and trepidation, I would not trade this life for the old one.

It's good I told Leon, not that he has any reason to know. It's damn good.

CHAPTER FIFTY FIVE

Julie

Well, here we are again, you and me, just like in the beginning. Things are going well. Sean and I are happy together, establishing a home, raising Alex. I quit my job at the restaurant. I have a real life and a real family now. I'm not a dumb kid anymore. So I found a job setting appointments at a dentist's office and that is all I do all day long, greeting patients and talking on the telephone. It is pretty easy, no stress, and I come home at the end of the day with energy for Alex. We live in Sean's house, which is a little white bungalow at the end of a tree-lined street. Sean built a play yard for Alex in back. We are thinking of getting a puppy.

Renae and Mark are going on a trip. This is their first vacation in I don't know how many years. They're going to Las Vegas and I think they plan on renewing their wedding vows while they are out there. They are probably pleased to have me out of their basement, finally, but I know they miss having Alex around so much. I make sure they see plenty of him.

All in all, everything has turned out for the best. Sean, who keeps his eyes and ears open when it comes to Angela and Rodney, tells me Angela is gone. She has family in Maryland and she left Springfield to go stay with them. Thank God that nightmare is over. Rodney and his boys are still living with his mother and he is still working in food service somewhere. I do not keep track of him. He seldom sees Alex now. I suspect he will stop altogether before long. In a way, I think it is for the best too. We have such a cohesive family unit, the three of us. No point in unsettling it. Maybe someday when Alex is older something will work out. For now, I just want him to be happy and secure, which he is. Right now, everything is perfect.

April, Sean's sister, had her baby at the end of August. She got another boy and I know she was hoping for a girl. If this keeps up, the Nichols family will have an entire football team sprouted.

Surprise, surprise, I am learning to cook. Nothing too fancy now, but I can make something besides spaghetti and scrambled eggs. The other day, I put a roast in the crock pot with the French onion soup powder. April taught me how. I actually did the carrots and onions and potatoes too. Sean thought it was good and that is all that matters. I love taking care of him. I love him so much and I am so lucky to have him.

So here's more news. You should probably know some bigwig from the biggest grocery store chain in town found his way to Claudine's bakery recently. His wife brought one of Claudine's baklavas home and, as they say, the rest is history. He is talking to her about selling some of her products in his stores. She told me about it when I took Alex in for a treat one day. How wonderful for her. I was so mad at Leon for firing her, but I know now I was being selfish. Now I see how Claudine blossomed since that awful time and how she's become what she was meant to be. I am a little envious. But actually, and maybe you have noticed, I have grown up.

I have one more secret left to tell. Tonight, I will tell Sean about the new life nestled deep inside of me. Sometime next May, Alex will have a brother or a sister. Sean will be so excited. Alex, well, Alex will be happy once he learns to share me. He'll like having a sibling. I know he will because he's bonded with April's family.

Thank you for coming along on this journey with Andrea, Claudine and me. I hope you've enjoyed the road trip with us. May all good things in life be yours. I bet Claudine would say the same. In fact, I know she would.

Let me tell you, she would hold her hands out and she would be holding some sort of treat on a pretty napkin, a blueberry muffin or a loaf of artisan bread, she's some sort of foodie refuge from the storm, and she would smile a smile so strong the universe could not duplicate it. Ever. You see how she is, don't you?

Acknowledgments

The words "Thank you" are not enough to convey my gratitude to all those who had a hand in crafting this book, whether literally or in the figurative sense. Crafting this book morphed into an enormous, phenomenal journey, and along the journey I found friends.

Thank you to my editor, Rebecca T. Dickson, who took my words and helped me pound them into something worth reading. Thank you for the "why," the "say what you mean," and giving the big picture a whole new meaning.

Thank you, Niki Bradley-Fowler, my cover artist, and someone dear to my heart. You rock.

Thank you, Paperback Press, for this opportunity, and a special thank you to Sharon Kizziah-Holmes for the unflagging support and the hugs.

Thank you to my beta readers without whom I would have never gotten this far: Ellen Harger and Sharon Kizziah-Holmes, two more rockin' chicks.

Thank you to Karla Olson, Gail Harris, and Yolanda Baldus, friends always.

Thank you to my family.

Thank you all.